Dark Crossings

A novel by

Gretchen Eick

Blue Cedar Press
Wichita, Kansas

DARK CROSSINGS, a novel

Copyright © 2022 by Gretchen Eick. All rights reserved. No part of this book may be reproduced in any form or by any electronic or mechanical means, including information storage and retrieval systems, without permission in writing from the publisher except for brief quotations in critical articles and reviews. Inquiries should be addressed to:

Blue Cedar Press
PO Box 48715
Wichita, KS 67201

Visit the Blue Cedar Press website: www.bluecedarpress.com

First edition August 2022

10 9 8 7 6 5 4 3 2 1

ISBN: 978-1-958728-01-7 (paper)

ISBN: 978-1-958728-00-0 (ebook)

Library of Congress LCCN: 2022940932

This is a work of fiction, the second in a series that began with *Maybe Crossings*. All scenes and characters are the product of the author's imagination. Historical events mentioned, including those in Cora's annual books prepared by her grandmother, actually occurred. Ida B. Wells-Barnett, James Forman, Leon Sullivan, Fred Hampton, Mike and Debbie Africa, Mike Africa, Jr., and people referenced as killed by police are historical figures. Their depictions are based on historical documents, as are the portions of this story referring to MOVE and the tragic attacks by police they experienced on August 8, 1978, and May 13, 1985. Keisha Johnson, Richard Allen, their family, George Marshall, Reggie Lewis, and his family are fictional characters.

Cover and interior design by Gina Laiso, Integrita Productions

Editor Laura Tillem

Copy editor Marilyn Bolton

"Funeral Blues," Copyright © 1940 by W. H. Auden, Reprinted by permission of Curtis Brown Ltd. All rights reserved. (ebook use)

"Funeral Blues," copyright 1940 and © renewed 1968 by W. H. Auden; from COLLECTED POEMS by W. H. Auden, edited by Edward Mendelson. Used by permission of Random House, an imprint and division of Penguin Random House LLC. All rights reserved. (paperback use)

"Anthem" by Leonard Cohen. Copyright © 1992 by Leonard Cohen, used by permission of The Wylie Agency LLC.

Printed in the United States of America at IngramSpark and Amazon.

Praise for Dark Crossings:

Gretchen Cassel Eick is a noted scholar, a historian, a talented and award-winning writer, and a person of conscience. In her latest book, *Dark Crossings*, Dr. Eick has crafted a riveting and rich story of love, family, and accomplishment with a dark overlay of grief and violence. This is a compelling story of lives connected by homicide in metropolitan Chicago in 2019.

~Ted D. Ayres, Vice President and General Counsel Emeritus, Wichita State University, host of *Inside the Cover* on PBS Kansas.

Eick is an expert storyteller. The storyline is rich, and her characters resist caricature and resonate. The backdrop penetrates so powerfully in part because it is so exquisitely designed by a trained and observant historian familiar with the era (1960s-2020) and what that era created as well as what it left behind. You will lose yourself in the story and in the intricate and immersive history.

~Mark McCormick, Deputy Director for Strategic Initiatives, ACLU Kansas, author of *Some Were Paupers, Some Were Kings: Dispatches from Kansas*

In her latest novel, *Dark Crossings*, Gretchen Eick weaves historic facts and fictional truths into a family tapestry ripped apart by a brutal, random tragedy. Readers will empathize with complex characters who struggle to make sense of it all. Eick displays her strengths as a historian and talented writer to explore themes of violence, racial discord, racial harmony, and, ultimately, enduring love. *Dark Crossings* is a page-turner that speaks to all of us longing for assurance in these uncertain times.

~Michael D. Graves, prize-winning novelist and author of *Shadows and Sorrows*, a Pete Stone mystery.

Historian and writer Gretchen Eick has crafted a story that will tug at your heart. With deep compassion she narrates how one man's untimely death impacts each of his loved ones in a unique way. Each path through grief is individual and every broken heart heals in its own way. Sometimes the path through grief takes unexpected turns and opens doors previously hidden as it does here.

~Ann Christine Fell, novelist, author of novels *Sundrop Sonata* and *Sonata of Elsie Leonore* and a memoir, *In the Shadow of the Wind.*

Dark Crossings features mystery, intrigue, and suspense tightly woven in a fictional fabric that leads the main character into 1970s and 1980s Philadelphia to the MOVE movement to discover her unknown father and his family. Gretchen Eick highlights with sensitivity the internal and external tensions of race, class and culture within an interracial family faced with societal trauma. *Dark Crossings'* characters keep readers guessing while also serving as a stark reminder of the tragic events surrounding MOVE.

~Reginald D. Jarrell, professor of communications, lawyer, clergyperson, and author of *31 Days (Nights): Memoir of Living Black in America* and *Wings.*

As a trauma counsellor who works with people affected by homicide, I look for realism, honesty, growth, and a unique quality such as a lovable quirkiness in characters. The characters in *Dark Crossings* ring true in their mannerisms, inner dialogues, interactions with loved ones, and self. I have been a fan of Eick's writings ever since I read her novel, *Finding Duncan.* Eick uses an unusual, highly effective way of connecting a reader with her characters. *Dark Crossings* is a brilliantly woven blend of lives, family connections, and history.

~Ronda Miller, life coach, teacher, poet, author of *MoonStain, WaterSigns, Winds of Time, I Love the Child, Going Home,* is on the board of the Writers Place.

Gretchen Eick writes another great novel that focuses on the struggles of an urban family dealing with loss. I also read the prequel to *Dark Crossings, Maybe Crossings,* and hope she will write a sequel as her third in this family saga.

~Primus Singleton III, a Philadelphia native and playwright, and Laboratory Sales Specialist at Ascension Via Christi.

~Other Books by Gretchen Eick~

Fiction:

The Set Up, 1984: Classified until 2064 (Blue Cedar Press, 2020)

> Britain's big drug bust in 1984 brought an investigation quickly classified by the government for 80 years. This is the story of five ordinary people caught up in an international intrigue the government has hidden since 1985. Based on actual events.

The Hard Verge, Britain 2025 (Amazon, 2019)

> When a woman journalist seeking asylum from Syria goes missing in a Britain governed by the Ultra Right, her partner and four sympathetic Members of Parliament search for her and unravel a web of state secrets that involve Saudi Arabia, a chemical weapons facility, and the international adoption market.

Finding Duncan (Blue Cedar Press, 2015)

> When Duncan believes his wife is unfaithful to him, he flees his life in the U.S. to disappear in a remote fishing village in Scotland. There, an old Scot, a Dutch woman, and her child "save" him, temporarily. Meanwhile, back in Wichita, KS, his abandoned wife Amy reinvents herself as a single mom. Then their paths cross. But can Duncan, haunted by depression and more losses, ever be found?

Maybe Crossings (Blue Cedar Press, 2015)

> The first book in the Crossings series is a historical novel that begins in the Sixties and follows white and Black activists in the Civil Rights Movement. Forty years later they reconnect. How will the children of Sixties parents define family and commitment in the early 21st Century? A forty-year family saga in Black and white.

Non-Fiction:

They Met at Wounded Knee: The Eastmans' Story (University of Nevada Press, 2020)

A history of the U.S. 1858-1945 from the perspectives of its impact on Indigenous Americans and other Americans of Color told through the lives of the best known Native American of his time, physician Charles (Ohiyesa) Eastman, and his Anglo wife, Elaine Goodale Eastman, each the author of eleven books.

Dissent in Wichita: The Civil Rights Movement in the Midwest, 1954-72 (University of Illinois Press, 2001/2007)

The U.S.'s first successful student-led sit-in, the first federal desegregation investigation of a Midwest school system, the founding of a rebel group within the NAACP [the Young Turks] that pushed the organization to address economic issues, and Chester I. Lewis, Jr., a national and local civil rights leader — these are some of the Movement's Midwest stories told in this prize-winning book.

Edited Book:

The Death Project: An Anthology for These Times (Blue Cedar Press, 2020)

Thirty-six writers reflect on grief, dying, and recovery through stories, poetry, memoir, and explanations of different religious traditions' practices at death.

In Memoriam

Roger Ames, Composer

and

David Cunningham Cassel, Conductor

The music remains.

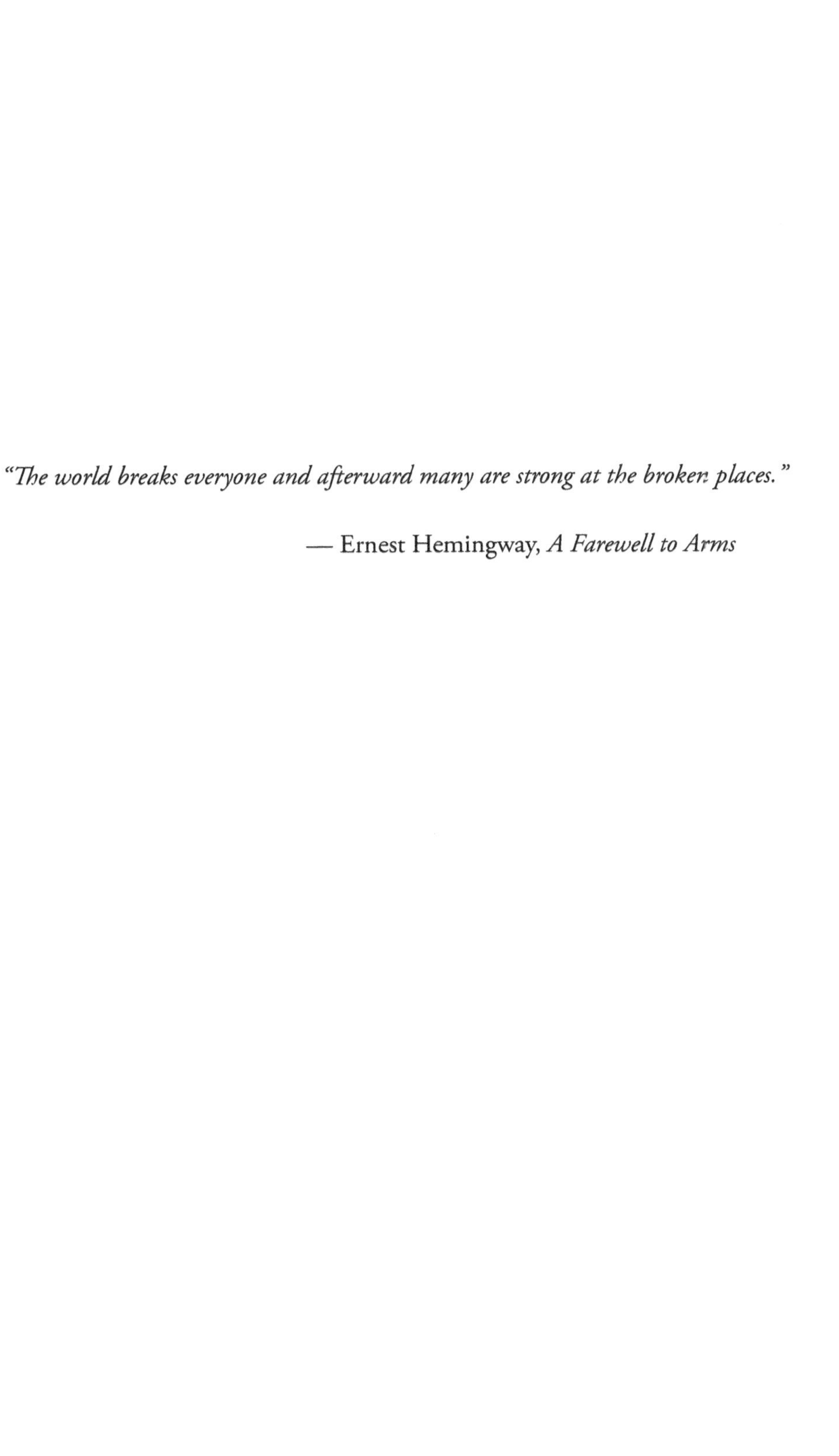

"The world breaks everyone and afterward many are strong at the broken places."

— Ernest Hemingway, *A Farewell to Arms*

The Characters in Dark Crossings and Their Relationships

Arthur Johnson	Cora Brown	Whitmore Parents	Lewis Parents
Son **Don** Daughter **My Young** Raised by Cora **Cora marries Arthur** Son **Richard Allen** unknown to him b. 1966; adopted **Don marries Ann and becomes Keisha's Dad**	Son **Edward** by first husband Booker (d. 1951) Cora becomes "Gran Cora" to Don's Family: Ann, Keisha, Richard, Cora, & Caleb.	**Ann** Daughter **Keisha** (b. 1965) Ann, Edward, and Reggie worked together in Mississippi the summer of 1964. **Ann marries Don who raises Keisha**	Son **Reggie** (d. 1985) Daughter **Keisha** unknown to him Son in New York Daughter **Femi marries Jacob** Son **Ajani** Son **Barron** Son **Aidan** Daughter **Joan marries Andre**
Richard marries Keisha 2003 Daughter **Cora** b. 2004 Son **Caleb** b. 2005		Note: This novel takes place during 2019 and early 2020.	

Part I

~Prologue~

The first warm weekend in Chicago followed a sudden spring snowstorm. The fickle weather was cautionary, an ominous foretaste of things to come. Twenty-four shootings and five murders in one weekend, including people attending a baby shower. It was April 2019.

In the Woodlawn neighborhood a group of men in their later teens leaned against the pockmarked wall of a defunct grocery store, smoking. Skulls and Gothic lettering etched into their necks and arms identified them. They were entrepreneurs, working out the details of their next hostile takeover, and they spoke the language of their business. The average person walking home from work, or school, or the corner store crossed the street, picked up their pace, and hurried away.

The two young men approaching from opposite ends of the block were not average. One was a PhD student at Northwestern University. The other was an ex-felon who'd fallen in with the Crips and done time as an adult when he was fifteen. Now released, he was trying to reinvent himself. Both were highly intelligent, from loving families, and motivated to succeed. Both sought to escape the group gathered in front of the boarded-up grocery.

They passed each other, not making eye contact, and hurried on. Not being seen was their salvation.

Had they worn different clothing (and been differently colored), the gathered Crips might have been mistaken for the moguls in Armani suits who dominated hedge funds, the arms trade, or the big banks. It would be an understandable mistake. They, too, dealt out death. But for the 510 families in Chicago who would lose a loved one to homicide in 2019, death by homicide carried an up close and personal punch they would never get over.

This is the story of one of those families, the family of Drs. Richard Allen and Keisha Johnson, who reside with their two teenaged children on Maple Avenue, in Evanston, Illinois, just north of Chicago.

Chapter 1

"*Damn it, there is no place for me in all this mess. I cannot compose without my own tidy uncluttered space. You thrive in this environment. I don't.*"

Richard paced the living room, his mouth closed so tightly it might have been wired shut, his right fist hammering the palm of his left hand. Then he tripped on the string of the xylophone pull-toy, the one with each metal bar a different color, the one way too young for Baby Cora. All 6'4" of Richard went down.

The crash startled the baby who began to cry. Keisha stood like a stone obelisk halfway to Richard to help him up and halfway to the baby to comfort her. She was paralyzed by indecision. Which of these unhappy people should take priority at this moment?

Sprawled on the floor, frustrated and fuming, Richard had had it. "Keisha, you work like a whirlwind and it's easy for you to multitask. *But you create chaos everywhere and you don't consider how that impacts the people around you, namely ME! Look —*" He pointed at the piles of articles, stacks of papers she was grading, dozens of sticky pads in neon colors on which she squeezed notes in her almost illegible scribble, stacks of books, mugs of pens and highlighters, cups half-full of cold coffee, and plates resting precariously atop her printer with bits of sandwiches leftover from days ago—not to mention the baby paraphernalia.

"I know you take pride in being Miss I-Can-Manage-It-All, but *I can't tolerate all this chaos.* It's like living where a tornado is touching down."

After the baby entered their lives on Valentine's Day, 2004, Richard's orderly environment had disintegrated into mounds of toys, boxes of diapers and wet wipes, bottles and baby clothes, trash cans overflowing and stinky. That Keisha's tolerance for spatial chaos greatly exceeded Richard's was no surprise. Keisha simply didn't notice. Her mind was elsewhere. Not so for Richard.

That afternoon, during exam week, he exploded. "*I just can't take this any longer.*" It was The Crisis of their first year of marriage.

They had consolidated their belongings into one apartment—his, because there were fewer stairs to climb, and they both loved the back porch that looked out on Lake Michigan. They could walk to the university where both were on the faculty. But nowhere in the apartment was there a space not littered with baby stuff and Keisha clutter.

Richard's musical Muse required his full attention. Chaos in his space fractured his concentration, blurred, even erased his ability to listen and notice the natural world that sparked the music that sang inside him, triggering soaring harmonies and clashing counter chords. Once he heard them, his challenge was to write them down before the light shifted, before the scene changed, and his opportunity to interpret what he heard and felt moved on.

His composing relied on being able to see patterns: the tidiness of notes on a page of composition paper, the nuanced shift of seasons, the progression of days that began with a stunning expansion of color across the morning sky and ended in almost imperceptible erasure of light gradually eclipsed by sprawling darkness. He was a connoisseur of patterns. They nourished him. And to see them necessitated an orderly work environment.

"I need order. It is nonnegotiable!" He pulled himself to standing and, unable to find a surface that wasn't occupied with baby things or Keisha's papers, stomped out of the apartment.

When Keisha had discovered she was pregnant with Cora, Richard had run from their relationship. He wasn't ready for that level of commitment. Having children petrified him. He feared kids would drain them of spontaneity and calcify them into automatons whose top priority was running to meet the needs of the children. They would lose the Best Friends and Lovers intimacy that he had experienced only with Keisha. During the difficult months before Cora was born, Keisha came to the sad acceptance that Richard would be "Uncle Richard" to their daughter, the man who dropped by occasionally but wasn't involved in raising her.

In the end, when she was seven months pregnant, Richard had come around. At her family's reunion on Thanksgiving Day, he'd presented her with a giant box in which, like Russian dolls, smaller and smaller boxes nestled. The smallest box held an engagement ring.

Every Thanksgiving after that, when the extended family gathered and they went around the dining table before eating, each naming something they were grateful for, someone said, "Thank you, God, that Richard *finally* married Keisha." They all would laugh, and Richard would beam and blush.

Now, as the door slammed behind him, Keisha expected to hear that he was done with marriage and children, and tried to prepare herself. She felt terrified and desolate imagining life without him.

When he returned two hours later, the baby was asleep in her arms, her face was blotchy, and her raccoon eyes with their spreading mascara circles told him she'd been crying.

"Is something burning?" he asked, looking alarmed.

Keisha passed him Cora and fled to the kitchen to turn off the fire beneath the pot of chili she was cooking for their dinner. The mess of onions, tomatoes, beans, and ground beef was firmly attached to the bottom of the pan. She opened the garbage can and scraped the black and crusty chili into it.

She hadn't yet shared with him what the doctor had told her this afternoon—that she was pregnant *again.* They would have two children eleven months apart: two children, two demanding careers, two quite different approaches to space. She moved back to the living room, taking the baby from him, watching where she placed her feet in the minefield of toys and wet wipes.

Richard stood in the doorway studying the scene.

Holding the still-sleeping baby, Keisha watched him warily, wearing the armor of past rejection. She waited for him to speak, trying to summon her usual confidence.

"I think we need to move to a bigger apartment," he said. "I must have one room that is orderly, one room that is my private space. And you need space to sprawl. We can afford it. We're both teaching. What do you think?"

It was so not what she expected. She sank into the sofa, staring at this man she had married. Instead of staying angry and blaming her, he had focused on what they needed to change. There was no ultimatum, no "my way or the highway." She began to weep. Which started the baby crying.

He sat beside her.

"I expected you would leave us," she blubbered into his chest as he held her.

That moment became the touchstone of their marriage, the model for how they would handle other conflicts. "We must remember today," Keisha had said. "It will keep us together."

Richard, whose father was a pastor, replied, "Dad would say we just experienced Grace, a holy moment."

"I think Grace just told us we can do this." Keisha was grinning through her tears.

He called for carry out Pad Thai and they sat, legs touching, discussing where they wanted to live and how many rooms they would need. They would look for a new apartment after they turned in their grades in May. And she told him what she had learned from the doctor that afternoon. He surprised her by saying two children so close in age would be good, easier on them as older parents. "We'll just have to hang in through the diaper years. After that, no problem, right? ...As long as I have my space!" For the next few months, Richard would use their bedroom for his (tidy) composing space. The crisis was resolved.

Of course, there would be plenty of other crises. Often replays. Richard would declare himself. Keisha would feel defensive and withdraw, which she did when she felt criticized. Richard would stand his ground and stomp off. Later he'd return, apologetic, but insistent that things must change. And they would negotiate. Both learned they could survive their flash points of difference if they named what they needed, listened without getting defensive, and negotiated a solution.

When they told Keisha's parents that another grandchild was on the way, Ann and Don stepped in with an offer to help with a down payment on a house in Evanston. "We are really privileged. You do know that, don't you?" It was important to Keisha, a biracial woman who had been raised by white parents, that her (white) husband remember that most families of color didn't have access to family money to help them buy a house.

"I do know that. Don't you know I married you for your money?"

"And I married you for your access to Grace. And she's shown up *again*," Keisha replied.

They started looking for a house immediately.

The sixth house they looked at was a foursquare, two-story, red brick built in the early twentieth century. It was within biking distance of

Northwestern University in Evanston, Illinois, where they both taught. An overgrowth of ivy covered the street side, and lilac bushes in prolific bloom framed the front door, exuding a fragrance so strong that even Keisha, who paid little attention to sensate details, gushed about the scent. The lilacs were the *piece de resistance,* they agreed. They both fell in love with the house.

There was so much more space. The house had a central hallway with walnut wainscotting and woodwork. The hall led past mirror-image dining and living rooms to a large kitchen at the back with an island for food prep and barstools along one side. Adjacent to the kitchen was a sizable family room that could also be accessed from the living room through an oversized oak door. A row of windows faced the back yard, making the room light and airy. Keisha pledged to confine the chaos of childhood to the family room and the children's bedrooms. Richard doubted she could keep that promise.

Upstairs four bedrooms and a small "sewing room" opened onto a hall lined with built-in bookcases. Those bookcases were even more enticing than the lilacs. Richard and Keisha would each have an office, the guest room doubling as Richard's study, and Keisha would use the sewing room as her workspace.

It was a serviceable house, practically arranged with whimsical touches that gave it personality. Like a balcony overlooking the back yard that could only be accessed from a window in their bedroom, and an enclosed side porch with toughened glass roof panels to let the sun flood in. On the sunny day when they first saw the house, the porch looked like a shiny prism some Greek god, exercising immortal pique, had hurled against the exterior wall.

"I can put our babies out here to nap!" she declared.

"Think you'll remember where you put them once you get into your research?" Richard was teasing her.

"You just want to bring your keyboard out here to work. Guess we'll have to do some heavy negotiating," she teased back.

The house was so perfect that Richard joked he wasn't moving ever again, not until they carried his body to "Boot Hill." Keisha rolled her eyes at him, but she felt the same.

To his surprise, Richard took to being a dad. He fell in step with the routines of raising children—especially after they graduated from bottles and diapers to reading, talking, and locomoting. Once they were school-aged, he enjoyed chauffeuring, attending recitals and science fairs, rescuing them from falls from ice and roller skates, teaching them to ride two-wheelers, and setting up a tent in the back yard so they could pretend they were Lakota and Northern Cheyenne camping out at Little Bighorn. "Accuracy is important. I *am* an American historian," Keisha had reminded him.

He also loved semi-annual gatherings of their large extended family— his and Keisha's parents, his sister and her family, Keisha's cousins, Gran Cora and Grandpa Arthur, the matriarch and patriarch on Keisha's side, and Gran's son, Uncle Edward. Family trips to Cleveland for Thanksgiving around her parents' large table, stopovers in Nashville to see Keisha's grandparents—these became the highlights of his year. Having grown up in a minister's home where crisis calls from church folk took priority, even at holidays, Richard discovered he loved having time with family that no one disrupted. "Family," he would say, playing his awkward Aw, shucks persona, "is the greatest."

Back at the beginning, when their relationship had been precarious, Keisha's Gran Cora had told her it would work out. She had been right, as usual.

Until she met Richard, Keisha lived in her head. The people she knew there fascinated her. She found historical figures and people from literature much more interesting than the flesh and blood people in her physical world. Where some folks would ask, What would Jesus do? Keisha asked herself, What would Ida B. Wells-Barnett do?

In her imagination she pictured Ida B. as a wise and energetic older Black woman who lived across the street and dropped in to visit and share her "take" on the latest political developments, what books were "must reads," and why Chicago was such a segregated city. Ida B. supplied Keisha with advice on child raising, having raised her children on a healthy diet of activism. A hundred years ago Ida B. took her children to protests— at least one accompanied her on the long train trip to Washington, DC to lobby for women's suffrage. Of course, Ida B. went alone to the sites of lynchings that she investigated and publicized. She had led an international campaign to end lynching. Ida had embraced the life of the mind as well as the life of caring for family. Keisha thought Ida would approve of how Keisha responded to her mentoring from the grave.

Ida B. Wells-Barnett wasn't Keisha's only mentor. Many women, some dead and some alive, played that role, including Keisha's mom Ann and her Gran Cora. She checked in weekly with the living, and as frequently with the dead. Once Richard entered her life, he joined the cloud of personal consultants who guided her through life.

Richard understood living in your head. He lived in his own interior world of historical figures, too, most of them involved in making music. He *"got"* Keisha. And she got him. When he came upon her intently working, brow furrowed and eyes staring at something no one else could see, he'd ask, "What is Ida B. telling you today?" She'd respond, "What are you learning from Stravinsky, my love?"

How did other people manage living on one plane, The Present, when there was such rich instruction to be had moving back and forth between The Present and The Past? On this they agreed. It made them odd and bonded them.

In the early days of their marriage, after Keisha's swollen body had pushed out baby Cora, they had walked along the lake shore pushing Cora in her buggy and discussing whether their head habitation would have to change now that they were parents.

"I think we'll both have to pay more attention to The Present while we are caring for small children. We do have to keep them warm, safe, and full tummy'd."

Richard suggested, "Maybe we should agree to let each other know when the world of Now becomes too much for us. We can take turns returning to our Caves of the Mind."

"I like that, only let's agree to be equal opportunity mind-dwellers. Needing to retreat is not gendered, agreed?"

"Agreed."

The day Caleb started preschool Keisha and Richard met for lunch on campus. The cafeteria was noisy with the clatter of trays and dishes and the animated conversations of students. Keisha suggested they reflect on how they had weathered the pitfalls of their children's early childhoods.

"I think we've successfully tag-teamed up close and personal parenting." Richard offered a high-five.

"It helped that we fell in love with our children."

"I confess I liked them better once they could talk and share their imaginary worlds with us."

Keisha gave him a gotcha grin. "That's because there's less mess and clutter. Seriously, we've been really lucky to teach at the same university with flexible work schedules and to live close to our work."

"It also helps that they're interesting small persons"

She nodded. "You're the better listener, I think. As a composer you listen for the mysteries of the momentary."

"I'll drink to that," he said, playfully toasting her with his coke. "That and the adorable way you scrunch your forehead when you're being analytical." He was smiling. "I do love you," he added.

"It's exhausting, right?" She grinned back.

Chapter 2

Cora was eighteen months old when Hurricane Katrina devastated New Orleans. The toddler sat surrounded by toys in front of her parents, whose eyes were glued to their television screen, watching the images scrolling: camera footage of Black people stranded on rooftops, clinging to trees, other footage of folks crowded into a stadium. Dead Black people floating in the swollen Mississippi River. Those images would remain forever in their memories, along with other pictures--uniformed military walking the hot August streets, hustling people off the sidewalk, cars floating down other streets, water surging through broken dikes, and rescue boats making their way to survivors through floating debris that included bodies for whom rescue was no longer an option. Later they wondered in hushed voices how the horror on the screen might affect their precocious daughter.

Cora was an early talker. By two she would chatter to her stuffed animals and imaginary friends. She memorized the books Keisha and Richard read to her. She repeated whole pages verbatim with precise inflections so that family members overhearing her could tell immediately which book her mother had read to her and which her father. She was a natural mimic, a vocal performer, a quality her introverted father found totally awesome and attributed to her mother's influence. Keisha was an animated lecturer.

Like her parents, Cora could entertain herself for hours. She was sufficient unto herself, needing little external stimulus. Realizing how bright her daughter was, Keisha used every opportunity to expand Cora's knowledge. Even when she was a nursing infant, Keisha talked to her, for example, telling the tiny being curled against her breast that, "Today Massachusetts made it legal for people to marry who they love. Your Aunty and her partner will be legally married next week! Ah, Baby Cora, it is a new world you are born into, a better world."

Cora was four when Senator Barack Obama ran for President of the United States of America. Finding the tall and beautiful Black woman who was the candidate's wife became a kind of Where's Waldo for Cora as her parents followed the campaign on the news. "There she is, there's Michelle, Mrs. 'Bama," Cora would say with great excitement, pressing her forefinger on the screen when Senator Obama and his wife appeared on television. Cora in her stroller went door to door with her mom to encourage people to register to vote that summer, and she was in the crowd at Grant Park, riding Richard's shoulders, her brother Caleb on Keisha's, when the announcement came that Senator Obama had been elected President.

From her elevated position, the park looked like a moving ocean of people for as far as she could see, jubilant people, all kinds of them. Many, like both of her parents, were crying. "Why are you crying?" the child asked, but her mother was too overcome to respond.

During Cora's childhood she spent a lot of time sorting pieces of information. Vivid photographic images fascinated her. Some things that she saw when her parents watched the news were scary, like people getting shot at school. Because Mama's friend taught at Virginia Tech, and Mama had talked with her about it, she especially remembered when thirty-two people were shot to death on that campus. Mama and Daddy taught at a campus. Might that happen to them?

She was eight when twenty children at a primary school in Connecticut were shot to death. The kids shot were younger than she was. It was all over the news. That same year, when she was in third grade, a young Black boy wearing a hoodie and eating Skittles was shot dead by a neighbor in Florida. Travon Martin could have been Cora's cousin by his appearance. Mama said his murderer was found not guilty.

Being eight, Cora thought a lot about what was fair and unfair. Travon Martin's murder was definitely not fair. She would remember his name and what happened to him. For several months she refused to wear a hoodie. Mama seemed to understand.

Despite the terrible things, Cora would view her childhood as an idyllic time. Her parents loved her and each other with a fierceness that she could see. The intensity of their connection made her feel treasured and distinctly special. Occasionally, when she was little, she would push her way into the circle they made as they stood holding each other. She thought they were like magnets when they stood this way and she wished to be in the center of such a powerful connection.

Mama answered her questions and listened to her seriously, but it was her mother's mother, Gran Ann, who most memorably reminded Cora that her childhood was a time when phenomenal changes were occurring all around her, globally and within the country she belonged to. Beginning when she was six in 2010, Gran Ann presented Cora with a handmade booklet each year on her birthday that had photographic images followed by paragraphs about the events that had shaped the world during the previous year of Cora's life. Cora was already reading chapter books and Gran Ann wrote short chapters describing the events that they read together.

The first booklet was titled *CORA'S WORLD IN 2009.* It featured the new president and his family. There were also pictures of doctors and nurses wearing full body covering and face masks while treating people with the swine flu. Gran had written about the H1N1 epidemic that had moved from country to country and took the lives of 12,469 people in the U.S. There were pictures of Michael Jackson, who died that year, and a photo of Cora and her brother Caleb doing Jackson's moonwalk moves. There was even a picture of former U.S. President Bill Clinton meeting in North Korea with the president of North Korea, and another picture of two American journalists being released from prison in North Korea after the President's visit. Gran wrote that she'd included this story because of Cora's cousins, whose father was in prison in North Korea. The family still hoped he would someday be released. Gran Ann didn't want Cora to forget him.

Gran's insistence that Cora remember an uncle she had never met intrigued the child. Whenever they visited Mama's grandparents, Gran Cora and Grandpa Arthur in Nashville, Cora would make her way to a wedding photograph that sat in a golden frame on the bookshelf in Gran Cora's bedroom. Uncle Son Chi was tall and handsome with smiling eyes and Aunt Mi-Young wore traditional Korean dress and looked beautiful and carefree. She had never seen her auntie in that kind of clothing other than in this picture. Nor had she seen her aunt look carefree.

Gran Ann's yearly booklets were a ritual that Cora looked forward to, a birthday present unlike any other. Mama called the booklets evidence of Gran's feminist consciousness. Cora wasn't clear what that meant.

Chapter 3

Having had children at the end of their thirties and being private people, Keisha Johnson and Richard Allen felt no need of a social life outside family. They were content within their bubble as their children grew through what Keisha called their latency years. Sometimes they wondered if their children found them weird. From the time Cora and Caleb were in school, Keisha and Richard had shared with them the historical figures who occupied their heads. They considered it part of their parental responsibility to expand their children's knowledge of The Past and the amazing people who shaped it. The kids made it a game.

"Who are you talking to today, Mama/Dad?" one of them would ask an obviously preoccupied parent. (Everyone understood the question applied not to living people but to the dead departed.) When Dad, or more likely Mama, went on too long explaining, and their young minds were losing interest, Caleb or Cora would interrupt. "________ is ready to take a break. S/he has other mortals to visit. Time's up!"

"I wonder what they say about us to their friends," Richard asked Keisha on a September Saturday in 2018 while the two of them were working the soil in the backyard flower beds, preliminary to planting bulbs.

"I overheard one of Caleb's buddies say we were different but 'dope,' whatever that means. They *seem* to be thriving, although I think they're about to outgrow our family bubble. Which makes me..." She was searching for the right word.

"Scared? Me, too. Time to hand them back? Or to fast-forward through the next four years? Any idea what Ida B. would advise?"

Keisha tossed a handful of mulch at him.

It was strenuous work planting bulbs—daffodils, tulips, and hyacinths. The beds were wide and long. They faced Keisha and Richard's bedroom with its odd little balcony and his study that doubled as their guest room. The yard would be beautiful come April.

She took a break to bring them tall glasses of iced coffee. Sensing

Richard's weariness, she proposed they hire a neighbor boy to finish the job, but Richard would not hear of it. "We're planting these bulbs so next spring and each spring—long after Caleb and Cora are through their teens—we will see their blooms from our windows. It will be *so beautiful*, and we'll remember our hard work getting them placed just the right depth and in masses of color. Dad used to say, 'Planting bulbs is coloring the future for those who come after us.'"

Keisha loved hearing her husband share his father's aphorisms. She loved his appreciation of his parents, especially his father, who had died five years ago and whose absence Richard continued to grieve. Richard called his father "a truly good man." Like father, like son, she thought.

Living together inside their family bubble was nourishing for the two of them. Of that Keisha was quite certain. Sometimes it stunned her how lucky they were, she confided to Richard months later while the kids played on their IPADS in their bedrooms, leaving Richard and Keisha an extra hour in bed one frosty Sunday morning.

After their leisurely lovemaking, Richard sat up and leaned back against the headboard. He watched his wife and savored the scent of Obsession that rose from her warm skin. He took pleasure from seeing her like this, the sheet covering her nakedness, one uncovered shoulder gilded by the morning sun. Out of nowhere he announced, "I think we should look for a church. My mother would be thrilled if we found a church. And it would give us a routine for expressing our gratitude."

"Your mother would not notice." She wasn't trying to be hurtful, just honest. His mother had Alzheimer's and was past tracking whether or not her son's family was part of a church. He could tell by Keisha's immobile face that she was dubious about his suggestion. Unlike Richard, she had not grown up attending church.

But church had loomed large in Richard's childhood. Attending every week and watching his father, who was the minister, lead the congregation had given Richard confidence and pride in who he was as the pastor's son. Of course, in his teen years he'd declared himself and claimed his right to stay home Sunday mornings, which probably embarrassed his father and set a bad example for the youth of the congregation. To their credit, his parents had acknowledged that religion, and how you express your gratitude for life, was different for different people.

"Just don't forget to *feel* gratitude, son," his father had said then, "and find your own way to express it." Richard *did* express it—with Keisha and, on occasion, with his students. Also, to his parents, and Keisha's parents, and their extended family. But now he thought it was time to expand that circle. Caleb and Cora were new adolescents. Their family bubble was, he acknowledged with regret, fated to burst as the kids hatched into young adults. Perhaps church could help them maneuver the rough seas of parenting teens?

"Let's ask around. Perhaps people in our departments have churches to recommend," Richard suggested.

"I doubt it. I don't know anyone who admits they attend church." Keisha was quiet, analyzing her reluctance. "My problem is, so many churches are segregated. I don't want us to attend an all-white church or an all-black church either. The world—*this country!*—is so mixed. I want our kids to experience "mixed" as the norm. *And* I don't want a church where they will be told how sinful they are or that same-sex relationships are against God."

"Well, Uncle Edward should be able to steer us to a congregation that meets your specs," Richard was smiling at his wife. It often surprised him how much he still had to learn about how she saw the world. Observing the world from within a brown-skinned body, you noticed different things, things that flew past Richard, as Keisha frequently reminded him when his whiteness clouded his perception. At least he'd been savvy enough to bring Uncle Edward into his church-shopping proposal.

Uncle Edward was a retired pastor. He was also brown-skinned and brilliant, the son of Gran Cora, who was Keisha's grandmother by marriage to Keisha's stepdad's father. It was a bit complicated, but they were all family and close. Uncle Edward lived in Chicago, so he knew the panorama of churches in their area.

Keisha seemed ready to change the subject. At least she hadn't rejected the idea out of hand. Give her time. He'd learned that. And if she didn't come around, maybe he'd invite the kids to go with him. If she saw her family going off to church without her, he knew she'd join them, not to miss anything.

He pulled her to him, loving the softness of her skin, the curve of her hips, how they fit together. They'd bought a king-sized bed years ago to have room for all four of them to snuggle. It had been their Sunday morning pattern for years. That communal cuddle had come to an end with the kids now teenagers, and the king-sized bed made the space between him and Keisha far too wide, in his opinion. Maybe it was time to downsize, trade the king for a queen-sized bed?

Richard planted a kiss on Keisha's forehead. "Have you any idea how much I love you?" he asked her. He burrowed his hands in her thick curls and she reached for him, smiling.

"I think I do," she said.

"More than the entire galaxy, more than infinity, more than Now."

Her eyes went suddenly wet, and her face shifted to serious. "And I love you back just as much."

Chapter 4

Two weeks after his fourteenth birthday, Caleb rode his bike to the Northwestern campus, parked and locked it to a bike rack outside the music building that housed his dad's office. It was a surprisingly balmy March day. Tomorrow temperatures were forecast to drop thirty degrees, typical of the Chicago-Evanston area. The forecast was why he'd taken his bike out for a ride before the brief warm spell died.

He was proud to be Dr. Richard Allen's son. He stopped here after school once a week, took the stairs to Dad's floor two at a time, and rapped their coded knock on Dad's door. The cafeteria in the building was closed but the vending machines dropped food 24/7, bags of chips, packages of cookies, and pre-fab cinnamon rolls, the food Mom didn't allow at home. "It's our guy thing," Dad said about their secret visits to the vending machines.

Today Caleb wanted to talk, so he and Dad sat across from each other, feet resting on the top edge of the desk, hands cinnamon roll-sticky, voices fuzzy from talking through all that sugar.

Caleb hesitated. He'd had the sex talk with Dad when he was twelve, but it hadn't come up since then. This was important. And awkward. He felt protective of Dad. Dad was a good guy. Innocent, kind of. Maybe even boring, at least to some people. Would Dad even know there were bad guys in his school? But this had been going on for a while, the locker room bragging and trash talking about girls, and it made him really uncomfortable.

Caleb licked his fingers and wiped his palms against his jeans. Then he took a deep breath. "Dad, there's a guy in my class who brags about all the girls he has 'had.' He says he's taken pictures of them and is going to post them on Instagram." Caleb had been looking at his shoes, but now he looked up to see how Dad was taking this news.

Richard set the remainder of his cinnamon roll on a napkin and looked at Caleb with a very serious look. Maybe Caleb should have kept this to himself?

The room was silent except for the sound of the wind off Lake Michigan trying to pry open the windows, a portent of the expected storm.

"Go on, son."

"I know some of the girls, and they are not like that. If he posts pictures and says they've done it with him, that would be awful! Some of the guys already treat them like they're sluts. This one girl, when I see her in the hallway, has this confused, hurt look and I feel really sorry for her and angry at him. But I don't know what I can do to stop him."

Dad took a long sip from his water bottle. He kept his eyes on Caleb. "What are you thinking about doing?"

"I could tell somebody at school, maybe the assistant principal? But if it got out that I did that, Ryan would make me pay, beat me up or tell everyone I'm a fag or that I can't get it up. He might say I'm doing drugs, and you can't trust anything I say. It could get nasty."

"That's a difficult situation. Have you had other run-ins with him?"

"Yes. When the new kid joined our class, the one from the Congo, I talked to him and invited him to sit with me at lunch. Ryan told everyone I was an emo boy."

"What's that mean?"

"One of those supersensitive people who is emotional, maybe cuts himself 'cause he *feels* things. Emos are goth. They wear tight black clothes, long black hair. They wear nail polish and makeup and are just out there. Moto, the new guy, came here as a refugee. I think he wears tight black clothes because that's all he has. Yeah, he is sensitive, but the counsellor told us he's been through a lot and we need to be kind to him." Caleb stood and began pacing, "And you can see *I* don't look emo, Dad—no nail polish, no makeup!"

"Whoa! Ryan sounds like a first-class jerk. I'm proud of you for wanting to challenge him. But it sounds heavy, like there could be serious consequences… Maybe I should talk with Ryan?"

"Dad, that would make it *worse*." Caleb was regretting talking about this with Dad. But it was too late to change the subject. "I just need your advice on how to handle it. I don't want him to get away with hurting other people. He's a bully, and the school has all these signs up about not bullying, but no one does anything about Ryan and his groupies who write stuff on the lockers and start all these rumors on social media."

"Stuff? Like 'emo boy' and 'fag'?"

"Even the 'n' word and 'trans.'"

"And that's happened to you?"

"U-huh." Caleb was looking at the floor.

"That is *not* OK. What would you think about Mom and me going in to see the assistant principal? She gets home tomorrow, and I can make an appointment for us to go in after school is out on Monday, when there are no students in the building, no one to see us. Do you think that would be a good plan?"

Caleb didn't know. His stomach was knotted. He wasn't at all sure this would help, but Dad was determined to protect him, and he didn't want to disappoint Dad.

Richard looked at his phone. "They've probably gone by now, but I'll leave a message. It's Mr. Carluzzi, right?" At Caleb's nod, Richard started punching the name of the middle school into his phone, then pressed the call icon. Caleb could hear the voice message, followed by a beep, followed by his dad's deep baritone voice leaving a message, requesting an appointment for late Monday afternoon with Mr. Carluzzi, and repeating his callback number.

He turned to Caleb, his brow wrinkled with worry. "No one should be treated like that, Caleb. No one. And you can't take on Ryan's bullying by yourself. Thank you for telling me what's going on. It's important."

Richard made a note in his phone to follow up with the school on Monday morning before his first class. Then he turned his full attention to his son. "Can you tell me more about the girl you are worried about him hurting?"

He was thinking, *Why are there creeps like Ryan in this world?*

Chapter 5

From the moment she began speaking in sentences, Cora questioned everything. Riding in her stroller she would turn to Keisha and ask, "Why is that tree green and the others yellow and orange?" Or, "Why don't pigeons use a toilet?" Curiosity was Cora's central attribute, one Keisha claimed came from her DNA. Both of them were full of questions. And impatient with facile answers. "I really want to know why, Mama." It was Cora's standard refrain. And her mama would suggest they look up the answers to her Whys, if Keisha couldn't supply them. It built a special bond between them. Cora, Keisha's oldest child, was the one most like her mother.

But, as Cora outgrew her childhood, she discarded her default way of learning, adopting instead a different way. Her father's trust in the universe, his mysticism, began to fascinate her. He was a composer. Where Cora's mother interrogated life, her father marveled at it. He didn't ask the origin of the notes that came together in his heart and spilled onto composition paper. He didn't ask why he knew to arrange them in a particular order, or which chords should flank them to make his melodies excruciatingly beautiful. He just paid attention to what the notes told him to do.

Richard's father was a clergyman. Yet Richard was not conventionally religious, not a church goer. He would say laughingly that he'd had enough of church as a child to see him through his adulthood. But church, the Bible, and spirituality were stored inside him in a reservoir. He could snack on them whenever he got hungry. No need to go to church. Cora remembered his saying, "Remember your grandma's cellar with all the shelves of her canned goods and baskets of onions and potatoes? Well, your grandpa made a cellar in me that he filled with his words and his teachings. It's like I have my own private root cellar. When crises come, I can draw on 'the Magic of God's World,' your grandpa told me."

Keisha agreed that the way Richard accepted without questioning the magic of his music had to come from his years of exposure to his father's spirituality. He had a personal depository, a deep well within himself that he unconsciously relied on to explain the world. When he sat at the table in their bedroom that overlooked their back yard where he did his composing, she could almost see him drawing possibilities from that well. He'd look out the window with that quizzical expression, not moving, and then turn to his keyboard, fingers racing his mind to capture the sequences, totally unaware that she or anyone else was present.

The change in Cora, the shift from examining everything to finding the magic without having to look for it, disquieted Keisha. She wished *she* felt more wonder. Sometimes she felt jealous of the growing bond between Cora and Richard, a bond she was constitutionally incapable of replicating. Sometimes she resented the growing closeness between father and daughter. When she confessed these feelings to Richard, he responded that he liked Cora and her mother just the way they are. Maybe as she matured, Cora's mother would acquire the ability to embrace life's magic.

Keisha was the epitome of a strong, independent woman. Their relationship felt reliably loving and attentive, but this difference between her husband and herself felt important and left her troubled. Could they accept that they were profoundly different in this way and let it go? She corrected herself. Not "they," for Richard clearly accepted and valued her different approach to life. *SHE.* She was the disquieted one. Especially so now that Cora had crossed the bridge to her father's way of seeing and left her mother behind.

Keisha left the bedroom quietly, closed the door, and descended to the kitchen mildly upset. Cora and Caleb were in the dining room working on homework and didn't look up when she walked past them. She began preparing dinner, turning on NPR to distract her from her unsettled thoughts.

Not long afterward Richard threw open the bedroom door and thundered down the steps.

"I forgot I have a gig on the south side. No time for dinner, Babe. Got to go. This will be a late one." He pulled on his wool pea coat, pecked her on the cheek, and strode out the door carrying his keyboard, his computer bag swinging from his shoulder.

"There's supposed to be a big snowstorm tonight. Will you be safe driving in the ice and snow?"

He was back in a few minutes. "I forgot to get gas. It probably is better to take the L if it's going to storm. No problem. See you after the bewitching hour, Foxy Lady." He grinned his bad boy grin. Then he was off, calling good night to Caleb and Cora as he hurried to the L stop.

Chapter 6

Richard stands on the subway platform above the street where the Red Line meets the Purple Line. It is nine hours after his conversation with his son. In nine hours the temperature has dropped from a balmy fifty to ten degrees above zero.

His gig at the Jazz Showcase in Chicago ended early due to a winter storm advisory. It is 1:30 a.m. and he awaits the last train to Evanston. He enjoys playing with this combo that has been getting some buzz of late in the local jazz scene. He is tired, but also exhilarated. It is so stimulating to play with these guys who respect each other's creativity and welcome innovation and experimentation. The energy blast he received from tonight will last him through the week! But now he is weary and ready to get home.

He stands alone on the platform, no one else in sight. The air is thick with ice crystals that bite his face. He winds his woolen scarf twice around his neck, tucking the ends inside his coat. There is clarity in the winter darkness and the one star that lights the night. The only sound is the slight rustle of crumpled potato chip bags blowing across the tracks and the few limp pages of yesterday's newspaper fluttering in the top of the trash can near him.

Being here alone would frighten some people, but for Richard, moments like this are sheer bliss. He rests his computer and M-Audio digital keyboard on the platform and gives his full attention to the darkness. He hears a faint clanging like chimes played from far away. It is a melancholy sound yet melodic, like a faint and fragile planetary conversation that he strains to overhear. From his right, toward the enclosed stairwell leading down to the street, he hears other sounds of the night, groans and sighs, mystical sorrow sounds that accelerate his heart. Most people would not hear them. They are barely audible but so poignant that he is overwhelmed with compassion and aches in his bowels for the unknown source of such sadness. Bass notes emerge from the darkness like phantoms, rise and fall back, howls become whispers.

When Keisha phoned him at dinner time, they'd talked about a story each had heard on NPR, a newscast about two journalists languishing in Saudi Arabia's unbearable prisons because of their coverage of corruption and violence within the Saudi government. They had wondered together how such people found the courage to continue their work, to keep broadcasting their words despite the danger, to accept incarceration, even torture and death, because of their beliefs. *I must write a piece about this*, he thinks as he stands on the platform surrounded by a night lashed with silence and sound. He is fifty, and an American composer with a genius for sounds and their stories. In the moonless night the stories of those journalists he has been thinking about are unleashed into the weighty darkness. It is not the first time he has felt the presence of the world's sorrow when he waits for the train in the early morning alone and apart from those he loves.

His attention is drawn to the one lonely star that seems to be holding up the sky. Now he hears the sobs of children imprisoned for throwing stones in Gaza, children Keisha told him about when she returned from a factfinding trip there. Keisha the historian maintains that all sorrow is one, be it the imprisonment of Oscar Wilde, the execution of Mary Dyer, the lynching of Michael Donald, or the millions carried to enslavement in the holds of slave ships. It feels that way to him now as sorrow sounds take over the sky. He feels momentarily overcome, only vaguely aware of the percussive click-clicking of the trains rushing through the station and the whoosh from the nearby factory emitting its nasty gases while no one is around to see.

He reaches into his coat pocket for a notepad and into his breast pocket for an ink pen. The pad is decorated with the logo of a charity that enclosed it with address labels in a recent appeal for funds. He'd tossed the labels—they paid all their bills online now—but pocketed the notepad. Never know when you need something to write on.

He scribbles rapidly to get down what he hears so that he can commit it to his keyboard and computer for a composition that will combine the human voice with piano and computer-generated sounds. Some say that this is not real music, only techy noise that is characteristic of 21st Century composers. Richard disagrees. Any true student of classical music knows that Beethoven also used the latest technology in his compositions—he used the new foot pedal and the extended bass notes on the forte piano that set the air vibrating with his sounds.

He finishes his scribbling, pockets the notepad and pen, and pushes away his nocturnal malaise. He is grateful for the lone star that keeps him company in the darkness. He lets his thoughts ramble.

Keisha got home yesterday from Memphis, Tennessee, where she'd gone to investigate the recent death of thirty-seven-year-old Sterling Lapree Higgins, a Black man arrested and subdued by the police until he went limp and foamed at the mouth. He died within hours. Keisha's mom Ann had flown in to stay with the kids while Keisha went to investigate. She's writing a book on the history of police killings. By now Ann will be back in Cleveland, asleep beside her husband Don.

My little family will be long asleep, too, he is thinking. That's the downside to these gigs.

He breathes in the cold air and holds it in his lungs overlong before sighing it out. There is much he is grateful for.

His daughter Cora at fifteen is a teenager and so bright they find her sometimes frightening. Cora has black hair that she wears like a curly halo around her face. She is inclined to speak her mind and challenge authorities of all dimensions. Richard finds her fascinating but exhausting, much like he finds her mother, Keisha, fascinating and exhausting. Cora's intensity is evident in the way she looks at you, her eyes boring through any surface reserve you put up, pressing forward into your soul, or whatever is within. The girl has no patience with people who live on the surface. She positively demands you let her in to your private spaces. She can ferret out inconsistencies and discontents within minutes of meeting you. Gran Cora, for whom she is named, says she has The Gift. Keisha calls her "our Modern Mystic." She is simply unique—wonderful and a bit alarming.

Then there is son Caleb, still a child in many ways. He is affectionate, quiet, and, like his father, fascinated by how things work—things like electronics and pianos, computers and cell phones. He can sit for hours listening to podcasts of Science Friday. He loves to take things apart and reassemble them. He reads science books for fun, something his father cannot imagine. Caleb at fourteen stands on the threshold of the escalator that carries one to teendom. Keisha says he is like Richard— scatterbrained and nerdy. *Un*like his father, Caleb heads out on his bike several afternoons a week to meet up with his friends in the park to play baseball, something Richard never cared about. The boy comes home habitually half an hour late with his shoes dusty and his jeans grass stained, his baseball mitt dangling from the handlebar. Caleb might be scatterbrained about some things, but one thing he'd never forget—his mitt.

He's worried about Caleb, about the bullying at his school. Day after tomorrow he and Keisha will meet with Mr. Carluzzi for his last appointment of the day. They chose the time deliberately. There shouldn't be students around the building that late in the afternoon, students who might tell the bully that Caleb's parents came to the school.

His mind shifts to his wife of fifteen years. Keisha continues to intrigue him. Not that she isn't predictable. Often he knows before she opens her mouth what she will say. He can read the way she crinkles her forehead, the way her eyes go slightly unfocused in the seconds before she responds to something he has said. His anticipation of what she will say is usually correct. But she is still a mystery. She looks at the world from a historical distance and at the same time peers close up and personal, taking in intuitively things Richard totally misses about situations and people. How he loves her! For a moment he allows himself to hold her gently in his heart, to remember their rocky beginning and the deepening magic of their connection. *Best risk I've ever taken, deciding to marry her despite my fears.*

Richard is smiling when his train pulls up. He hears the slightest whisper of brakes and a swoosh as the doors click open. He picks up his keyboard and computer and steps into the train. The last thing he remembers is a sharp, crippling pain across his right shoulder before he slumps to the floor of the empty subway car and the jarring, discordant noise his computer and keyboard make colliding with the aluminum armrest.

Part II

Chapter 7

Keisha woke up early, feeling disquieted. Richard had not come to bed, or had he crashed on the sofa, too tired to climb the stairs? She pulled on jeans and a sweatshirt and made her way down the oak staircase to check on him. No, he wasn't downstairs.

She'd left her cell phone in their bedroom. She ran back up the stairs, retrieved it, and called Richard's cell. No answer. She moved back downstairs to the living room, where the children would not hear her. From there, she phoned the Evanston police.

"My husband, Dr. Richard Allen, didn't come home last night. He was playing a gig in Chicago, and I expected him at least by 2:30 a.m. This has never happened before. Can you help me?"

The woman who took her call put her on hold for too long. Then someone else picked up to say that they were dispatching officers to her home. They would be there soon.

She fought the fear that flowed through her body like ice blood. She sat on the sectional sofa staring at the carpet, trying to marshal her resources. It wasn't working. When two police cars pulled up to the curb carrying four officers, she moved soundlessly to the front door to admit them, determined not to awaken Caleb and Cora. Seeing them standing together on the front stoop, dread filled her stomach and her mouth tasted of bile. When she tried to speak, she couldn't get any words out.

She ushered them into the living room where, after passing her their business cards, they sat stiffly, upright and solemn.

"We've located a man who fits your husband's description," the Deputy Chief of Homicide for Evanston said. He was tall and portly, a grandfatherly man. His eyes meeting hers were kind and for a moment she felt reassured and safe. "Apparently, he was mugged on the L, on the last train to Evanston. Probably about 1:30 this morning. Few people ride the train that late. He was found by the cleaning crew about 5:00. Whoever did this took his wallet and his phone, so we didn't find any ID. CCTV cameras show this man boarding the train with a digital keyboard carrying case and a computer shoulder bag, and three young men exiting at the next stop carrying what appears to be the same keyboard case and a computer bag."

"That must be Richard! Because of the storm and no gas, he took the L. Can you take me to him? Please?" She didn't recognize her own voice. She wanted the space between her questions and his answer to continue forever. She was holding her breath, her arms crossed over her chest, holding herself together against the answer she feared.

She was right.

An officer in a different uniform—Chicago PD?—spoke up. "Ma'am, I am sorry to tell you that he didn't make it. By the time the cleaning crew boarded that car to clean it and found him, he'd lost too much blood. We're working together, the Chicago and the Evanston PDs, and we will find the men who did this, ma'am. I am certain of that."

The Evanston Chief's look at the Chicago cop said, *Don't promise what you know you can't deliver.*

A female cop moved toward Keisha and lowered herself onto the sofa beside her. She was a substantial woman with a caring face, and the way she occupied that space communicated that she might protect Keisha. "I know this is terrible news, ma'am, terrible." There was something rote in her voice, like she'd been here before, saying these same words.

Keisha exhaled audibly. She unfolded her arms and cradled her head in her hands, which had begun to tremble. *This cannot be happening. It cannot be real.* Through the thick silence in her head, she heard the Chief ask, "Is there anyone here to stay with you?"

"My children."

Cora and Caleb! She must get control of herself. She didn't want them to awaken to this horror.

The female cop passed her a packet of tissues. Keisha wondered *Do all police officers carry packets of tissues?*

"Can you call a friend or older family member to come, ma'am? You should not be alone right now."

Keisha stood and nodded, grateful to be told what to do. She stumbled to the house phone and pushed autodial for her parents.

Mom answered cheerily. "Just a minute. Putting you on speaker, honey." Mom loved it when her only child called, regardless of the time.

"Mom, he didn't come back last night. The police are here. Richard was mugged. He was…*murdered*. Can you and Dad come? *Now?*" She looked at the man with the kind eyes for affirmation. He and the female officer on the sofa were nodding approval.

She was whispering, and Mom couldn't hear her, asked her to repeat what she'd said. She carried the phone to the living room so the sound would not carry up the stairs to the children and spoke again. She heard her mother's voice crack and then Dad's voice as he took the phone from Mom.

She heard her dad say, "Your Mom is gathering some things together. I'll call Lyft as soon as we hang up and get us a ride to the airport. We'll let you know what flight we're on. Hang in, Keisha. We will be there as soon as possible." He sounded very far away. As he clicked off Keisha thought she heard a low-pitched moan that must have come from Dad.

The Chief motioned for her to sit down. She moved to the sofa and lowered her body, still holding the phone, which had begun to talk: "If you'd like to make a call, please hang up now and dial again."

Another cop spoke. "Did your husband call you before he boarded the train?"

She mumbled "No."

"Were you home all night?"

"Yes."

"We're going to need you to come down to the station to identify your husband, ma'am, after one of your friends or family arrives to stay with you."

"My parents are coming, but they live in Cleveland, Ohio, so it will take them time to get here."

The officers exchanged glances. The Chief motioned to the other female cop, who stepped forward. "Officer Martinez will stay with you until they arrive. We'll be holding your husband's personal possessions as evidence while we investigate."

The Chief spoke again. "We'll need to interview you later in the day." Then they all stood, and Officer Martinez took a seat in a chair across from Keisha.

Keisha set their cards on the table beside the sofa and walked them to the front door. "Someone from the Evanston patrol will call you later today, ma'am. They will be coordinating the case. We are so sorry for your loss." In no more than ten minutes they had walked into her normal life and shattered it.

She sat in her usual place on the sectional sofa, unable to think or move. Officer Martinez brought her a glass of water and asked if she wanted anything else. She didn't. The officer stayed busy on her phone.

Both women were still seated across from each other when the doorbell rang two hours later. It was Uncle Edward, who lived in Chicago. Mom must have phoned him and caught him before he left for church. It was still Sunday morning, and the kids were still asleep. She collapsed into his arms, her face against his chest to muffle her sobs. They sat together on the sofa in silence while Officer Martinez let herself out.

Chapter 8

Don Johnson, technically Keisha's stepdad, had grown into himself after Ann and three-year-old Keisha had entered his life. He had learned from them that there were safe people in the world with whom he could be happy.

Three decades later, all in one year, Keisha had fallen in love with Richard, and Don had located the father he had not seen since his twelfth birthday. His family expanded to include his father's wife, Cora, and her son, Edward, who became the one person other than Ann with whom Don could talk freely about his life.

Thanksgiving, 2003, was the day Richard proposed to Keisha. That afternoon while the women cooked, the men went for a walk. Richard had talked with Don and Edward about his being adopted. He told them that he had just learned who the woman was who gave birth to him.

Listening to him, hearing her name, Don had felt suddenly breathless. His head ached and he felt panicky. *He knew the woman Richard was talking about*, Richard's biological mother. She was the woman he had loved one summer when he was home from college.

Not until decades after that summer had Don learned that she had had a baby, his son, and, unable to provide for her baby, had placed him for adoption. Richard was that baby. *Richard was his child.*

Richard was still talking. He was telling Don and Edward that he was about to propose to Keisha, apologizing for taking so long to reach this decision, saying he now was certain that he wanted to spend the rest of his life with her. Don's biological son would marry his stepdaughter!

There was no genetic reason for them not to marry, but Don had flooded with fear that it would weird them out, cause Richard to change his mind, make him run from such an unusual marriage. If Richard ran, Keisha would have to raise the child she was carrying on her own. If Don told them that he was Richard's biological father, Keisha, the daughter he had raised and cherished, could lose her chance to share her life with the man she loved.

In that moment of panic Don had decided to keep secret his biological relationship to Richard… In retrospect it seemed to have been the right choice. Keisha and Richard had been happily married for more than fifteen years. And Don had loved Richard like a son-in-law and, secretly, like a son. All along he had intended to one day tell Richard and Keisha, and his wife Ann, the truth. But the right moment had never arrived. Now it was too late.

He sat alone in United's last available seat from Cleveland to Chicago on this early April morning, surrounded by strangers. The truth felt like a weight he could not possibly lift. Richard was dead. Murdered. Gone. There would be no more time to listen as Richard talked about his family, his love for them, his delight in the new pieces he was composing. No more time to marvel at the sounds Richard conjured in his head. Never again would he sit in the audience, listening as Richard conducted, feeling deep pride in this man, his secret son.

Just before the plane to Chicago took off, he felt his phone vibrating. He'd forgotten to put it on airplane mode. It was a text from Edward. Short and simple. "You will get through this. See you soon."

His eyelids felt gritty, and his heart literally hurt. Ann sat three rows behind him, in a middle seat, too far away to reach for her hand, too far away for her to steady him, or for him to steady her. Neither of them had cried. There was no time for tears. They had to get to Keisha and the children. *I must focus on my responsibility for my remaining family. For Richard's sake, for Keisha, for the grandchildren, for Ann.*

When the Lyft deposited them in front of Richard and Keisha's home, Ann took his hand. Edward stood in the open doorway, supporting Keisha. Her face was distorted by dread.

Chapter 9

To the mourners gathered at the cemetery that gray April morning, Keisha looked like a solitary pine tree, tall and strong against the wind that withered everything in its path. She wanted desperately to be that tree, to be her fierce self, able to withstand anything. She was a woman who could move mountains, Richard had said of her, only partially joking. Wasn't that how she had met life, head-on with brutal honesty?

She could feel her bones softening, becoming gelatinous, incapable of holding her upright. She forced her thoughts to latch onto what she was experiencing like a baby to its mother's tit. This was something entirely new. She felt more ancient than a petrified forest. She took up residence inside her head, her default response to pain. She became Keisha the observer, Keisha the curious, monitoring her own responses, detached from what was happening in front of her on this expanse of farmland dotted with stone markers, where her dad Don had hurriedly purchased a burial plot.

She noted that the skin over her face was taut like the head of a drum. That tears froze vertical bars across its unfamiliar surface. She noted the cold of early spring penetrating her torso. She should have worn long underwear today as armor. Her hands and feet were icy. It was difficult to curl and uncurl her fingers. She forced them to clench, then used one hand to force the other hand to unclench. It was possible.

She willed her right leg to lift its foot from the frozen, mud-ridged grass. Using that will power, she reset that foot and did the same with the left leg and foot. The feet needed to be carefully placed to keep her jello body from collapsing. She would do this—for Richard and for the children. She must continue as Keisha Who Overcomes. She focused on the details—where to sit and when to stand.

The crowd moved closer together in the cold, slow rain. On either side she felt someone reach for her, felt spots of distant warmth where their hands curled around her forearm, touched her back, rested on her shoulder. They distracted her. She glanced left and right, startled to see her children beside her, their faces stricken and barely recognizable.

At some point, after what seemed like a long time filled with words she could not comprehend, the children moved forward, gently bringing her with them. Daughter Cora picked up a shovel and folded her mother's hands around the handle, helping her lift a small spade-full of dirt and turn its face downward so that the dirt rained into the hole and landed with a spattering of hollow sounds on the casket, a brush on the drumhead, Richard would call it. Uncle Edward, wearing a black robe, said, "This is loneliest sound we will ever hear." Richard the composer, a connoisseur of sounds, might have argued with him.

Then Cora passed her mother to Caleb so she could take the shovel and repeat what Keisha had done with it. Then it was Caleb's turn. Then Don and Ann, Richard's sister, her husband and children, other family members.

Somewhere in the recesses of her researcher's mind, Keisha found this ceremony oddly interesting. She observed the rest of the huddled people moving forward, each dropping a shovel-full of dirt into the hole. Richard's sister was guiding their mother to the graveside, patting her back and hushing her when she asked in a confused voice what they were doing. Richard's mom didn't understand what had happened. Of course not. Perhaps his sister was right that they should have left her back in the memory unit. Keisha reached out and touched his mom's arm, smiling at her. "I don't understand what is happening either," she said.

When everyone had filed past the grave, some tossing flowers along with their shovel of dirt, the mourners formed two rows, lining the path across the prairie to the road that led out of the cemetery, which was cluttered with cars. They walked in the middle, between the rows of grieving friends and family, colleagues, and students. Keisha, with Caleb and Cora on either side of her, forced her knees to bend, her feet to lift, her knees to bend again as she resettled each foot forward. It required enormous concentration. Again and again, until they reached the yawning mouth of a black limousine and entered its dark cave. On its leather seats she gave her bones permission to dissolve. As they did, she promptly fell asleep. She could feel the children's eyes on her but could not rouse herself. Not until they reached the church hall Uncle Edward had arranged for. There, church ladies served them sandwiches and coffee. People came up to take her hand and mumble things she couldn't quite make out.

The time since the morning when the police arrived at her home erased itself from her memory. It must have been full of phone calls, conversations with lawyers, work colleagues, extended family, and people bearing colorful plastic containers of food. She would not remember.

The one thing that she did remember was hearing Caleb say to his sister, "Mom seems to be doing amazingly. But we'd expect that." She was surprised to hear Cora reply, "I don't think so. Mom is good at being super competent on the outside, but Dad once told me she's soft as jelly inside."

Mostly, "Mom" drifted from room to room, chair to chair, task to task. Her ability to focus had run out.

One morning several days later, Cora knocked on her mother's bedroom door and called her to get dressed. They had a meeting at the lawyer's office for the reading of the will. Keisha did not shower. She had not had the energy lately. She struggled into jeans and a sweater, pulled on boots, and attempted to run a pick through her curls. She drank the coffee her daughter brought to her, ate a piece of toast, and brushed her teeth. Then, with Uncle Edward driving Richard's car, they drove downtown.

The lawyer's outer office was all shiny dark wood and armchairs with plump leather seats. The meeting room was more practically furnished--captain chairs ringing an oblong table and a big screen on which the pages of Richard's will were projected. There were no surprises. They had come here together twice before to work out their affairs "in case," exercising prudential responsibility.

At the end of the meeting their lawyer and friend said he had one more thing for Keisha. He brought out a small, tattered, ring-sized jewelry box tied with an orange bow and handed it to her with a note in Richard's handwriting.

My dear Keisha,

Do you recognize this box? It's the one that held your engagement ring all those years ago.

There is no ring in it now, just years of living together and loving each other.

If you are opening this, I will have been the first to "move on."
I know this will be a very hard time, but I know you, and I know
you will find your way.
My life with you made me a better person, inspired my music,
and blessed me. You will always carry my love with you.
No more words except, I love you forever.
Richard

"He brought this to me a month ago," the lawyer told them.

"Do you think Dad had a premonition?" Caleb asked.

The lawyer moved his head noncommittally. Then they went home.

She would not remember the weeks that followed.

Mom and Dad remained, sleeping in the guestroom. Sometimes Keisha wept, overhearing the intimacy of their muted, unintelligible conversations seeping through the wall. Sometimes she was angry that they had each other to talk to while she had no one.

Sometimes she was glad for their presence, for Mom preparing meals for Cora and Caleb, and Dad shopping for food and taking out the trash. Normally she would feel gratitude for them checking on the kids. Now her gratitude—like every feeling other than grief—was stillborn.

She ate little. She barely remembered the children. She remembered only her pain as the days ran together. She closeted herself in their room where she talked to Richard in her head and sometimes out loud. She refused Mom's offer to wash her clothes, do her laundry. She would not surrender the sheets and towels that carried his scent.

She forced herself to shower and then put on Richard's favorite shirt again and curled her body on his side of the bed, worn out with grief, her thoughts jumbled and unreliable.

Frequently her mind inventoried how she might end her misery. Pills? Pills and alcohol? Not a gun. She and Richard were pacifists and had written their state legislators in support of gun laws. Richard's voice in her head reminded her that she could not do anything violent, couldn't do that to the kids, to Mom and Dad, to his mom and sister.

Most days she stayed upstairs with her door locked against intrusion.

Dad checked on her three times a day, bringing the paperwork that she needed to fill out and send to the various accounts along with copies of Richard's death certificate. He seemed to sense how long she could focus on the work he set before her. He seemed to understand her hibernation. Of course, he would.

She hurt physically, her stomach, her head, her heart. Yes, her heart.

Richard came and went. She could sometimes feel his arms around her, lying beside her curled and aching body. They lay together like two spoons in that special intimacy they had when she was full blown pregnant. She held her breath and let herself relax into the feel of him, his warmth, the sweet scent of his skin. But when she turned and reached for him, he was not there.

One of those blurred days when she lay in bed all day looking for her erased life, her mom knocked softly on her door. Ann sat on the edge of the bed watching Keisha, who lay in the fetal position. After a time, she stroked Keisha's shoulder rhythmically.

"Keisha, honey, the children need you. They are grieving, too, and they need to know you won't abandon them."

Keisha opened her eyes with reluctance. She was looking through a dark tunnel seeking a spot of light, any light. Everything felt confusing. She mumbled something but her mom could not understand.

"Honey, I didn't hear you."

"I can't now, Mom. I just can't."

"Can they come in and have a cuddle with you? We are talking with them and reassuring them, but I think just one cuddle would help keep them going."

Keisha did not reply. She didn't turn toward her mom. She didn't notice when Ann stood and left the room.

A while later Ann returned with Cora and Caleb. Their faces were stark as they viewed their mom lying on Dad's side of the bed, her face to the wall. Cora stepped closer. "Mama, we're here. We can help you." Then her voice broke and she threw herself on the bed, her arms reaching out to hold her mom. Caleb hung back.

Ann spoke to Keisha in her mother voice. "Keisha, you can do this. We all know you. Caleb, get up there next to your mom. She needs you and you need her. I'm going downstairs to finish making dinner."

Caleb followed his grandma's instruction, perching on the opposite side of the bed, his eyes appealing to his sister to help him know what to do.

Keisha stirred and rolled onto her back. Her eyes scanned the faces of her children. Her arms emerged from the covers to receive theirs and they cuddled, listless and still against her body. There was no sound but weeping.

An hour later Ann climbed the stairs and opened the bedroom door, trying to make no noise. She saw the three survivors huddled together, asleep.

It was morning when Keisha awoke feeling the warmth of her children's bodies and imagining Richard's arms around the three of them, like their Sunday morning ritual since the kids were toddlers—all four of them piled together on the bed, warm and safe.

She felt Caleb stirring and heard his raspy puberty voice. "Mom, I could feel Dad here with us. Is that crazy?"

"No, Caleb. I felt it too. Even though I don't understand it. I think if there is any way possible for him to be with us, he will be. He is. Maybe we just have to let ourselves feel his presence, even when our minds say it can't be."

Cora was still asleep, her gentle breathing lifting the edge of the sheet and letting it drop.

"Mom, would you fix us pancakes like before?" Caleb's eyes bored into her.

She thought about it, debated, a huge part of her unwilling to leave the cocoon of this bed, this room. "I think I can do that," she whispered to Caleb. "But we don't want Cora to wake up alone." Caleb grinned conspiratorially. He leaned over his sister and blew gently on her eyelids until her eyelashes fluttered and her tongue licked the small puddle of saliva at the corner of her mouth. Keisha smiled. Cora always drooled when she slept. She and Richard had found it endearing.

"Mama?" Cora opened her eyes and anxiously scanned the room alighting on her mother's face. Mama looked tired with dark circles under her eyes, but she was smiling. It seemed a halfhearted smile to Cora, but at this point she'd be satisfied with anything other than that vacant, haunted look. It would suffice for now.

Chapter 10

Richard had so loved waking to birdsong—the bedroom window open and sun motes dancing in the air as a dozen birds of all colors and sizes chatted at the feeder below their room. Others splashed in the birdbath, seeing who could throw sparkling drops the farthest. He had found such spring mornings magical and inspiring. Often he would climb out of bed quietly to take his seat at the window and write the melodies in his head that swooped and careened as carefree as the birds.

He watched his wife who lay beside him, turned on her side, turned away from the light, her body compressed into a fetal ball. He wanted so to drape his arm across her shoulder, to nuzzle beneath her curls until his lips found the slender column of her neck. Since the first time he had lain with her, he had loved the vulnerability of her neck, hidden by the thick mass of her amazing hair that she wore like a warrior princess. Ah, the abundance of her. So much everything. Brilliant and feisty, witty with a confidence that sometimes bordered on arrogance, stunning, and somewhat aloof. But underneath the self-reliant way she often presented herself, a gentleness and caring and vulnerability that totally disarmed him.

He loved her without reservation. It had taken him nearly a year to trust that she would be his safe place, that she would never leave him. And now, after more than fifteen years of marriage, he had left her. Not by choice, no, never by choice. Watching her now curled into her misery, a wave of compassion swamped him. It was all he could do not to wrap her in his arms and carry her with him away from her Pit of Despair.

His peripheral vision noticed the box with the faded orange ribbon on the bedside table and beside it the photo of Cora and Caleb. She'd taken it on one of their trips to see her parents, Don and Ann. The kids were clowning around in the back yard, posing like rock stars with imaginary guitars and wide grins. Keisha had it enlarged and framed. "It captures their happiness," she'd said.

He could not touch her, could not take her with him. Cora and Caleb needed her more than ever, and she needed them. He could only watch and love.

Chapter 11

It was Keisha's first day back on campus after her compassionate leave. As she fumbled for the key to her office, she noticed one of her favorite grad students sitting stiffly on a chair next to her door, waiting to speak with her. Ronald stood as she approached, tall and lean, respectful and uncomfortable, *young.*

She ushered him into her office. "Do you want a bottle of water?" she asked him. It was awkward.

Her office felt oddly familiar. For seventeen years she'd sat at that same desk, facing the door. She inhabited this world of books, surrounded by the stories of the men, and especially women, whose lives inspired her, who she talked with inside her head, the people she relied on. Or used to.

Now nothing felt familiar. She glanced at her books, but her historical friends inside them seemed to have deserted her. Or she hadn't the energy to summon them. She followed Ronald's eyes to a cup of coffee overgrown with mold that sat next to her computer.

The young man was clearly uncomfortable. He opened his briefcase— the loud snap of its locks startling in the cavernous silence of this space. He pulled out some papers. *Who carried a briefcase these days?* He cleared his throat and jumped into the void.

"Dr Johnson, as you know, for my dissertation I have been researching the development of Black capitalism in the 1970s, and I've discovered that Philadelphia was the center of a movement to develop Black entrepreneurs." He was formal and nerdy, but his excitement was palpable. She wanted to tell him that her husband, the love of her life, had been murdered four weeks ago and, frankly, she didn't give a damn what he had discovered.

Of course, she wouldn't say that.

Ronald passed her an 8 x 10 black and white photograph of a large shopping center, along with a copy of a *Philadelphia Inquirer* story on the collaboration between a downtown Black church and the Wharton

School of Business at the University of Pennsylvania. The young man was trembling with excitement.

"That's Progress Plaza. It was training hundreds of young people to start and manage businesses *in the Seventies!* Most of the shops in this shopping center were Black-owned." He raised his head from the papers on his lap and grinned. He didn't look so nerdy when he smiled, Keisha observed.

"Dr. Johnson, my auntie and uncle live in Philadelphia. They've offered to let me stay with them during the summer so I can do my research on site."

Ronald's delight in what he was learning moved her. "I found stories in the press that indicate the Nixon Administration supported the programs for Black economic development. The Philadelphia program came out of a church, assisted by the business school. Did I say it was Zion Baptist Church? My grandfather is a Baptist preacher. So is my uncle. The one in Philadelphia. I can stay with him and run what I learn through his network of pastors. I imagine I'll find that other Black churches ran similar programs in other parts of the U.S. in the Seventies and Eighties."

Keisha smiled, but not too broadly. She said she was happy his research was proceeding so well. She did want to encourage him, but she did not have the energy right now for his young excitement. He reminded her of herself a lifetime ago.

She commended him for his plan and then stood to indicate their meeting was over. He could leave now.

Ronald scrutinized her. "Dr. Johnson, you don't think this is a big find, do you?" His eyes stayed on her while she sagged back into her desk chair and took a deep breath. *How much do you confide in your students? They carry the worries and expectations of their families. They don't need the added weight of yours.*

"I *am* excited about what you're finding." She pulled herself back into the confines of this small office, into the world of research and pursuing curiosity. Her responsibility was to encourage the future. What would Ida B. do, she asked herself. *Encourage him.*

"Ronald, your research trip sounds excellent. It's great you have family there who can help you network. I know a professor who has a new book on Black capitalism. Perhaps you'd like to interview him? I met him at a conference before I came to Northwestern. I can give you his email. It should still be good. Dr. Robert Weems, Jr. I could send him an email introducing you to him and you could follow up and find a time to interview him?"

"That would be sweet. I found contact information for Prosperity Plaza, the shopping center. Thought I'd email some of the merchants. Maybe some of them are still owned by the same families, although fifty years is a long time. I guess that's a long shot."

"I like the way you approach research," she replied. She noticed he was beaming. It took so little to make a young person's day. She and Richard had agreed that was why they loved teaching.

"Have you identified the questions you need to answer? Do you know what you need to know?"

"Yes. I want to know if the programs like the shopping center remained successful over all these years and if not, why not? What records did they keep on the people they trained? Can I access them? Can I find some of their graduates and interview them?" He was on a roll, the ideas tumbling from him.

"Also, when Nixon ran for re-election in 1972, did he continue to support Black economic empowerment? I've learned that he adopted his Southern Strategy in 1972, appealing to white Southerners by using racially coded messages to tell them he was protecting their interests. I remember you lectured on that topic in March right before…"

It was the first reference either of them had made to Richard's death. The young man couldn't look at her after stumbling so awkwardly into her loss. The whole campus had been abuzz with it. But talking with other students about Dr. Allen's murder was one thing. Talking with his bereaved wife was something else entirely.

Ronald gathered up his papers, the photo, and the *Inquirer* article. He backed toward the door. "I'm so sorry." His voice was so quiet she almost didn't hear him. "Can I come see you in two weeks to report on what more I've found?" She could feel his discomfort.

He's only six or seven years older than Caleb, she thought. *He probably hasn't tasted grief yet, doesn't know the protocols. Are there protocols?*

Looking at her from the doorway, Ronald's facial expression changed. His brown eyes softened behind his thick glasses, and he appeared older than his early twenties. Perhaps she had misjudged him. Perhaps he *was* acquainted with grief.

She was still seated as he reached behind him, not taking his eyes off her, and found the doorknob. "You know we all are rooting for you and your children. We respect you so much and we don't want you to be hurting," his voice was low, intense. Then he left her office.

Ronald had said what she needed to hear. People cared about her. She was not alone. Even though she felt alone. It helped her get through the morning.

Chapter 12

Ronald had been raised by his grandmother, his mother's mother, along with his younger sister. He was in middle school when he and his sister came to live with their grandma in her red brick duplex that looked identical to all the other red brick duplexes in their south Chicago neighborhood. Identical except for Grandma's porch boxes. Those porch boxes were her delight, overflowing with pansies in the early spring, geraniums for most of the summer, and mums in the fall. Grandma watered and fertilized them, and they paid her back with colorful abundance.

When he first moved in, those porch boxes had showed him which house was his new home. He'd walk from school looking for their splash of color. But in his second week living with Grandma, after walking several blocks he saw no geraniums, and his anxiety grew until he began hyperventilating. He kept walking, scanning the sameness of the street. He feared running into the wannabe gang members who hung out on the block behind Grandma's and sometimes strutted the street, attempting to look threatening.

After walking several more blocks, he saw Grandma sitting on the porch, her hands in dirt-stained green garden gloves and her face scowling. As he moved toward her, he noticed four small pots of red geraniums lined up next to her rocking chair.

Being passed from relative to relative in his early childhood, he had learned the unspoken rules of each household that took him in. He practiced close observation of those on whom his life depended, alert to picking up clues that showed what counted with whomever he was living with.

That day Ronald observed that Grandma's mood darkened when her porch boxes held only a few scrawny weeds. "My porch boxes are 'in transition,'" she sighed as he climbed the steps to her porch with its flowerless boxes. "Like us, they must have time to catch their breath before they put out glorious blooms." Her face showed she didn't like these transition times, didn't like the absence of color that made her home appear just like the others on the street.

Grandma valued standing out, not for show but for excellence. She raised him to work harder than other people. "You have to be better in order to be taken seriously," she told him, a message she repeated several times a week. He didn't think about what her own growing up years had been like, or why working hard and rising above others was so important to her. Grandma was Grandma. He assumed she'd always looked the same—soft, mahogany brown skin, dyed black hair straightened and curled under, clothes tidy, colors matching, face fluctuating from scrutiny to satisfaction.

Half of his growing up years he'd spent trying to live up to Grandma's expectations. When he graduated high school with a 3.8 grade point average and was granted a scholarship to Northwestern, he knew he had done it. As he walked across the stage at graduation and they announced his scholarship, her face had radiated "satisfied." He attributed it all to her, the woman who wouldn't let him fail. Not just by setting high expectations, but by loving him quietly, without being demonstrative. Excellently.

Just before the end of the spring semester Ronald sat on Grandma's porch reading. He'd learned how to block out the sounds of the neighborhood, the chatter of children playing in the vacant lot across the street where another row house had burned down several years ago, the loud music blasting from the house next door, the squish and screech of cars braking to a stop. He'd learned how to focus, how to live in a zone, how to transform noise from a distraction to an indistinct, barely audible buzz that did not interfere with his concentration. Why was it called "white noise?"

He held a book he'd checked out from the university library. It was worn, but he held it with reverence and read intently.

"Looks like you've found a fine book," Grandma said as she pushed open the screen door and stepped on the porch. She often found quality in old things. She lowered herself into the porch rocker, pulling her cardigan around her. "What are you learning?" The question was her standard way of engaging him in conversation, drawing him out, and learning from her smart grandson.

"*Build Brother Build,* Reverend Leon Sullivan's book about his work in Philadelphia building Black businesses and training Black people for professional jobs. It's really interesting. He had his church members build an investment fund by pledging ten dollars a month for thirty-six months and used the money raised to purchase land to build the first Black-owned shopping center in the U.S. The rest of the funds he used to train young people for skilled jobs and business start-ups."

Grandma's face showed interest. Led by her questions, he went into more detail. She remembered Reverend Sullivan, and thought she had a glossy copy of *Ebony* that featured his work in Philly, with a photo of him on the cover. Later they'd look for it in the trunk in her bedroom.

Ronald had not been separated from Grandma since he had moved in with her at age eleven. Next month that would change when he moved to Philadelphia for a couple of months to do research for his thesis. This would be a major change for Grandma and Ronald, something he avoided thinking about. She had taken him in and raised him for over a decade, provided for him, encouraged him. She said his time in Philadelphia would do him good, show him how capable he was of living on his own in a new city, show him what she already knew—that he was ready to fly solo successfully without her nearby.

Maybe so, but her kind of support was scarce in his life. For the moment he didn't want to be anywhere but here on her porch while she planted geraniums and they talked. He let himself enjoy the late afternoon warmth that settled over the porch. It nourished Grandma, Ronald, and the geraniums that fluttered when an occasional breeze found them.

Chapter 13

Caleb opens his eyes to birdsong floating into his room on shafts of slanted sunshine. The light glitters and flutters in the late spring air as it walks across his bed. Its brightness surprises him, and he closes his eyes to keep it from burning him awake.

He doesn't want to wake up. He needs to finish his dream, to find out how it ends. Will his father see him sitting beneath the giant old oak tree? Will his father walk across the space that separates them, his arms outstretched, and find him?

He squeezes his eyelids closed, trying to get back to this crucial moment in his fourteen-year-old dreamlife, to answer the question that has circled his brain for the past two months.

The dream only partly returns: Dad is nowhere in sight. Caleb is alone beneath the oak tree, and it has started to rain. He hears the pings of raindrops against the metal gutters. He hears the whoosh of wind across the suddenly darkening sky. The shafts of sunlight are gone, like his dream, like Dad. Now all he sees is the gloomy grayness of a stormy May morning. His stomach is growling. His head hurts. He is alone, truly and completely alone.

Too many mornings he awakens with that same dream and that same loneliness, uncertain whether Dad will ever find him.

Dad gone. Again and again. Just gone. He was supposed to go to Caleb's school the following Monday to meet with the assistant principal, to talk with him about Ryan, the bully. But Dad left Saturday night, suddenly. Caleb never got to see his body.

What did Dad look like dead? Was his face all purple and blue from being beaten by some group of wannabe gang members and left to die in the empty elevated train in the middle of the night? Caleb had insisted Mom tell him. She had not said much, only that he looked like a shell of himself, that Dad was no longer residing in that shell. "Like a cicada that leaves its shell house behind." Where did she come up with this crap?

"Caleb, want some eggs and bacon?" Mom's voice comes through the heavy door to his room that he keeps closed and off limits.

"OK." He knows he needs to get up and shake off his funk. Dad taught him that word. "It's a great word when you feel so low you could be halfway to China. It's also a fun word to say. Say it with me: Funk, funk, funk." Dad had made weird poses that he changed with each repeat. They'd fallen out laughing.

Caleb's feelings keep switching—from angry to sad to depressed and back to angry. He feels like electric current is running through him when the anger surges. It is so unfair. If he had a dad like Bruce's, who spent most of his time drunk and who got mean and hit them, it might be fair, even *good*, for Dad to die. Or if Dad died from cancer like Joe's uncle, he might be ready to see him go to end his pain. But to be murdered? To simply *disappear?* One minute strong and healthy and joking around, the next, gone?

He plays on his phone for a while, then reads some websites. His mind returns to the question, *WHERE IS DAD AND WHY DID HE LEAVE US?* He picks up a book Granddad had given him. He throws it hard at the wall across from his bed. The wallboard crumples where the book hits it. It looks like an old person's mouth, all wrinkled with lines radiating out, the way little kids draw sunshine.

What happens now? The last six weeks have dragged on. He thought they would never end. And that afternoon when he and Dad sat in Dad's office talking about how to handle bullies—the day before Dad died— seems a hundred years ago.

He recognizes his sister's footsteps coming down the hall. There is only one year between them, but you'd think she was five years older by how she acts. She stops at his door and yells, "Bruce is on the landline for you. *Do you hear me?*" Everyone thinks she is "such a good girl." They don't know her up close. She can be so irritating. Like now.

"Come get the phone, Caleb... OK, I put it on the floor outside your door. Don't trip on it, and *talk to Bruce!*" Her footsteps make the wooden floor squeak as she hurries back to her room.

Caleb pulls on his jeans and T-shirt. He makes his bed and opens his door. No one is in sight. He picks up the receiver, but Bruce is no longer waiting. He takes the stairs in a great rush, challenging himself not to trip, and enters the kitchen where Mom is spooning eggs and bacon and English muffins onto a plate for him.

"Thanks, Mom. I gotta call Bruce." He doesn't make eye contact.

He and his plate go to the back yard where he sits on a step, drawing his knees level with his chin, and begins shoveling in food. Then he clicks on Bruce's number.

"Hey, dude, can you meet me in a half-hour? I got something for you." Bruce's voice sounds different. "I'll come by your house, OK?"

"OK."

When Bruce arrives, he has two guys with him who Caleb doesn't know. Caleb feels disappointed that it's not just him and Bruce. They are wearing similar shiny blue jackets and L.A. Dodgers baseball caps.

"Let's walk to the park." Bruce starts walking without waiting for Caleb's answer. He reaches into his pants pocket once they turn into the park. He looks around, like he's watching for someone. Then he pulls out a plastic bag. It holds a bunch of pills about the size of aspirin but all different colors, bright colors, like Smartie candies. The other two guys grin at each other. Caleb thinks they look stupid.

"OK, happy pills for each of us. Take one." Bruce passes the bag around and everyone takes a pill. Except Caleb. "Don't be a jagoff! They're happy pills. Fuck, man, X won't hurt you. Or are you wanting something else?" Bruce reaches into his other pants pocket and brings out another plastic bag with two hand-rolled cigarettes. "Just to show you what a good friend I am, I'll share one of my joints with you." He passes the bag to Caleb.

Caleb feels uncomfortable. He wants to get out of there, to walk away from Bruce and go home. He wants his phone to ring. It doesn't.

Bruce dangles the bag with the cigarettes under his nose, waiting. He is smiling, confident that no fourteen-year-old would turn down an opportunity like this. The weed smell drifts up from the mouth of the bag.

Caleb still doesn't move. His brain is racing through his options.

"Where'd you get the Molly?" one of the guys Caleb doesn't know asks Bruce.

Bruce shakes his head. "For me to know, man." Bruce ties the bag of pills with a twister and puts it back in his pocket. He is still holding the weed.

"I've read they lace that stuff with really dangerous shit, man, like ground glass and other stuff." Caleb is trying to sound authoritative.

Bruce knows he likes to know how to make things. He's hoping to distract Bruce so he'll stop pushing him.

It seems to work. For now, anyway.

"Don't waste your good stuff on this nerd," says the other guy, the one who hasn't spoken.

Caleb can tell they want to move on.

"Wanna shoot some hoops?" Caleb suggests, then feels utterly stupid. No one has brought a basketball. This idea is out of nowhere. Out of his discomfort. He's sure they can tell he's out of their league.

Bruce turns to the other guys. "We need to give him a break. His father died and he's pretty messed up." Bruce and the other two start walking together, a threesome, toward the other end of the park, leaving Caleb behind. Caleb walks in the opposite direction, toward his lonely house where his lonely mom is probably sipping red wine and crying as she grades papers.

Bruce is right. He is messed up. They all are.

Chapter 14

The Monday after graduation, Keisha spent all day in her office entering grades in the computer for underclassmen. She was exhausted. At the end of the day she sat in her car watching the sky fill with orange and pink. She should be home preparing supper but resisted starting her car. Did she have the courage—or the energy?—to face her life?

She had phoned the police from her office to ask what progress they had made on finding Richard's killers. They had passed her off to someone skilled at pacifying victims' families who gave her the same response she received every week when she called. "Dr. Johnson, we have nothing to go on. Chicago PD has only murky gray footage of three young men exiting at the University of Chicago station in a snowstorm, two-and-a-half hours before your husband was found, long gone by the time a patrol car pulled up to the L station. And there were no witnesses." She felt enraged. What were the police doing? Were they even trying to find who killed him? Who destroyed her family?

Graduation had been an ordeal. A substitute conducted the choir as they sang the university anthem. As though someone else could step in and replace Richard and life would continue as usual. She hated the young man conducting. Yes, hated him for not being Richard.

Lately, in addition to anger, she'd felt fear growing inside her. Like a malevolent plant sending out runners to her arms and legs and, especially, to her head. What was she afraid of? That she'd run away, not be up to moving on with her life? That she'd fail her children? The rest of her family?

The fear plant had been there a long time, nourished by assorted disappointments and betrayals. When it had hold of her, it distorted her behavior.

She remembered feeling its presence acutely her junior year in college. She had been sitting in the university library's special collections room, researching the Reagan Administration's relationship to African

Americans. She had found an article from 1985 about the Philadelphia police burning down several city blocks. They killed eleven members of MOVE, what the paper called a revolutionary African nationalist group. The article mentioned that another man died that day, a Reggie Lewis. A witness reported seeing Lewis on the street, arguing with the police, trying to stop their attack on the MOVE house. Reggie Lewis was the name of her biological father. The coincidence grabbed her attention.

The obituary in *The Philadelphia Inquirer* was sketchy. This Reggie Lewis had attended graduate school, but had dropped out to be the administrator of a shopping center. What had caught her attention was a reference to his civil rights activities—working with Dr. King in Chicago and registering voters in Mississippi. Keisha's mom Ann had met Keisha's biological father in Mississippi. They'd been volunteers with Freedom Summer, two of the thousand young people who went South to register voters and teach literacy.

Mom had told her only that her birth father was a civil rights activist working in Philadelphia when he died. Nothing more. Could this Reggie Lewis be her Reggie Lewis? If so, why would Mom, the person who meant the most to her, not tell her more than his name and the fact that he had died? Why hadn't she told Keisha *how* he had died? Prior to that moment in the library, Keisha had never acknowledged, even to herself, her anger at Mom for preventing her from knowing him. This withholding of important information about her father felt like betrayal. Anger and fear mixed. It was scary. If she couldn't trust her mom to be truthful with her, who could she trust?

Keisha had driven home from the university that afternoon and confronted Mom, who was standing in the kitchen making tea. All these years later Keisha could see Ann standing beside the kitchen sink holding a tea bag and turning toward Keisha, looking stricken, caught, and uncomfortable, as she confirmed that Reggie Lewis, who died in Philadelphia on May 13, 1985, shot by police, was Keisha's biological father.

"How could you do this to me? How could you keep me from knowing my father? How could you lie…"

"I didn't lie. I just told you he was a major leader in the Movement. And he was. I didn't want you to be hurt or disappointed."

"Why would I be hurt or disappointed?"

"Because he told me that his family were followers of Marcus Garvey, even decades after Garvey died. I knew they never would have accepted his having a child with a white woman. That's why I never told him about you."

"Mom, you are white! I've known lots of Black families with multiracial relatives. You made the decision for both of us. You withheld our ability to know about each other or to meet each other…I am so angry with you. Do not make decisions that belong to me. It's too late for Reggie Lewis to say this to you, so I'm saying this for me and my father."

"I was trying to protect you."

"Well, you didn't. And I don't think I will ever be able to forgive you for this betrayal."

Keisha had stomped out of the house and driven back to her college. For many months she had existed in a very dark place, crippled by anger and fear. If she could not trust her mother, whom could she trust? Betrayal was unforgivable.

During those months, Keisha's rejection left Ann frozen in despair. Don had kept the connection. He launched a one-man campaign to hold on to his wife and daughter. He refused to let Keisha go. An introvert with a troubled family background, he always said Keisha and Ann had saved him. Now it was his turn.

He kept her from sinking by his own quiet accompaniment. He sent her cards with only a few words. Just the most important ones. "I love you." "We love you." "You cannot go where our love won't find you." He'd sent her flowers on Valentine's Day, and at Easter, when she'd refused to come home, he'd brought a basket of her favorite chocolate truffles and driven several hours to leave them outside the door to her apartment.

Then one evening Don had phoned, and Keisha had answered. His voice ragged, he shared the terrible news that Mom's parents—Keisha's grandparents—had died in a fiery car crash on a lonely road in Upstate New York. "Please come home. Your mom needs you," he'd said to her stunned silence. And she had gone home, gone to Mom, the breach repaired.

Now, nearly three decades later, Keisha was the one living with the sudden, violent erasure of the person who was the center of her world. It felt crazy but part of her felt betrayed again. Not by Mom this time. By whom? By Richard? By God, if there is a God?

All of the family were trying to help. The children stayed away from her, sensing she had no energy to help them cope when her own needs were so overpowering. Her parents and Gran Cora called regularly, and Uncle Edward brought them dinner once a week that first month.

Still, Death covered each of them like a caul. They saw everything through its opaque membrane. Like looking through a special lens that alters what the camera of the mind sees, toning down colors and blurring images. Death had crept into the home they had loved. It lurked in dark corners, under beds, in closets, in familiar smells and favorite foods. It undermined each of them. It severed them from their traditions, now too painful, from the familiar patterns of family connection. From everything connected to Richard.

The sky was dark purple now, layered with random streaks of light. It must be late.

The faculty parking lot was nearly empty. She felt the chill of mid-May at dusk. Her mind seized on a poem she'd learned when her grandparents were killed.

> "Stop all the clocks, cut off the telephone,
> Prevent the dog from barking with a juicy bone,
> Silence the pianos and with muffled drum
> Bring out the coffin, let the mourners come…."

She spoke the familiar words aloud sitting there in her car in the faculty parking lot. W. H. Auden understood. He, too, must have experienced time stopping with the death of the one he loved, so that everything existed in Before or After, and nothing was ever the same again.

> "He was my North, my South, my East and West,
> My working week and my Sunday rest,
> My noon, my midnight, my talk, my song;
> I thought that love would last forever: I was wrong."

Was Auden right? What about her children? Did they now believe love could not last? The thought troubled her. She wiped the back of her hand across her eyes. If their children felt this way, she had betrayed both them and Richard. She must find the strength to keep going. For them.

She looked at her digital phone glowing in the early dusk. It was late. She drove out of the parking lot as the last streaks of light made the sky breathtaking.

The house was mostly dark when she arrived fifteen minutes later with two large pizzas. Balancing her laptop case, purse, and the pizzas, she somehow opened the door and stumbled into the dark hallway, calling out, "Cora? Caleb? Can one of you get the lights, please? How about pepperoni pizza?"

Caleb sat in the dark in the living room with his large headphones on nodding his head in time with the music only he could hear. He didn't look up. Cora must be in her room. It was late and they had to be hungry.

Carrying the pizza, Keisha turned on the hall lights with her elbow, which attracted Caleb's attention. He was beside her in a minute, taking the pizza from her and pecking her on the cheek. "Welcome home, Mom," he said tentatively.

Seeing the hall light creep under her bedroom door, Cora emerged, looking questions at her mom. "We thought you decided not to come home." She turned away and followed Caleb to the kitchen to set out plates and napkins. "Someone delivered this for you." Cora indicated a large plant wrapped in florist's purple cellophane sitting on the kitchen counter. "There's a note. It's from Uncle Edward, I think."

Keisha opened the small envelope taped to the cellophane. The note was written in Uncle Edward's unique, graceful penmanship. He wrote, "I'm discovering one new thing each day. Today it was this Weeping Iris. Blooms only one day a year, but oh what a day that is."

Keisha read it aloud. Enigmatic and symbolic. Typical of him.

"So we have to wait a year to see it bloom? A lot can happen in a year." Caleb looked at her skeptically.

"I think that's the point," she replied. She moved the plant to a southern window in the family room after giving it a drink.

They munched their pizzas without much conversation.

"It's awfully quiet in this house since Gran Ann and Granddad went home to Cleveland." Caleb's voice was at the cracking stage. It was hard to tell if he was emotional or just adolescent.

"Caleb thinks we need a dog." Cora kept her eyes on Keisha. "What do you think, Mama?"

"Let me think about it," she replied. Something else to take care of, she thought, when I can barely take care of myself, much less them.

Chapter 15

A melody slid down the scale, then repeated. It took her some time to identify its source.

Mom and Dad had taken her to the musical *Jesus Christ, Superstar*. She must have been nine. It was her first off-Broadway theater experience, and she'd laughed and wept and loved the fast-paced drama and the young cast. A line kept circling her mind like a mantra. Something like "Everything will be all right."

She needed those words tonight, after the homicide detective had come by to report on their progress, or lack thereof. Until tonight she'd forced herself to shut out the images of Richard's battered and bruised body; she'd banished what she'd seen when she and Uncle Edward had identified him—this big, gentle, loving man, reduced to a carcass, almost unrecognizable. The visit from the man from homicide brought those images out of hibernation.

She and the detective had sat in the living room, taking the same seats they took that early morning hour when her world, as she knew it, had imploded.

"This has the markings of a gang initiation killing, but we have no evidence that points to specific persons. No witnesses at that hour of the night. No weapon, no fingerprints. Unless your husband had enemies? Any you've thought of?"

"No enemies. He was a good man, a kind man." Her voice was monotone, her body rigidly upright. She was unable to be helpful.

Unhelpful. Like she'd been the day her husband's life was taken from him, when she'd suggested he take the subway rather than drive to his gig on the Southside because the forecast was for a surprise spring snow. At least she thought it was her suggestion. She'd relived that last time she saw him again and again, trying to remember. It was so typical of her to think she knew best. So typical of Richard to follow her suggestion. If he'd driven to the gig, he would still be here. Instead, the straight, uncomplicated road their family had followed had hit a dead end, and they were stuck, unable to see any other roads to move down or across.

The homicide detective did not stay long. He said something about their investigation hitting a dead end. That phrase again. She should come to the station to collect Richard's things. Dead end. Road to nowhere.

Then he left.

She closed the front door, locked it behind him, and made her way to the kitchen to start cooking dinner. At least she was cooking. That was something.

Everything will be all right.

The words ran like a dripping faucet. A mantra of false assurance, circling the drain.

Chapter 16

Ronald returned from campus one ethereal June day elated. He'd had another meeting with Dr. Keisha Johnson who had approved his dissertation proposal and even seemed excited about it. He had also heard from Dr. Brown, the archivist emeritus at the Bostwick Collection, the man he'd phone interviewed last week. The archivist invited him to rent a room in his house while he was living in Philly for the rest of the summer. They had connected well on the call and, thanks to his years living with Grandma, Ronald was comfortable being around old people. But he wouldn't have a paying job in Philadelphia, so he didn't know how he'd afford to pay rent.

The retired archivist had sounded interested in what Ronald was researching. He'd suggested a dozen people Ronald should interview. Being able to use his name would help Ronald gain their trust. Very helpful.

The archivist lived in Yorktown Village, the middle-class Black housing development that was started by Rev. Leon Sullivan in the Seventies to keep middle-class Black families from fleeing the city and to keep housing in North Philadelphia economically diverse. His first face-to-face interview would be with Dr. Brown, which should give him access to families living in this Sullivan housing development. He couldn't wait to tell Grandma of this good news. She was playing cards with her women friends at the moment.

It was a quiet Friday evening, surprisingly quiet for the start of the Memorial Day weekend. Maybe the higher temperatures kept people indoors. Ronald found the quiet disconcerting. He scanned the street in front of him looking for anything that would indicate a problem.

From the end of the block, just before his grandma's house, he heard a loud, persistent thumping bass and saw a group of young men clustered together foot-working to the beat. They wore black Juggernaut T-shirts, jeans, and showy sneakers, and their voices were raised in animated conversation. He crossed the street to avoid walking through them.

"He be in trouble if he snitch on Tyrone." Ronald heard one of them say.

A late model Lincoln pulled up to the curb beside the young men and the tinted driver's side window slid down slickly to reveal a man, probably in his late thirties. One of the men approached the driver, handed him something, and received an envelope in return. Then the Lincoln pulled away, soundless as a hybrid. The man with the envelope was passing something out. Then they dispersed.

Ronald worried about those men. They had begun to appear around this time most evenings. They disappeared after 2 a.m. He worried they might bother his grandmother when he was not living there. His sister had moved in with her boyfriend earlier this year, so Grandma would be living alone once Ronald went to Philadelphia. He thought the men resembled a colony of bats in their dark clothes, or maybe a claw of panthers? He smiled, remembering how he'd learned that meaning of "claw."

Ronald loved trivia, as did Grandma. One of their favorite games was naming an animal or bird and challenging the other to use the correct word for a group of that animal. A pride of lions was easy but a clowder of cats—that was more impressive. A murder of crows, a streak or destruction of tigers, a leap of leopards, a jamboree of jaguars, a coalition of cheetahs, a scurry or dray of squirrels? Grandma and Ronald competed to see who could stump whom and it was always close.

Once he was well past the men, he crossed the street again and walked briskly up the sidewalk, taking the steps to the porch two at a time. His peripheral vision caught the last two men heading down the cross street. When they were out of sight, he unlocked the front door.

Chapter 17

At fifteen Cora wasn't clear about a lot of things—foremost, why someone had killed her father? He was the gentlest of men and would never hurt anyone. Several years ago, when she and Caleb had first beseeched their parents to add a dog to their family, Dad had agreed, on the condition that they adopt a rescue dog, preferably one who would otherwise be put down. Which was how Jemison joined the family, a scrawny pit bull the Humane Society would not accept. When Dad turned out to be allergic to dogs, coughing and sneezing and itching, he toughed it out *for six months* until they could find another family willing to take Jemison, who by then looked sleek and preferred Dad over the rest of them. *Why would anyone murder such a person?*

In the almost two months since her father's murder, Cora had put away childish things and tried to accept the reductions of her new life—no more hugs and cuddles, no more fun movie nights or cooking elaborate meals whose origin was some country they would learn about as they ate, no more laughter. She had become the super-responsible eldest child.

Being the eldest, Cora felt responsible for her mom and Caleb, especially with Mama sunk so low in despair. Would she ever return to being her fun self? It really wasn't fair on any level. She and Caleb still had to finish growing up. *We need our parents for that,* she and Caleb agreed one Friday evening when Mama was closeted in her bedroom, stifling her tears under the false assumption that the kids could not hear her through the thick oak door and the memory-foam pillow.

The two of them had gone downstairs into the family room, stopping to dish up mounds of Moose Tracks ice cream, their compensation for parental neglect. It was June and the sky was still light as they stared into the overgrown back yard and savored their ice cream.

"Do you think this is the rest of our lives?" Caleb turned to face his sister, looking unusually earnest and intent. "I mean, is Mom just *gone?*"

Cora felt squeezed between her mother's need to disappear and her brother's need for reassurance. She'd been asking herself the same question. Choosing her big sister role, she reassured her brother, doubting as she spoke that anything she was telling him was true.

"She just needs time. It's not been that long. Now she's done with her classes and not working, except for her research. She'll probably come around soon."

She was uncomfortable lying to Caleb. And she resented having to be the grown-up in the family when he was only a year younger and Mama decades older. Responsibility left Cora no space for her own grief.

Most days, Cora felt like she had become the parent. She woke Mama each morning and reminded her that she had to be at the University, or the lawyer's, or wherever. She set out Caleb's clothes so he wouldn't look ratty. She made breakfast, three bowls of cold cereal that she put on the counter in front of the barstools ringing the island in their kitchen. There was only room for three barstools. When Dad was there, they sat at the dining room table to eat. With Dad no longer there, Cora had decided: they would eat in the kitchen. Maybe they wouldn't notice he was missing? Fat chance.

Most evenings they ate frozen food meals or pizza. It was so unlike Mama to not care about healthy eating. But Mama was unlike herself in many ways now, and it didn't look like that was changing in the first weeks of her summer break. Gran Ann tried to make up for Mama's neglect by calling daily, but she was in Cleveland, far from Evanston, Illinois, and they never talked for long.

Cora thought other voices in the house might help make things seem more normal. She wished their grandparents would return. The silence was deafening. None of the three of them said much. Ever.

"So, what are we going to do if Mom stays like this?" Caleb's voice sounded like he had a mouth full of gum. She had to listen closely to pick up the consonants through the ice cream.

She had no answer. Even trying to come up with something plausible terrified her. So she didn't respond.

During the last months of school, her closest friends had tried to include her in their conversations, but she could tell everyone was wary, treating her carefully, as though she might break. She saw the way they avoided asking her anything that might possibly unwind her. She was also quick to feel this as rejection. Since early April, she'd avoided her friends so she wouldn't be treated this way. So, this summer she had no friends to hang out with or confide in.

In the past, when she was feeling insecure, she would talk to Mama about it, but not now. And as annoying as Caleb could be when he went out with his friends biking and came home late, she understood why he didn't want to be here. Mama's depression crowded every room in their house, like one of those blow-up figures that gets bigger and bigger, pushing everything aside until you think it will explode.

None of it was fair, not Dad's death, or Mama's retreat, or Cora's being forced to become the adult. But what could she do about it?

She had had enough trouble keeping her grades up last semester and getting herself out of bed every day. She didn't want to be the responsible one. She wanted to be a carefree teenager like her friends. And she wanted her Daddy.

No one talked with her about what had happened. The police had come once or twice after he was murdered, but they never stayed long and only talked with Mama, their voices low and unintelligible.

At the end of the school year her class took a field trip to the Science Museum downtown on Lake Michigan. They were taking the L, and, as much as she wanted to go, she stayed home. Daddy had been killed on the L. She didn't know the details, but that was enough to make riding the L, even in the daytime, terrifying.

She hadn't told anyone why she wasn't going on the school trip, like she hadn't told anyone that walking to school made her nervous. She'd look over her shoulder, watching for anyone who might want to kill *her*. She wasn't being paranoid. Just realistic. If someone wanted to kill her Daddy, they might want to kill the rest of the family, too. Each night she double-checked that all the doors were locked. Mama hadn't noticed.

Sometimes she thought she saw Dad walking up ahead of her. She recognized his ambling gait and the way his arms swung with his steps. He was so tall you couldn't miss him. She would feel her heart beating fast and would pick up her pace to reach him without drawing attention to herself. Each time when she was abreast of him, she'd discovered the person was not Dad, only a look-alike, and not even very close to what her daddy had looked like. Her heart plummeted and she couldn't catch her breath, as if she'd fallen hard and had it knocked out of her.

Sometimes she saw his face when she opened her school locker, right there inside the tan metal door. It became a game she played, keeping Dad incognito inside her locker. If he was there, he'd be safe. He wouldn't be able to truly leave. But by the time school recessed for the summer, he had stopped showing up. She was frantic not to lose this small connection to him, but what could she do?

In P.E. class in the locker room on the last day of school, a girl was showing pictures of her boyfriend to a cluster of other girls in Cora's class.

"Have you done it?" another girl asked. The question brought nervous laughter. Some girls acted so sophisticated, like they'd been sleeping with boys for years. To Cora's surprise, the girl with the picture on her phone said, "No. We just cuddle." Which brought more laughter.

Standing in front of her locker, away from the others, Cora felt tears start and willed them to dry up. "We just cuddle." That's what she missed the most. Just cuddling. Dad's long arms wrapped around his family on the king-sized bed, his neatly trimmed fingernails tapping a melody on her arm that only he could hear.

Chapter 18

Caleb kept in contact with his group of friends. Boys didn't talk much about their lives outside of school, so they didn't put him in uncomfortable situations. As long as he kept busy, he was OK. So he played ball and went to the after-school program for wannabe engineers led by Mr. Tunde. Mr. Tunde taught them to make all kinds of things, starting with an engine that powered a homemade car with a remote device. There was a lot of math involved in the things they built. Caleb liked math.

Dad was good at math, too. He used to say that math and music went together.

When Caleb was at school where he had to sit still for hours, it was harder. His mind would wander and sometimes he would feel mad, really mad. For no reason. He'd want to hit someone. He controlled it most of the time, but sometimes he couldn't. Like the last week of school when a bunch of kids on the track team were talking about the latest shooting of an unarmed Black man by the Chicago police. The other guys' voices got loud as they stood beside the track before their practice half-mile run.

"Fuck white people, fuck them all!" The guy's voice was loud and angry. There were nods and sounds of affirmation.

Before he knew what was happening, Caleb had hit the boy who had spoken. Hit him once and then again and again. The boys yelled at him.

"Hey, man, what's up with you?"

"Get off him, man?"

"You got something wrong in your head?"

"Doesn't he know he's Black, too?"

"Yeah, but I heard his dad was white."

"Don't go acting all crazy, dude. You're gonna get us all in trouble."

"Get off him!"

The other guys pulled Caleb off and held him as he squirmed and tried to jerk free. When he got loose, he ran off, out of the school yard and down the street toward home. He didn't stop until he got to his house. He took the key from the flowerpot where Mom hid it and let himself in. He didn't even stop for a drink. He hurried to the safety of his room and crashed onto his bed, his body convulsed in sobs. He felt so angry, so *ANGRY*, and he still wanted to hit someone. He sat on the edge of his bed and began to pound the wall with his forehead, over and over, while the pain in his head intensified and drops of blood began to drip onto his jeans. When he'd used up his anger, he fell asleep, his head buried in his Black Panther pillow.

Keisha found him huddled on his bed, the position of his head disguising the blood stains. A pinkish splotch on the wall beside the bed attracted her attention. So did the voicemail message from the assistant principal on the house phone.

"But Caleb doesn't get into fights," she told the assistant principal when she called back.

"He did today, Dr. Johnson. Your son is acting out his confusion and anger at what happened to his father. It is understandable, but we can't allow it to happen again. He needs to see a counselor. Do you want to make an appointment with our school counselor, or do you prefer to use your own professional?"

So Caleb began seeing Dr. Mehta twice a week. Dr. Mehta told Keisha there was no quick fix for such grief and she should plan on his coming for at least a year.

Caleb had resisted, even in the car as they arrived at Dr. Mehta's office. "Mom, I am not some weirdo. One fight! Come on, Mom." Then, as she opened the passenger door to show him there was no turning back, he used his biggest guns: "*Dad* would never force me to see a shrink."

"Well, Dad isn't here, so I am the boss, and you will see Dr. Mehta. And it will help!"

"So why aren't you seeing one if it's so helpful? You're more messed up than me."

She pulled his arm to get him out of the car, stung by his comment and the truth of it, angry at her smartass son. "OK. We will *both* go, starting *now*."

The therapist was surprised to see both of them entering his office together. It was what he had suggested, but Dr. Johnson had rejected the idea. At the end of the session, he proposed they each come separately. Keisha would see another therapist in the practice. "You each have your own individual issues to work on. You'll be giving each other—and yourselves—a gift. Caleb doesn't have to feel responsible for your wellbeing and you can feel less responsible for his."

Cora sat at her computer. Summer had arrived with a vengeance. The heat seemed to crawl across the grass, under doorways, through the air conditioning. It seemed to fill the air to suffocation. While Caleb and Mama were at therapy, she sat scrolling through articles on grief. Beside her was a bowl of vanilla ice cream with hot fudge sauce and whipped cream. Ice cream had become her solace. Why not? She wasn't going anywhere. She had to watch out for Mama and Caleb. She had little to occupy her time during the long, hot days, so she gave herself the pleasure of ice cream. The days she thought she'd overdone it, she'd go to the bathroom and barf it all into the toilet bowl, flushing twice and wiping her face and the edge of the bowl with toilet paper that she'd watch swirl away on the final flush.

She knew there were words for what she was doing, medical words like bulimia and eating disorder, but she didn't care. Mama wasn't noticing how quickly their stock of ice cream disappeared. Caleb wasn't around more than absolutely necessary. No one noticed and no one cared.

They'd asked if she wanted to do therapy also. They seemed to be glad to go now that the first weeks were over. But she wasn't interested. What had Marie Antoinette said about her suffering people? Let them eat cake? Today she'd say, Let them eat ice cream.

But at night, after they had all gone to their rooms, ice cream didn't stop her tears. She'd lie in bed, the edge of the top sheet stuffed into her mouth to muffle the sound of her sobs, and cry herself to sleep. It was going to be a very long summer.

Chapter 19

The Cora for whom Keisha and Richard named their firstborn had left her family's farm at thirteen to live in Nashville, where she could attend high school. No high schools in rural east Tennessee admitted Blacks. She'd excelled as a student and developed talent as a musician. She'd met Booker, whose ambition and devotion matched her own, married him, and given birth to their son Edward. Then Booker went to fight in Korea, leaving his wife and son behind.

When a Korean landmine blew apart her beloved husband, she was twenty, a single mom with a young son to raise. With financial help from her husband's best friend and war buddy, Arthur Johnson, she returned to school and acquired a college degree. She agreed to take in Arthur's Korean daughter, Mi-Young, and raised her alongside her son Edward. Somehow she managed raising two kids, earning an MA, and teaching at Tennessee State University, a historically Black college. Eventually, Arthur moved to Nashville, and, in 1967, when it finally became legal for Blacks and whites to wed, they married.

That she'd coped and excelled she credited to Arthur's help, her church, and the Civil Rights Movement, into which she poured her considerable energy and devotion.

At ninety-one, Gran Cora was still a Force of Nature. She knew what was going on in the world and in her country, and she spent her time resisting the roll back of progress underway at the state and national levels. She organized her church ladies to register voters, like they'd done in the Sixties, and to speak out, going in groups to the state legislature to demand their representatives and senators support bills that protected and expanded voting rights.

Gran Cora valued family, which she defined by love, not blood. When Arthur was reunited with his son Don, in 2003, she'd welcomed Don, his wife Ann, daughter Keisha, and the man Keisha married into her family. She became "Gran Cora" to Keisha and Keisha's children, the family matriarch. She loved it.

Gran Cora was a disciplined woman, disciplined about listening to the Lord and about listening to the people she loved. She observed people, intuited their trouble, shared their pain. Those qualities—she called them "gifts"—had brought her and Arthur together decades ago. Now, on a late June Saturday morning, eleven weeks after Richard's murder, she put those gifts to work.

She texted Keisha, her granddaughter. *You available for a chat?* When the thumbs up icon quickly appeared, Gran Cora phoned.

At first, she didn't recognize the sandpaper voice that answered the phone.

Haltingly, Keisha talked about how hard it was just getting out of bed in the morning, how absent she felt from her children and her students, how Caleb had beaten up a boy at school, how the days crawled by. Gran Cora listened. When Keisha wound down, Cora took a deep breath. She hoped she was doing the right thing.

"Keisha, you've known me as Grandpa Arthur's wife. But before that I was married to Booker, Edward's father. He was the love of my life. I think you know Booker and Arthur fought together in Korea, and Booker was blown up. He was just twenty. The pain of losing him burned out my insides. I literally felt seared. I'm not saying it was worse than or the same as your pain. Pain is individual. It belongs to us uniquely, which is why it's so awful—no one else can know what you are going through."

She felt a shift in Keisha's attention and heard the weary anger in her words. "Thank you for saying that. So many people say they know what I am going through, but *they don't.* They didn't know Richard like I do—*did.* They can't know what it is like to lose him." Cora heard an audible intake of breath. She waited. "People tell me I'll get through this, get 'closure,' but I don't believe that. Our family will never really recover. Even if they catch who did this, and I have no confidence they will, that won't take away our pain and anger. It won't bring him back. I can't be sure of anything after this." She stopped speaking. Perhaps she remembered that she was talking to someone who had also experienced the sudden death of the person she loved most. When she resumed, her voice was subdued, quiet.

"Gran, I feel like my heart is truly broken. There is so much I want to talk over with him. I need his counsel, his confidence in me, his love." Her voice trailed off.

"Pay attention, child. Pay attention to the people who come into your life in these days. God doesn't leave us alone even in the loneliest moments. People appear who help us heal, people whose own pain calls us to reach out from ours and connect. 'You will be lifted out of the Pit where your feet are stuck in the muck. You will be set upon a rock and given a new song to sing.' Do you know those words? From the beginning of Psalm 40?" Gran paused before speaking again. "What are you afraid of, Keisha?"

"I'm afraid I won't hear any new song."

"That was my fear, too. Maybe it still is. Funny how we can see other people so much more clearly than ourselves. I absolutely know you *will* hear it. When you get as old as me, you have a lot of living to look back on. You can look for patterns, see how you made it through this and that terrible time. Looking for what you've already survived is helpful discipline. It's your history, your survival story. It gives you something to hold onto until you can hear the first notes of your new song."

Keisha stopped talking altogether.

Gran feared she'd gone too far, said too much. It was time to end the call, let the conversation stew inside Keisha a while. Before she signed off she asked, "Will you let me know when you hear them, those first notes? Will you tell me when you hear the first notes of your new song?"

"Yes."

"I'll be waiting." She wanted to help Keisha watch for the newness that wasn't yet conceived, much less born. She wanted her to trust that it would come, was already beginning to take shape inside her. Maybe Keisha would think she was a demanding busybody for asking Keisha to share such a personal moment with her. That was OK. *Just don't miss it because you're not looking,* she thought.

After they rang off, Cora left the kitchen to waken her husband Arthur, who was napping in his recliner while a news show on TV scrolled photos of Britain's new Prime Minister, Boris Johnson. Arthur's head sagged on his chest and the cup of coffee beside him had gone cold.

Gran Cora savored the scene—their one-bedroom, senior living space crowded with the clutter of their retired life, plants next to the door waiting to be repotted, mail stacked on the round table that did double duty as both a desk and eating space, Arthur's walker wearing its tennis ball shoes, their respective pills lined up on a painted metal tray that had seen better days. She thought of the time they'd nearly lost Arthur, just before young Cora, her great granddaughter, was born. *I'm so grateful for these years,* she thought.

New summer sun shone through the blinds and striped the room with possibility. Involuntarily Gran Cora smiled. Growing old together was a blessing. Her smile faded. It was a blessing Keisha and Richard would not receive.

Sunday morning, after listening to her favorite TV preacher, Gran Cora called Keisha's daughter Cora, her namesake. The fifteen-year-old sounded hesitant as she answered the phone.

"This is your Gran Cora calling to see how you're doing. So, how are you doing, young lady?"

There was no response. Was the child afflicted with teen angst or was it more serious?

"I spoke with your mom yesterday. She sounds pretty blue. I figured you might be pretty blue too. And maybe you'd be willing to talk to me about it." Then Gran waited for Cora to speak. She forced herself not to jump in even when the silence stretched out. Finally, she heard a fragile eggshell voice.

"We're all blue. This house is a graveyard and we're each marble monuments."

She's going to be a writer, Gran Cora observed to herself. "That's a powerful statement. Marble monuments can't move. They're stuck in one spot and all looking in the same direction rather than at each other. Am I getting the picture?"

"Yes."

"Is everybody dead in the house?"

"Well, mostly. Mama does her work, but she rarely talks to us. Sometimes we hear her crying. It's like she died, too. Caleb and I don't know what to do since Gran Ann and Granddad went back to Cleveland and it's just us here. Sometimes Caleb says he's going to run away. But I can't leave Mama. I'm the oldest. I'm responsible for her."

"Have you told her you need her to be present?"

"Not exactly. It's like she's hiding in her room. She doesn't give much opportunity for us to talk to her."

"Do you have meals together?"

"Sometimes. She doesn't cook much. Mostly brings home carry out. We serve ourselves and take it to the TV. Mom goes upstairs to her room."

"Have you tried writing her a note, telling her what you're feeling?"

"No. If she knew that we feel she's just *gone,* it would put more stress on her, and it seems like she couldn't handle one more stress. Maybe we've watched too much TV, but Caleb and I took the sharp knives from the kitchen and hid them under his bed."

"She noticed they were missing?" Gran Cora concentrated on keeping her voice level to disguise the alarm she was feeling.

"I don't think so. Like I said, she's not cooking much anymore."

Gran Cora was lying on her bed, back against the headboard. Young Cora's account felt like a boulder lowered onto her chest. This was too much for these young people to cope with.

"I am so sorry," she said, unable to find any other words. "Is it better when someone else is in the house with you?"

"Yes, but they can't stay forever."

"Is it OK with you if I talk with Uncle Edward and your grandparents about our conversation? I think together we may come up with some ideas about how to help."

"You can talk with them, but it won't do any good."

"You took the knives away because you thought she might be suicidal?"

"Yes. But what do I know?" The girl stood on a high wire, afraid to upset her mom with this revelation but terrified to continue handling the situation by herself, just her and her brother.

"You know a lot. Remember, you are a Cora and that means wisdom, courage, and skill. OK if I call you later today or tomorrow morning? I should be able to confer with the others by then."

"I won't be going anywhere. Caleb goes out with his bike and his friends. I babysit Mama. It requires a lot of energy."

"See what I mean about wisdom?" the old woman wanted to elicit half a smile. Nothing indicated the girl was smiling. "OK, I'll call you tonight or tomorrow. Remember who you are, Cora, and whose you are. Bye for now."

Cora puzzled over Gran's last comment. *Whose you are? Besides the daughter of the brilliant Dr. Keisha Johnson, no longer the charismatic person she had been, and Dr. Richard Allen, recently departed for parts unknown? Maybe it was some of Gran's church talk?* They'd only started attending church the couple of weeks before Dad was murdered. Of course, they didn't go after... She hadn't had enough exposure to pick up the lingo. Oh well.

Tomorrow. She calculated how many hours away Gran's next call would be. At the most, twenty-four hours, give or take, before the family Jedi just might send help. Or not. Meanwhile she would get herself a bowl of ice cream.

Chapter 20

Don and Ann stood in the shade of the open garage, a can of black paint between them. They were painting their wrought iron yard furniture on this hot afternoon, sweat coating their faces and sliding down their arms, making it hard to hold onto the paint brushes.

"I hate it that we came back here. We belong with Keisha and the kids." Ann's voice was intense and worried.

"Without Sam, we can go back anytime." Sam the Dog had left this life two weeks before Richard died. He'd lived a good, long life for a big dog, but Don missed him terribly. The timing of Sam's death was fortuitous, however, allowing them freedom to travel back to Chicago whenever they were needed.

"I keep calling and texting Keisha, but she rarely replies. I don't know what else to do." Don stopped painting and sat on a folding chair, not noticing or caring that black paint dripped thickly from the brush he still held, puddling on the newspapers that covered the floor of the garage. "The only other time we've known her to be so remote and depressed was…"

"When she learned that I hadn't told her the truth about Reggie's death." Ann often finished his sentences. She thought it was a sign of the depth of their connection. Don thought it irritating. Sometimes he'd say so, but not today. Today he was too immersed in his own grief. And his own secrets.

Ann's cell phone made the squawking chicken sound she'd chosen for her ringtone. She set down her brush and wiped her hands before picking it up. She felt quite smug about her choice of ringtone, though they all teased her about it. It grabbed her attention when all those sound-alike ringtones didn't.

It was Gran Cora. They looked at each other with trepidation. Always when she called, they feared she was calling to tell them that Don's father, Arthur, had died. Please, not another death. Not now.

But she was calling about Keisha. On speaker, they listened to Gran's account of her conversations with Keisha and Cora.

Ann fidgeted as Gran Cora's report spilled out. *They hid the kitchen knives?"* She struggled to remain composed. According to Gran Cora, Ann's granddaughter and grandson were drowning in their grief-flooded house while trying to keep their mother afloat. Sadness overwhelmed Ann, sadness and hopelessness. She was a problem solver, but she felt submerged in helplessness.

Gran Cora proposed a Skype call with the extended family—Edward, Arthur, Don, and Ann. Edward would be finished with church and his lunch by 2:00 today. Would that work for them? Two was three in Cleveland, just enough time to put away the paint supplies, clean up, and get out of the heat.

Don had time for a quick shower before their Skype call. He needed time alone to think. He emerged wrapped in a blue bath sheet, feeling grateful for air conditioning. That other time Keisha had left them— when he had stayed in touch with her, leaving care packages at her dorm and sending flowers and brief notes that said he loved her--she had eventually come around when she learned of Ann's parents' sudden deaths in a car crash. She'd taken off immediately, driving most of the night to get back to them. What might call her out of her isolation now?

He pondered whether to tell Keisha what he had intended to tell Richard, that Richard was his biological child. The shock of this new knowledge might distract her. But it might make her feel sorry for *him*, put the focus on *him* when it needed to be on Keisha and the children as a family unit. Richard's wife and children were the ones most needing help and attention. Besides, his secret might feel like betrayal and make her angry.

By the time he dressed and went downstairs to sit with Ann for the call with the extended family, he had relocked the box inside his heart that held his secret. It could and should wait.

By the end of the Nashville-Cleveland-Chicago group conversation, the family had come up with a plan: the situation merited a family intervention. Edward, who lived nearest Keisha and the kids, committed to spending Monday evenings with them. He would come on the L for weekly family dinners and lead check-in conversations, giving each a chance to share what was percolating inside. He was a good listener and a good cook. He would bring the ingredients and prepare supper at their house in Evanston with Keisha and the kids helping. That would provide consistent weekly support.

The others would engage in one-on-one defense. Ann and Don would leave tomorrow to drive to Chicago for a prolonged visit. Ann would focus on Keisha while Gran Cora would check in every few days with her namesake, and Don would stay close to Caleb, assisted from a distance by Arthur. He would also keep calling the police. Perhaps locating the people who killed Richard would bring a little solace?

They phoned Keisha and announced they were coming. They'd expected she might resist their intervention, but she sounded listless and apathetic.

Ann had the hardest assignment: to find a project Keisha could sink her teeth into that would provide a new direction and reawaken her curiosity.

That was their plan, a way they could collaborate and be supportive, *something*, anyway.

Ann and Don sat up late that night staring at the TV. They kept losing the plot of the British mystery that was their Sunday evening ritual, Ann asking Don what had just happened. "I'm not paying attention," he confessed. Finally, they turned off the television and the lights and headed to bed. But sleep was elusive.

Don lay on his back staring at the nightlight that cast long shadows across the ceiling. He longed to tell Ann of his own special grief at Richard's death. He fell asleep wondering if Richard knew without the words having been said, if the dead can access what is happening with those they leave behind.

They were very clear when they arrived that they would stay as long as she and the kids needed them. They cooked, cleaned, hung out with Cora and Caleb, did everything they could to hold back the tide of grief swamping Keisha and sweep the debris it carried out of the house.

Except they couldn't.

In the few moments when she was able to see anything other than her own pain, Keisha noticed how much older her parents looked. Richard's murder had aged them.

On July 4th, Caleb and his grandpa prepared breakfast for the women of the family. The temperature had retreated from the 90s and there was a pleasant breeze, so Don suggested they serve breakfast in the back yard. Caleb told Granddad he doubted Mom would respond positively to being invited to breakfast at the picnic table. *Oh, well. If she chooses to stay in bed, there'll be more for me, more food and more airtime,* he was thinking.

He liked spending time with Granddad, although there was only so much time with old people he could take before heading off on his bike or going to his room to play video games. Granddad didn't pry like Gran Ann, who asked a lot of questions about his life that he wasn't sure he wanted to answer. Granddad just stayed quiet most of the time, quiet but friendly. Caleb was pretty sure his grandpa enjoyed being with him.

When they finished the fruit salad and the bacon and assembled the chocolate and almond croissants from the bakery in a basket lined with a cloth napkin, Granddad suggested Caleb run upstairs and announce that the eggs were cooking; they should get up NOW and come in their pajamas to the back yard for a picnic breakfast. "Tell your mom we've made strong coffee with real cream that she can have either iced or hot. Make sure she tells you which. That way she's committed."

To Caleb's surprise all three females responded positively to being summoned. Even Mom. Within ten minutes they were in the kitchen, drawn there by the smells of bacon and coffee more than by Caleb's knocking on their doors. Don added onions, spinach, mushrooms, and Swiss cheese to the eggs and dished up generous portions on large paper plates. He turned on the radio, setting it to the classical music station, and ushered them out the door and down the steps to the picnic table. Caleb thought it was going to be a good day.

Right after she sat down Keisha stood up and returned to the kitchen. The music, Beethoven's 5th, abruptly ended. When she returned, she carried a tissue and her eyes looked red. They watched her, waiting for some explanation. She'd become the emotional barometer for each of them. She sat down and picked up her fork. "This looks delicious. Thank you, Dad and Caleb. A real treat."

She gave no explanation, and no one asked for one. They treated her with default super-sensitivity. But none of them liked the power she had to ruin their days, nor did they know how to change it.

Gran Ann was the most intrepid. She wanted conversation. "Did your army of tulips bloom this year? I remember how hard you worked filling that bed with them last fall." She stopped, realizing too late that she'd brought up *BEFORE*. Then she resumed, looking for a way out of stirred memories. "Granddad and I thought we could plant some perennials in that bed so when the tulips die it won't look so barren." *Whoops. "Die."* She'd done it again.

Tension around the picnic table, nervous sideways glances to check Keisha's responses.

"Would you like us to plant perennials in that other bed? They're much more practical since they don't...they're not like annuals that have to be planted every year."

When Gran Ann started again, Caleb rolled his eyes at Granddad. *Would the woman never learn to shut up?*

But Ann tried again. "I have something for you, honey. I thought it might interest you. It's summer, your classes are over, and you have more free time. I'll go get it. Be right back."

Granddad attempted to distract them. He directed a question to Keisha. "Are you on campus this week? I know you're not teaching summer classes, but do you have advising or research you do there?"

Caleb thought Mom could hardly ignore this direct question. He was correct.

"I'm meeting with a couple of my grad students this week, conferring with them about their research. I've not been doing any of my own research. Can't seem to focus enough. Why do you ask, Dad?"

"I thought Caleb and I might visit the science library, maybe find some books he'd be interested in."

Gran Ann came out the kitchen door holding a box and the pot of coffee for refills. She slipped the box to Mom and poured the three adults more coffee.

Keisha stared at the box.

"What is it, Mom?" Caleb was impatient as usual.

"It's a DNA kit."

Caleb: "Dope!"

"No, Caleb, it's actually pretty cool. You use it to locate others who share your DNA. It helps you learn about your heritage. You put a sample of your saliva in the tube and send it to them."

Caleb: "*MOM! Get with it!* Dope means awesome. Don't you already know your heritage?"

"Yes, but I have a birth father who died when he was thirty-nine who I know little about."

"The one who was shot by the police?"

The adults seemed surprised he knew this. Gran Ann gave Caleb a stern look that he thought was unfair. *She can stumble repeatedly into what is taboo, but the one time I mention a family member murdered, she looks daggers at me?*

"I thought your mom might be interested in finding some of her relatives on the Lewis side of your family. She loves doing research and might locate cousins or aunts and uncles. I thought it might be interesting for you and Cora too. Your other grandpa and I worked together registering voters and teaching literacy in Mississippi more than fifty years ago."

"Uncle Edward was there, too," Keisha added.

Cora perked up, interested, but Caleb felt protective of Granddad. "Granddad, are you OK with Mom finding about this other man? Doesn't it hurt your feelings?"

"Grandpa knows he is my Dad forever and ever." Keisha reached out to squeeze Don's hand.

"Just kidding," Caleb said. He felt relieved.

Granddad smiled at Caleb, appreciating the boy's concern. "Grandma and I talked about this before she bought the kit. I know your mom is my daughter. I also know that some of her wonderful attributes come from her biological father, and I support her searching out his family if she wants to. It is fine by me."

Caleb watched his mom closely. She appeared conflicted, half intrigued by the box next to her plate, half wary. He expected her to be truthful. She usually was. "Thank you, Mom and Dad," she said. "I will pursue this, but I can't promise to do it now."

Caleb changed the subject, turning to Granddad the scientist. "Would the library have much on DNA? Do you know much about it?" His interest was growing.

"I think we're all on the same learning curve and the library will have a lot to help us with," Don reached for another two pieces of bacon. "Please pass the croissants," he said.

Later, while Ann and Keisha did the dishes and Cora carried out the trash, Keisha whispered to her mom, "I can't listen to classical music these days without getting sad. I didn't want to explain because Cora is playing violin. Of course, she has a number of classical pieces she practices for orchestra. I don't want her to know that hearing them is hard for me."

They heard the door from outside opening. Cora, back from the yard carrying the last dishes from the picnic table, eyed her mother and grandmother warily, trying to read their whispered words she'd heard and not heard. It was what she did each day. Trying to sort out what people weren't telling you took a lot of concentration. But the conversation had ended, and Cora was left to guess. Again.

Part III

Chapter 21

On Wednesday morning Keisha drove to campus to meet with Cassandra Brown, one of her PhD students.

Cassandra was a strikingly beautiful Black woman who carried herself with confidence. Her hair was in long braids, beaded and with extensions. She wore big earrings and stylish clothing and always drew attention when she entered a room. Cassandra's PhD was on Black nationalism and the Nation of Islam during the Seventies and Eighties. She sat facing her advisor, leaning forward and talking animatedly about her research.

"Dr. Johnson, I think I'm going to focus on Philadelphia. It had active Nation of Islam and African nationalist groups and was the center of Black Capitalism in those years. I want to find out if Reverend Leon Sullivan's Zion Baptist Church and Jeremiah Shabazz's chapter of the Nation of Islam were connected. Also, the MOVE organization. It really interests me that all three were in the same place with very different approaches, but they all were teaching Black folk how to thrive and be independent economically, culturally, and socially. Do you think this will work for my dissertation?" Cassandra was pumped and her eyes shone. "I don't think anybody has studied these intersections."

It interested Keisha to hear about Cassandra's research. Cassandra kept talking, her excitement about what she was discovering obvious. "MOVE was this sort-of African nationalist group that lived communally, grew their own food to avoid chemical additives, and homeschooled their children so they wouldn't grow up learning trash about Africa and Black people's past. They were *not* popular with the city police."

"Frank Rizzo." Keisha named the notorious Philadelphia police chief and mayor who openly despised his Black constituents.

Cassandra nodded. "You know he's the only police chief in the city's history who the city honored with a statue?"

The conversation made Keisha recall the research she had done in grad school for a paper she wrote on Black nationalist groups. She opened her laptop and began taking notes. Cassandra was on a roll.

"In 1974 MOVE started to speak out against police brutality. During seven months in 1975, MOVE members were arrested on misdemeanor charges more than 150 times, and some of them were sentenced to several years in jail and given steep fines. They ran a Black-owned business, a car wash. It was their major source of income, but the city closed it down. At their trials they insisted they had done nothing wrong and asserted that their members had been arrested 'more than six hundred times.' The city charged them an outrageous one million dollars to get out on bail!"

Keisha was more familiar with MOVE's struggle with the Philadelphia police in the 1980s. This was new to her. "So what happened?"

"Some MOVE members were released from bail in March 1976, and a fight broke out with police that resulted in more arrests. MOVE charged that a baby, Life Africa, was stomped to death by police. The courts refused to hold the police responsible for the baby's death, using the excuse that there was no birth certificate for the child. The baby had been born at home. MOVE didn't trust the health care system, so they took care of their own. They didn't fill out government forms like birth certificates. They didn't pay taxes. Also, the cops beat a pregnant woman with MOVE so badly that her baby was born with a fractured head. You can't make up this stuff, Dr. Johnson!"

"What do you think of MOVE?"

"They're complicated. At first they were nonviolent, but after this, John Africa called for them to defend themselves if attacked."

Keisha needed clarification. "I knew about the police attack on May 13, 1985, but you're saying the police were out to close them down years before then?"

"Yes." Cassandra pulled up her notes on her tablet. She was excited to share what she'd been learning with someone who was interested. She scanned her file on 1976 and continued.

"In July 1976, the city announced it was inspecting the MOVE house and the condition of the children who lived there. They would remove the kids if conditions were unsanitary. MOVE erected an eight-foot wall and refused to let them in. The sanctity of private property and all that. There were arrests and MOVE members who were arrested received long sentences. Two hundred cops staked out the house, and one hundred plainclothes police. This was during the summer of 1977.

A MOVE member who had been a police informant led the police to an arms cache in a nearby apartment that he said belonged to MOVE. The police arrested six MOVE members on federal firearms charges.—Are you following all this?"

Keisha felt numb. Why didn't she know about this? She was writing a book on police murders of Black people, but this larger story of MOVE had not been on her radar.

"For ten months the police laid siege to the old Victorian house that was MOVE headquarters, stopping all food and water from going into the property, turning off utilities, and allowing no one to leave. It was a full blockade."

"This is incredible! Didn't MOVE have supporters to come to their defense?"

"People in the neighborhood were divided. Some wanted MOVE out and others thought the police were violating the basic rights of MOVE members, treating them this way because of their color. Some supported a court case to challenge the city's decision to blockade the property."

Cassandra stood and began to pace. "The Pennsylvania Supreme Court agreed to hear the case, but eventually supported the police blockade. By March 1978, *one thousand cops were involved*, and *it was costing the city $1.2 million!*"

Keisha stopped taking notes and just listened.

"The city said MOVE had to evacuate the premises in ninety days, but MOVE couldn't find anywhere to go. They tried to purchase a farm in Virginia, but that fell through. It seems someone got to the owners and scared them off. So, the deadline for their evacuation of the West Philadelphia property came and they were still there. Judges issued contempt charges. The police attacked the building with water cannons and fired their rifles into it."

Keisha's hands were trembling. "Are you saying the police fired upon and poured water into a building with *children?*"

"Yes. Some later testified they were hiding from the gunshots in the basement and the water was up to their waists. They were holding the children up so they wouldn't drown. If this was a movie, people would never believe it really happened. When the assault ended, nine MOVE members were jailed and charged with murdering the one policeman who was hit in the barrage of bullets. Witnesses disagreed whether the first shot, the one that killed the police officer, came from inside the building or from outside. The MOVE Nine were found guilty of firing the bullet that killed the policeman—nine people guilty of firing one bullet!—and they were sentenced to *thirty to one-hundred years in prison* for the murder of that officer. They maintained their innocence all through their decades in prison. Two of them are still in prison, after more than forty years!"

Cassandra brought up a series of images on her laptop: young Black men and women standing on the porch and balcony of an old Victorian house holding guns. "Some of them testified that they carried toy and nonfunctional guns that would not have to be registered, but the police thought their guns were real. For demanding their rights to live as they wanted, those folks lost decades of their lives."

Keisha stared at Cassandra. "Imagine suffering all that violence and harassment for living in a commune in the 1970s—a time when communes were growing like dandelions all over the U.S. Young *white* Americans were forming communes because they were disillusioned with the government after the Vietnam War," she said. Keisha had not felt interested in much of anything for the past four months. Now, she was riveted by Cassandra's account, eager to know more.

"And you're connecting all this MOVE material with Jeremiah Shabazz, the head of the Philadelphia Temple of the Nation of Islam? I thought he was working with Malcolm X?"

"At first, yes, but after Malcolm made his pilgrimage to Mecca, and saw that good Muslims come in all colors, he broke with Elijah Mohammed and formed his own organization. He no longer believed that all whites were devils."

Keisha was trying to recall what she'd read about Jeremiah Shabazz. "I think I remember reading that some scholars think Shabazz was part of the group that planned Malcolm X's assassination. Shabazz was so committed to the separation of the races that he attended a KKK rally."

"No way!" Cassandra was shaking her head. The beads in her braids made small musical sounds clicking against each other.

"These intersections are really interesting and important to document. So, you're finding strange bedfellows among those who supported Black economic development? The Nation of Islam, MOVE, and Reverend Sullivan, all pursuing it with different approaches?"

"Yes. There's a similarity in their naming, too. Many MOVE members replaced their last names with 'Africa' the way the Nation of Islam members replaced theirs with 'X' or took African names. Both groups worked for Black *self-sufficiency*. Isn't that similar to the philosophy behind developing Black Entrepreneurship, Black Capitalism?—'We take care of our own?' Rev. Sullivan was training Black people in the skills that brought higher salaries and a capacity for self-determination. It sounds to me like the same goal. Am I right?"

Keisha smiled, "Yes, at least in part. But think carefully about whether Black capitalism required separation of the races. I believe both Sullivan and MOVE included whites, unlike the Nation of Islam. Explore how the U.S. government related to all three. I think you know Richard Nixon's Administration funded some Black Capitalist ventures in his first term. I think he even went to Philadelphia to see Rev. Sullivan's Black-owned shopping center. Nixon also introduced Affirmative Action. Then he switched to his Southern Strategy and courted White Supremacist voters in the South in order to win re-election. With the Alabama segregationist, George Wallace, running against him, he feared Wallace would take votes from him, so he 'out-Wallaced Wallace,' playing on white fears of Blacks."

Cassandra's forehead furrowed. "But I thought Nixon funded Black entrepreneurship because he wanted to keep residents of urban areas from rebelling?"

"Some scholars say so. I don't know enough to say. But this is amazing material you've gathered. I'm proud of your work. You're going to Philadelphia next week to do more research, right? Ronald is there now working on Black Capitalism. I think your work is complementary. Why don't you meet with him while you're there? You could probably really help each other. I'll check with him and send you his contact info."

Keisha closed her laptop, suddenly feeling exhausted. "I'm sorry that my personal life has prevented me from being more involved with your research. I am so happy to see that my neglect hasn't held you back."

Cassandra had been talking almost nonstop. She, too, looked weary. "Dr. Johnson, I couldn't be doing this research without what I've learned from you in our seminars. I hope I can be half the scholar and teacher that you are. Thank you for encouraging me to pursue this."

Driving home from campus, Keisha mulled over what Cassandra

had taught her about MOVE. She knew so little about her mysterious biological father, Reggie Lewis. She owed it to her students as well as to her children to learn more.

She was glad she'd sent in that DNA sample.

Chapter 22

By mid-June Ronald had arrived in Philadelphia and moved in with his uncle and aunt who invited him to stay for free. Dr. Brown seemed to understand his change in plans.

They ate breakfast in the back yard his first Saturday with them. June in Philadelphia was still pleasant weather-wise, although his uncle cautioned him not to take the nice weather for granted. "You can fry eggs on the sidewalks in July and August. When your cousin was five, he actually tried it!" His uncle laughed, remembering.

"Most of the summer you feel you're on the inside of a cow," his aunt joked, "damp and hot and traveling from stomach to stomach." They chuckled at her imagery.

His uncle retorted, "Ronald spends his days in the Temple library where the air conditioning is so strong, he wears a winter sweater. We'll probably have to inform him when July and August arrive."

Ronald liked the easy repartee between his uncle and aunt. They had the knack of making room in most conversations for laughter. He also liked his room in their house. It was on the second floor, had good Wi-Fi, and a window overlooking the back alley.

When he'd first arrived, he'd experienced a holdover from his childhood, the feeling of walking on eggshells, anxious not to offend these folks who were taking him in. Despite living happily with Grandma for eleven years, the first time he stayed somewhere else, that old stomach crunching fear of offending and being rejected returned. It was one of those default fears no amount of achievement could banish.

That afternoon, he walked around Progress Plaza and the Yorktown Community behind it, built by Rev. Sullivan to recruit middle-class Black people into the city to live in suburban luxury in the heart of North Philadelphia. His uncle's and Dr. Brown's connections were helping him locate elderly North Philadelphia residents who'd lived there since the early 1970s and who were willing to be interviewed. His uncle vouching for him paved the way. He had also attended Yorktown's neighborhood association meeting earlier that week and located a few people to interview there. His research was going quite well, he informed Dr. Johnson in an email.

One afternoon an email popped up from Cassandra, Dr. Johnson's other advisee who was also researching in Philadelphia. She suggested they meet to share what they were learning.

Ronald found Cassandra intimidating. In class she never held back, jumping into discussions with vigor and challenging others to take apart her arguments. The woman was so confident and intelligent. And attractive. He wrote back suggesting they meet on Friday at the Du Sable Museum of African American History. There was an inexpensive café down the block where they could talk over coffee. When she texted a thumbs-up, his confidence soared. He told himself he would not walk on eggshells with Cassandra.

They met outside the café and found a booth in the corner where they could each open their laptops and still have room for coffee and pie. Their conversation was easier than Ronald had expected. She seemed genuinely interested in what he was finding.

Chapter 23

Paris was silent at 5:30 a.m. on Bastille Day. Most Parisians were still asleep. But by 8:00 the air in their St. Deny neighborhood would vibrate with the sounds of its polyglot immigrants' lilting and guttural voices, chatting as they set up their stalls in the open-air street market below Joan's apartment. The sound of health care professionals scurrying along the sidewalk to check in or out of their shifts at the hospital would float up to her window, too. By late morning, children's laughter would be heard, as families set out with picnic lunches and bottles of wine to lie on the grass of parks or sit on the curbs along the parade routes to observe this holiday.

But this early in the morning, the neighborhood was mostly silent, except for the occasional hum of car tires against pavement still wet from the early morning shower and a few trucks wheezing to a stop, shifting gears, and groaning as they picked up speed to cross vacant intersections.

Joan lay on her side of the bed, her hair spilling over her pillow like a dark cloud. In the mid-July heat, she'd pushed off the top sheet, which lay bunched at her feet. Too early to rise. Too early for anything but the procession of quandaries that marched through her mind.

The ceiling fan stirred the thick heat. Beside her Andre, the Frenchman she had loved for twenty years, shifted to his side, hugging his pillow. That little boy habit made her smile. She resisted patting his back, although a current of maternal feeling surged in her momentarily. Since her son was launched as an L.A. lawyer, she'd not made much room in her life for maternal. Her career and her man had taken up all the space.

For an hour, she lay there contemplating: A performance in three days with her band. A song she needed to practice that she hadn't sung in years. The man Andre had called to fix the air conditioning in the apartment— was he coming today at eleven? Her drummer, diagnosed with Coxsackie virus and quarantined with his young family, who all had contracted it. The arrangement she needed to finish. Andre's disappointment at having to cancel their Croatian seaside holiday. The email from her sister.

She got up, careful not to disturb Andre, and slipped into jeans and a tunic, bunching her runaway hair at the nape of her neck. Femi's email was the most pressing. She opened her laptop and found it.

> *I heard today from a woman who claims to be Reggie's daughter! She lives in Chicago, Evanston, actually. She found me through 23andme, the DNA test. She says her mom told her only that Reggie was a hero in the civil rights movement. Then in college, somehow, she discovered his obituary while doing research. Recently, she decided to try DNA analysis to see if she could locate any of his family, and that led her to me. She suggested we might meet on Skype or Messenger. I'm debating whether to invite her to the house. Reggie's child! It makes me happy to know he has a child in this world, something good to live on after him. I thought maybe you and I could talk tomorrow?*

She reread the email. They rarely mentioned Reggie, but he was always there. She resisted an impulse to reply, fearing the ping of incoming mail might awaken her sister, as it was seven hours earlier in Chicago and Femi would be in her REM sleep.

When she looked again at the message, she saw Femi had attached the woman's email. She opened it. Fairly terse, like someone hesitant, perhaps afraid she would not be welcomed? She had inserted a photo of herself (presumably) with two teenaged children: a tall girl, attractive, wearing her hair in a soft 'fro, and a boy, who might be a bit younger, darker-complected and serious looking. Each had an arm wound around the woman's waist. The woman staring out bore some resemblance to Reggie. She had that serious, intelligent gaze Reggie had, but something in her expression conveyed...was desolation too strong a word for the aura she gave off?

When Andre woke up two hours later, Joan was still there, in the oversized leather chair, asleep, the open computer on her lap, long dark.

Chapter 24

On the fourth month anniversary of Richard's death, Keisha stood beside the table in the bedroom where Richard's keyboard had found its home, where he sat so many hours while complicated harmonies played in his head and descended through his fingers onto composition paper. If only he were here now, face intent, eyebrows raised in that expression that told her he was onto something new. She could see his long fingers playing across the keyboard, trying out the harmonies he heard, gentling new combinations of sound, then scribbling notes on the staff, smiling to himself, delighting in the music only he could hear.

She missed him so much. She wanted to share her search for Reggie's relatives with him. She needed his focused attention that erased everything else but her and the problems she was pondering. Unlike Richard, she needed to talk her way to understanding. How often he had made room for her to do that with him, listening closely, even when her needs were pulling him from his own creative work. How often she'd gone on and on, talking through something puzzling her, until, like a kaleidoscope, the shapes found their way to a new configuration, and she knew what to do. *Oh, Richard! Why did you leave so soon?*

She walked to his chair in front of the window, moving like a much older person, her grief fresh again. She slid into the chair and ran her fingers over the grain of the oak table that served as his desk. Years ago he had given her his study and had begun using the table in front of the window as his work space. He had joked that would keep her chaos in the other room and ensure their bedroom was orderly.

Her favorite photograph of Gran Cora and Grandpa Arthur stood on the right side of the table in a rugged wooden frame. It arrived a month ago with a note in Gran's distinctive handwriting: "Raw wood, Keisha, like all of us, still becoming. You're still becoming too, my lovely grandchild. You will get through this. You will make a new way. Paths are made by walking."

She let the new information simmer. She had just spoken with her aunt, a woman she had not known existed, a woman who lived in Paris with her French husband, singing jazz in the clubs Josephine Baker sang in nearly a hundred years ago.

Their conversation had been less awkward than she would have expected. But what do you say about your half-century life to a stranger who happens to be your unknown father's sister and who never knew you existed? They spoke of the other aunt also, Femi, who lived in Chicago, who had three sons and grandchildren. And an uncle in New York. But Reggie's parents—Keisha's biological father's parents—had died years ago, according to her Parisian aunt.

She'd learned about this extended family so quickly after sending in her saliva sample in the 23andme DNA kit her mother had given her last month. "Something to distract you. You always wanted to know more about your father, and maybe this will help," Mom had said.

The report said she was half Jamaican with roots to Sierra Leone and other roots to Scotland, as well as a dash of Slavic and German. Nothing concrete about her father's people. Then an email had arrived from a woman in Chicago named Femi who said she was Reggie's sister. Keisha had replied, and then, this morning, the phone call from Paris, from the singer who said she was Reggie's baby sister. Said she had idolized her tall, handsome brother who was so courageous, who died far too early, far too violently.

Keisha's hands were trembling. The first time her hands had shaken was when, in college, she'd come upon that newspaper article about the police raid on a row of houses owned by Black middle-class families in West Philadelphia. It was dated May 14, 1985. The notes she had taken that day were barely legible, the wiggly letters betraying her terror. She had read that the police, with the approval of the city's first Black mayor, had ordered the families who lived there to evacuate their homes. Then, at 6 a.m., the police had begun to fire on the allegedly armed group inside one of the rowhouses.

Newspaper photos showed a nice neighborhood, two-story rowhouses with crisp white trim and columned front stoops, across from Cobbs Creek Park. Journalists wrote that the 6200 block of Osage Avenue was a place where people knew each other, shared barbecue, let their children play ball in the safe, quiet street.

Then, five hundred police had gathered in the street ordering the

MOVE members to come out and surrender. Gunfire from inside met 10,000 rounds of ammunition fired by police outside the MOVE compound in the space of ninety minutes. The police had to send for more ammunition as the shooting continued all day.

In the late afternoon, a police helicopter flew low over the rooftops and dropped a makeshift bomb onto the roof where MOVE folks had constructed a kind of bunker. The bomb was C-4 explosives provided by the FBI, and the explosion shook the entire neighborhood.

Within an hour and a half, the entire north side of that block of Osage Avenue was on fire. The fire consumed three blocks of houses. Sixty-one homes were completely destroyed, and 250 Black people made homeless. Police Commissioner Frank Rizzo had ordered the firemen not to put out the fire. It killed eleven MOVE members, five of them children.

Only two MOVE members survived, one woman and one child. The woman was convicted of riot and conspiracy, and imprisoned. Four years after her release in 1996, a jury ordered the city to pay her half-a-million dollars for its violations of her constitutional rights.

It was the largest residential fire in Philadelphia's history. And it was deliberately set by the police. No one was ever punished for the killing of eleven people and the destruction of so many people's homes.

And on the street, another Black man lay dead: Reggie Lewis, shot by police when he tried to stop them from firing all those bullets into the MOVE home. He died not knowing he had a daughter in this world named Keisha.

Would he have died so young if Mom had told him she was pregnant? It was the thought she had suppressed for decades. *What would Reggie have done if he had known Ann carried his child?* Did Mom ever feel responsible for his death? Keisha's body shivered. No point in going down that road. That was then; this was now, and now, thirty-four years after his death, Keisha had just spoken to a member of her biological father's family.

She needed to get control of herself before the children came looking for her. Cora had dance class until one, and Caleb was still at a sleepover at his friend's house. She looked at her phone. There was probably time for a conversation with Uncle Edward. She fetched a glass of water and sat at Richard's worktable, her eyes staring at the back garden, unfocused. Then, she called Uncle Edward. His voicemail kicked on. "If I've given you this number, then please leave me a message and your number and

I will call you as soon as I can. If I <u>haven't</u> given you this number, please hang up and don't call again." His message always made her smile, but today she really needed to talk with him.

"Uncle Edward, this is Keisha. I need to talk to you. Urgently. Please call me. 312-978-1257."

Within minutes, he called back, apologizing. He'd just returned from a bike ride along the lake shore and had been in the shower. Now he was clean and dry and ready to listen.

She could picture him in his leather recliner. A video chat would be distracting, so they simply talked.

"Reggie's baby sister Joan just phoned me from Paris. She sounds nice, but I keep seeing that rowhouse blazing, imagining him trying to stop the police, and being shot dead for trying to intervene. I can't stop shaking. Other than Mom, you're the only person I know who knew him. Please help me."

"No wonder you're shaken. Talking to her made your father's death real." He didn't add, "so soon after Richard's terrible death," but Keisha was sure they both were thinking that. "Tell me about the sister."

"Her name is Joan, and she lives in Paris with her French husband. She's a professional jazz singer. Grown children, I think. She said she was fifteen years younger than Reggie. Said she idolized him."

"Did she mention the MOVE raid?"

"Only vaguely. Something like, 'his violent death.'"

"I remember how close he was to his family. He was the eldest and very responsible. His parents were from Jamaica, strong people, Garveyites, as I recall. Raised him to be a strong Black man, a 'race man' who would dedicate his life to helping his people. When I knew him, he was struggling with their expectations, I think because of your mom and the feelings he had for her. He didn't think they would accept his falling in love with a white woman."

"I think Joan married a white man."

Keisha heard Edward sigh. "Fifteen years can make a big difference in people's attitudes. Maybe because she was the youngest? They can get away with a lot more than us oldest and onlys. Did you learn anything else about the family?"

"Yes. He has another sister here in Chicago. She's been in touch with me by email. And a brother in New York. Apparently, I have a bunch of cousins. She said she'd email me some photos. Both of their parents are dead, but Joan, the woman in Paris, talks to her sister Femi in Chicago every week. She said she'll be coming to the States on tour in November and will be in Chicago. She suggested we meet up. She'll send me tickets to one of her Chicago gigs. Uncle Edward, I haven't said much to the kids about Reggie. Caleb was protective of Dad when Reggie came up in a conversation this summer. I think he thought I was being disloyal to my dad by being interested in learning about Reggie. I *am* interested in pursuing this, but the kids have been through so much this year."

"If you decide to talk with them, I'd be glad to be there, in case they have questions about him. You know, he was my hero. I can come out on the L without much notice. I'd be pleased to introduce Reggie to his grandchildren."

Keisha heard a catch in his voice. She'd never thought about how Reggie's death might have affected Uncle Edward. Her trembling subsided.

"Keisha, you will know when it is time to talk to Cora and Caleb and what to say. Is there more you want to know from me?"

She was silent, sorting through her questions. "Yes. Why would my biological father go from being a civil rights activist with the Student *Non-Violent* Coordinating Committee to joining what sounds like a cult, an *armed* cult? What did he hope to achieve 'for his people' by being part of MOVE? Had he become a revolutionary? And if so, why?"

"I'm afraid I lost contact with him before he moved to Philadelphia and met MOVE. Maybe those are questions you can ask Joan and the other siblings?"

"I don't know if he stayed in touch with them when he got involved with MOVE."

"They can answer that. The historian Keisha wants details, dates, and places. I can only give you feelings. Your father was a good, caring man, a dedicated man who was determined to do something to further the Movement. After 1968, strategy disagreements at the national level and Nixon's crack down saw the Movement shift its focus back to its origins in local grassroots communities. The country fell in love with 'Law and Order,' and the Movement became mostly local in the Seventies and Eighties. My guess is that Reggie remained a Movement activist and shifted his own work to Philadelphia because Philly had become a leading area for creative organizing. But how he ended up with MOVE? That's a mystery. It sounds like you have some research to do, real and important work you can throw yourself into. It may help you to pursue this."

"Uncle Edward, I don't know what to do about Mom. Should I tell her about this contact? Will it upset her?"

"What do you think?"

"Well, she gave me the DNA test as a gift so I could find out more about Reggie, so I think she wants to be supportive. But if his family would have rejected her, she might not be able to go with me on this journey. That would be hard on her."

"One step at a time, Keisha. Bringing her along is a way of showing her—and your dad—that you love them. But it is *your* journey, and they both will understand that. You will figure it out, who to talk to, when, what to say. You are your parents' daughter—all three of them."

Keisha heard the front door open and Caleb calling up the stairs. "Mom, I'm home." His voice wavered between tenor and baritone. "I'm in the bedroom," she called back. "I'll be down soon."

"You know where to find me, Keisha. Your young man needs you now, and I need a bathroom break. We'll talk soon." Uncle Edward clicked off before she could reply.

"Coming," she called, stopping first at the bathroom sink to splash cold water on her face. Mom had been right about the DNA results distracting her.

The following morning, the telephone dragged her from a fitful sleep populated with dreams that she was drowning. She picked up the phone too late, but whoever she missed left a voicemail message. It was Uncle Edward.

"I didn't sleep well last night. I realized you and I had never talked about your birth father before. Maybe I could have saved you some pain if I had told you seventeen years ago, when we first met, that I had been close to him and would be available to talk with you about him. In typical introvert fashion, I left it up to you to initiate that conversation. This call is to say I'm sorry I let all this time pass without our talking about Reggie. Oh, and I did think of one thing that might help answer your questions, so let's talk when you're up to it. I love you, Keisha. Reggie would have loved you, too. Like your mom and dad, Richard, the children, and your students love you."

She felt the hot smart of tears as his message ended. She knew she was lucky to be loved by these people. It didn't take away the pain of her losses, but it was important to remember.

She zombie-walked through her shower and pulled on jeans and one of Richard's flannel shirts that he wore around the house on Sundays before they had started to go to church. She and the kids hadn't gone to church since his funeral.

She tucked her hair into a hair clip, seeing with chagrin a steak of white she'd not noticed before. She didn't bother with makeup. She made herself coffee, and, carrying her phone, moved to the front porch, where she sat in the rocker waiting for Cora to wake up. Caleb was playing a video game in the family room.

She felt listless. It was like she'd gone down a rabbit hole and, like Alice, found the world reversed, everything a mirror image and asymmetric, vaguely familiar, but perplexingly "off." She didn't have the energy to return Uncle Edward's call.

"Mom? Are you alright?" Caleb's voice. He'd come looking for her. Her coffee was stone cold.

"I'm okay. Do you want pancakes?" She had intended to revive their family traditions.

"Naw. I already got myself some cereal. The guys are meeting in the park to shoot hoops. Okay with you? I'll be back by one. Can I get you something?"

He was being so grown up. Before, he would not have asked that. It was so like Richard. He's trying to be the man of the family, she realized, riding a wave of salty sadness.

"I'm fine," she lied. "Be careful out there."

"I'll be fine, Mom. See you." He turned and was gone, leaving the screen door to bang shut behind him.

"See you." Did he see her? Probably more clearly than she'd realized. Since her parents had returned to their Cleveland home after a three-week visit, she'd vacillated between feeling she was getting a grip on her life and feeling devastated. Just when she'd thought things were improving, grief had returned with a vengeance. Her therapist said to beware of the familiar—in this case, grief. It was seductive. It could suck you back into patterns that you embrace simply because they are familiar.

Her children witnessed it all, and it must be so scary for them, especially when grief had her in its talons. Could they even remember her as she had been, now that they saw her stumbling through her days, silent and sightless, leaving them to take care of themselves? She couldn't go on like this. The children deserved better.

Two hours later, she phoned Uncle Edward. "Could you come?" was all she said, surprising them both. He was equally cryptic. "See you around 4."

Cora was in her room listening to music through her headphones when Uncle Edward arrived. Caleb had come home from basketball and left again for a friend's house. Keisha had barely stirred from the porch rocker.

She noticed how white Uncle Edward's hair had become and the way he watched his feet when he stepped up onto the porch. He must be in his seventies now. She suggested he sit in the rocker and fetched a bottle of Merlot and two wineglasses. She settled herself on the wicker chair across from him and poured them each a substantial glass of wine. The crimson wine sparkled in the late afternoon sun.

He waited for her to speak.

"I haven't talked to them, but I think I must. I've drifted so far from them, into my own wounded world. It's not fair to them."

"Are you able to focus on your teaching?" His face veiled his feelings. He was just listening.

"The semester starts in three weeks. I'll use last year's syllabi. I managed to get through my classes in the spring. I've taught the material many times. It probably seemed to my students they were listening to extended robocalls. Not my usual charismatic style!" She grinned.

She could see it made him happy to see this glimpse of her former self.

"All I've been able to read, when I could focus at all on someone else's words, is biography. I've been reading how historical figures coped with loss. Lincoln, Teddy Roosevelt, DuBois—mostly men losing children and spouses. Not much written about women surviving loss historically."

"How about Caleb and Cora?"

"Neglected. I recognize it, but don't do much about it. Caleb is in therapy to work on his anger. He says it helps. I am too. Cora's alone most of the time. Doesn't seem to have friends."

"And you're hoping that if you include them in discovering your other family, it could knit you back together?'

"Yes." Keisha laid her head against the back of the wicker chair. Within minutes she was asleep.

Edward rocked slowly watching her sleep and then nodded off himself. They sat for some time, both dozing, until the soft rhythm of Cora's feet padding down the wooden stairs inside the house pulled Edward awake. He opened the screen door and followed Cora into the kitchen.

"How is the smartest fifteen-year-old at Evanston High?" he bantered. She turned from the kitchen counter and extended a plate with cheese and crackers, smiling warmly. "It's so good to see you," she said.

When Caleb rode up the driveway on his mountain bike and parked it in the garage sometime later, Edward and Cora were working on supper. Edward called it creative cookery. Pasta with whatever veggies could be found, and a piquant, aromatic peanut and ginger sauce. A real homecooked meal.

They carried their plates to the side porch—Edward's idea. The early evening sun through the glass roof of the porch made everything brighter. Hearing them, and smelling the aromas of garlic and peanut butter, Keisha stirred and joined them.

When they finished eating, Edward asked if Caleb and Cora could take time for a family meeting. Both looked surprised but said yes. He asked how each of them was doing. He was family but not every-day-living-together family. Caleb went first.

"We're OK. Actually, we're not. Mom goes in and out of being a zombie. Sometimes it feels like we've lost both our parents."

Cora jumped in to defend Keisha. "It's not her fault. Everything is different without Dad. It's like an amputation of an essential body part. You don't know how to get around without it, without *him*. We each stay to ourselves. Caleb and I try to help, but Mama is just far away. I think we're both scared. We're focused more on her than on Dad, which feels weird. We don't want to be home 'cause there's such a heaviness here. But we feel responsible for Mama and want to help her get through this. It was better when Granddad and Gran Ann were here. They protected us."

"From what?"

"From feeling hopeless, maybe? Gave us someone to talk to who was interested in us."

"And sometimes we all laughed," Caleb added.

Keisha could see that Edward was moved by their honesty. She felt proud of her children.

"Is anybody angry?" Edward looked at each in turn and all three nodded.

"Furious." Keisha said. "It is so unfair. Why Richard? Why pick on such a good person? Why destroy our happy family?"

Caleb raised his voice, his eyes shining with emotion. "*Mom, our family is NOT destroyed,* not unless you want it to be. We are still here, all three of us. *We are still a family. Don't do this to us.*" He stood and left the room. They heard a sharp sound as his hand slammed against the wall.

Uncle Edward spoke in his voice of authority. "Your children are truthtellers, like you. I need a little more time with all of you. Come back and join us, Caleb. Our family meeting isn't over."

When Caleb returned to the doorway, eyes down, Uncle Edward continued. "You are courageous and strong people. Getting through this starts with being honest with each other. So thank you for your honesty. Your mom has some things to tell you and to ask you."

All eyes were on Keisha.

For an hour they talked. Keisha told them about the DNA test and her contact with Reggie's sisters, about Joan's call from Paris, and Uncle Edward's connection to Reggie when they roomed together in Mississippi during Freedom Summer, 1964. She told them they had a whole other family with cousins and great uncles and aunts, some just an hour away in south Chicago. She asked what they thought of this information, and how they thought she should respond.

"So, Mom. Remember how you used to talk to historical people? It sounds like Uncle Edward is one, since he was part of Freedom Summer. We learned about that in U.S. history last year."

Cora corrected her brother. "Gran Ann was, too. Guys are so macho."

There was energy in the room and real conversation. There was also caution.

"How will Gran and Granddad feel if you get all cozy with Reggie's family? *They're* your parents, after all." Caleb was looking out for his loved ones.

"Do you think we could go to Paris to meet Joan? I've always wanted to go to Paris." Cora was seeing opportunities.

"What if they are criminals or just want to take advantage of us?" Caleb, cautious. Then he spoke again as though pushing RESET. "Does the idea of meeting them make you excited, Mom? Cause if it does, I think you should go for it. We want you back, and if sharing you with them is how that happens, I'm good."

Keisha didn't talk about how Reggie had died, and no one else brought it up. That could wait for another time.

Later, after the kids had returned to their rooms to work on homework, Edward reminded Keisha of her question to him on the phone: Why had her father gone from nonviolent civil rights organizing to supporting an allegedly armed community in West Philadelphia?

"At my age, I'd better tell you this while I'm able to remember," he joked. "The last time I saw Reggie was when 'Snick'—the Student Nonviolent Coordinating Committee—met in 1965 to vote on who they wanted to lead them—John Lewis, the short, humble, religious guy who had been their leader, or Stokely Carmichael, the tall, outspoken guy from Trinidad who advocated the organization expel whites and let SNCC be an all-Black movement. It was a fractious meeting with strong feelings on each side. Reggie sided with Stokely Carmichael, and I sided with John Lewis. Carmichael won, not by much, but all the whites in SNCC had to leave. Stokely's argument was that racism was a white people's problem, and whites should work on that problem among their own people—where the change had to come." Edward poured himself another glass of wine.

"Reggie had grown up in a family that followed Marcus Garvey, leader of the largest mass movement of Black people in American history. Reggie was raised to believe in building the economic, political, and psychological strength of Black people. Get your Black economic act together and let whites work on white folks."

"Do you think my birth father became a Black Panther? They were brokering peace agreements between gangs and feeding and mentoring poor kids in central cities. Seems like he'd be drawn to that."

"I suspect you're right," said Edward. "The Panthers met a lot of hostility, though. It was dangerous being a Panther. They were viewed as militants, radicals, and enemies of white folks in those years. I once met Fred Hampton, the head of the Chicago Panthers. An amazing young man working successfully with gang members to stop gang violence."

"*You met him?*" Keisha was obviously impressed.

"He was gunned down by police as he slept. *He was only twenty-one!* All that talent wasted by police bullets." Keisha had never seen Edward so grim.

"You know, in hindsight I think Reggie, Stokely, and Fred Hampton might have been right. In those days, and ever since then, I followed the integrationist, nonviolent route. I became a church pastor and Reggie and I lost contact. I wish I knew how he made sense of his world. Lord knows, I find it challenging to make sense of mine, especially recently."

They both were quiet for some moments.

"Thank you for mediating this conversation."

"Thank you for including me. You know I need you and your children. The need goes both ways." He looked embarrassed, like he'd said too much.

"Will you come cook on Wednesdays again? I promise we'll Oooo and Ahhh."

"I'd like that."

As Uncle Edward started down the front steps, placing his feet with care so he wouldn't fall, Keisha called to him.

"I'd forgotten that we are still a family."

Caleb appeared as she was closing up the house. "I have an idea," he said. "Uncle Edward isn't married, and he's not your uncle by blood. Why don't you marry Uncle Edward?"

For the first time in a while, he heard his mom's old laugh.

Chapter 25

Femi and Jacob's house was a three-story, sandstone walk-up dating from the 1920s, its entrance a dozen steps up from the street. Femi had lived in the West Woodlawn neighborhood since 1975, when she moved to Chicago from New York to attend the University of Chicago. There she met Jacob, who became her husband two years after she graduated. In 1981, they had purchased this brick rowhouse on South Champion, a half-dozen blocks south of Washington Park.

They bought the house from an elderly white woman whose family was moving her to a nursing home. It was a dump, but Jacob and Femi worked on their fixer-upper house for twenty years, replacing the lath and plaster walls with wallboard, stripping thick layers of grayed paint from the woodwork, tearing up the awful shag carpet to uncover beautiful oak floors that they sanded and polished. On most weekends they'd worked on the house, moving from room to room, project to project, until it was a showpiece. The extended family teased them that the house was their favorite child.

At first, they shared the house with Femi's brother and his small family. What her brother contributed to the rent allowed Femi and Jacob to save money for renovations.

There were five bedrooms—or spaces they made into bedrooms—but only two baths, one on the first floor where Femi and Jacob lived, and one on the second floor where her brother and his family stayed until they moved to Brooklyn.

Femi had taught in the Chicago public schools all those years to pay the mortgage, taxes, and insurance. Jacob's day job as an electrician took care of the rest of their bills.

Their family expanded. Ajani was their firstborn. His name, meaning "the one who wins the struggle," seemed appropriate for an oldest child. Barron arrived two years later, "a noble and free man." They planned to have no more children, but thirteen years later, when Femi was forty-one, along came their change-of-life baby. Jacob named him Aidan because it meant "little fire." "My sperm had a little fire left, I guess," Jacob joked. Aidan never liked his name.

With the three boys sharing one bedroom, no matter how hard they worked, they could not make that bedroom presentable, which was one reason they never sold the house when the neighborhood deteriorated and the crime rate climbed.

In 2019, Femi was sixty-two and still teaching at Till Math and Science Magnet, which was just down South Champion. She planned to retire in a year or two. Of their three sons, only Aidan, twenty-one, was living at home. Aidan's "little fire" had gotten him into big trouble when he was fifteen. Unlike his older brothers, Aidan got involved with the gangs that had moved into West Woodlawn. His homies were closer than family and required him to perform an initiation rite—participating in an armed burglary of the Jamaican Jerk restaurant a few blocks from his home.

In the midst of the burglary the cops arrived. The rest of the Crips scattered. Aidan, the novice, was frozen with fear, caught in his first and only illegal activity. He was sentenced as an adult and sent to prison for six years, although he was released early for good behavior.

He'd been back on South Champion for a year now, living with his parents and trying to recover his life. It wasn't easy for any of them. Femi and Jacob had been trying to help him find a job, difficult with a felony conviction.

On a warm Saturday in July, Femi and Jacob sat on the back stoop soaking up the last rays of what had been a glorious day, puzzling over what to do about Aidan. The back yard was strewn with desiccated leaves prematurely fallen—"like Aidan," Jacob observed to his wife as he nursed a ginger beer.

Aidan appeared in the doorway. "Going out," he said, not making eye contact. Had he heard them discussing him?

"Come join us for a while, son," Femi's voice sounded artificially cheery. Jacob pulled a folding chair from under the steps. Its green plaid woven webbing looked sorrier than Aidan's face as he reluctantly took a seat.

Aidan usually kept to himself, and never said much. When they were together, like now, he kept looking behind him, first to one side and then the other. It annoyed his father, who insisted he look him in the face. Aidan mumbled something about prison making him watch his back.

Can't trust people. Femi's firm hand on Jacob's knee cautioned him to let it go, and he did. They sat silent in the white noise of children playing a couple of yards to the north.

"Joe says he can get you a job as janitor at The Jamaican Grocer." Jacob looked at Aidan to see his response, but Aidan's face remained impassive. After ten minutes, Aidan excused himself, put his chair back under the stairs, and went "out."

A few days later Aidan came to the kitchen for a beer when Femi was starting supper. "What did you mean about prison making you distrustful of people?" she asked him.

He sighed a drawn out do-I-really-need-to-do-this sigh, followed by more words than she'd heard from him at one time since he'd moved back home. "I was a Crip, right? And your brothers are supposed to look out for you. But when others started beating on me one time in the yard, the Crips who saw it just looked the other way. I learned no one's going to help you but yourself."

"We're your parents, Aidan. We want to help you." She could hear in her head Jacob finishing her statement, "but you've got to help yourself."

Aidan seemed to hear the unspoken words. "Yeah, Mom," he said, "I know I've messed up, I'm your number one disappointment." He turned and took the stairs to his room two at a time, shutting the door with a smack.

The following Saturday, Femi and Jacob raked leaves out back together. Working on Saturday projects was the most intimate time of their week, the time when they shared what was going on inside and out.

"Ajani called while you were napping," Femi told her husband. "He has a friend who's hiring and who's willing to overlook Aidan's conviction." She took a long sip of her strawberry pop.

Jacob turned to look directly at her, then turned away, his eyes on the neighbor's cat. "You know if we suggest it—or if Ajani does—Aidan will drop the idea like a hot potato. What kind of influence do we have over him, Femi? None at all."

She was massaging her left calf, trying to release a cramp that made her grimace. "Should we give him an ultimatum? Get a job or find somewhere else to stay?"

Jacob's irritation showed. "We tried ultimatums when he was in high school, and his response was to hang with the Crips and get himself six years. He's the only one of our kids with a GED instead of a college degree. I really don't know what we *can* do. Feels like we're as stuck as he is."

They raked in silence. A black cat stealthily patrolled the top of the wall at the rear of their property that hid the alley. The middle of its body swung back and forth as it moved. A nearly dead blue jay lay amidst the fallen leaves, quivering now and again, its fires almost out. Its struggle with death disturbed Femi. "Our yard is just like the world, predators and victims. Not a good thing to see. Mama would suck her teeth and say this bird is an omen." As a young woman Femi had found Mama's Jamaican folk beliefs amusing. Now they took up space in her head. She tried to dismiss her foreboding.

She took a detour. "I spoke with Joan this morning." They both loved her baby sister who lived in Paris, a city that treated its artists like celebrities. "I told her about the woman who emailed about being Reggie's child. Joan has probably called her by now. I know you're skeptical, Jacob, but Joan and I think we should meet her. What is there to lose?"

"What are you thinking? You want to invite her to our house? Pretending like Reggie's craziness and the shame he brought to this family never happened? What?—We gonna butcher a goat and put on a grand celebration for the prodigal niece? Invite the boys and their children?" His anger surprised her.

"We lost Reggie so long ago—thirty-four years now! If he has a child in this world, it means some part of him still lives. It's a blessing. I just wish Mama and Papa had lived long enough to know her. She's a piece of Reggie, honey. It's not like she's wanting to use us to get some inheritance. She's a university professor with two children, Reggie's grandchildren."

Jacob was silent for some time.

"Why are you so critical of Reggie? It seems you always want us to forget him." Femi sat down heavily at the picnic table under the maple tree.

"Baby, I know you loved your big brother. I know Joan did, too. But I wish you would be realistic about what he did to your family. They were immigrants, facing prejudice every time they opened their mouths and let their patois out, prejudice from white and Black Americans." Jacob tied up the black trash bags full of leaves, moving in bursts of speed that signaled he was upset. Then he stopped and looked directly at her.

"They worked hard to prove their worth, like we have. Then Reggie takes his good brain, all his degrees and charisma, and throws it away on a crazy group of wannabe Africans. Talking against this country. Talking back to police and to the businesses that had made him prosper. He brought it on himself." Jacob threw down his rake. "The way he died—shot by the police for defending those crazy people—it was terrible. It about killed your mama and papa. All those reporters trying to interview your parents, trying to blame them for Reggie's joining that group, saying he had taken up arms against the government... *They could have been deported!*"

"You forget the years he worked nonviolently to improve this country. He was registering voters, for goodness sake! Besides, most of those 'guns' the MOVE people had turned out to be *toy* guns!"

"Okay, I'll give you that. But Reggie could have been a doctor or a lawyer. Man had a brain for anything he wanted to do. Hell, he was managing a shopping center! Instead, he became a political organizer, living poor in West Philadelphia working with a couple dozen crazy Black folks."

"We don't really know what he was doing those last years. Anyway, what does that have to do with Reggie's child? I want to meet her and her children. Joan does, too. She's coming 'across the pond' in November for a series of gigs, including several nights here in Chicago performing at the Jazz Showcase. She can take a few days off before flying to L.A. *We want to meet the woman.*"

Jacob wasn't listening to her. "Living poor, challenging the cops for how they treated Black people. What good did that do? *It got them all killed,* gunned down and then burned to death when the police dropped a bomb on the roof. Got lots of other folk injured too, and their homes burned to the ground. Reggie may have been a hero in the mid-Sixties, but twenty years later, baby, he'd lost his way. And no amount of your romantic remembering will make that heroic to me."

They had never talked so frankly about Reggie. Jacob's evaluation of her brother's life left Femi shaken. She stood and brushed bits of leaf off her jeans, then turned and entered the house without speaking. She needed to think about what Jacob had said.

If she was serious about meeting Reggie's daughter, Femi better know how to answer the woman's questions about Reggie. She could not think straight. Reggie's death and the terrible deaths of the people he defended and called "my family" had made him a mystery to the younger sisters who adored him. She wanted him to be a hero who stood up for those who were mistreated, a legend, not a man who'd lost his way. Even all these years later this conversation hurt.

They'd been so much younger than Reggie. The age difference too great for them to remember much about the years they lived together as kids in the apartment in Brooklyn. She had been seven when Reggie went south to Mississippi for Freedom Summer. The only thing she remembered from then was sensing that Mama and Papa were terrified about his safety, though they didn't speak of it. She remembered the tightness of their faces and how the news preoccupied them. All those young people living with those poor folks in rural Mississippi, teaching them to read and write and registering them to vote.

She remembered Reggie coming home for Thanksgiving that year, 1964, discouraged. Telling them that those "crackers" were determined Black folk would not vote in Mississippi. She remembered that his words got on Mama's last nerve. Mama had told Reggie he could not to talk like that in her house. "Mr. Garvey never saw the use of name calling." *I wonder what Mama would have said had she lived to see Joan marry a white Frenchman.*

Femi recalled no details from that Thanksgiving. Just her feelings. Joy at seeing him safely home. Delight that he still wore his big toothy smile, that his eyes still danced, despite whatever had happened in Mississippi. Her admiration for him was unqualified, and all these years later nothing could change that, not even her husband's harsh assessment. Reggie walked on water. He had been *for* them unconditionally. That was sufficient.

Of course, they all knew he was their parents' favorite. But none of them were jealous. Reggie's specialness gave them bragging rights.

Femi last saw him at Christmas in 1983, when her parents and siblings had gathered in Chicago at her and Jacob's new home to greet Ajani, their first child and the newest grandchild. When she tried to remember the details—what Reggie wore, what he said about his life in Philadelphia—her mind went blank. She'd been preoccupied with the demands of hosting her extended family and being a new mother.

But by that last Christmas together, her parents' faces and body language when they were in the presence of their eldest and most beloved son gave away how they felt. Jacob was right about Mama and Papa being disappointed in Reggie. Like Jacob said, he seemed to have lost his way.

Femi had been standing in the doorway. Now she stepped into the kitchen and pulled the screen door closed behind her. Without making eye contact with her husband, she called over her shoulder, "I'm going to work on supper."

While she was peeling potatoes, it struck her that Jacob's frustration with their youngest and prodigal son might be connected to his feelings about Reggie. Perhaps Jacob was afraid that Aidan might follow Reggie's path. Naming that fear was powerful. Yes, she could see why Jacob was afraid. Maybe she should be, too? For a young man of twenty-one Aidan lived a withered life after prison. None of his homies came around to thank him for taking the rap for them. No evidence of any girlfriends or even boyfriends.

She'd allowed herself to think that maybe Aidan preferred men. (She'd never mention that to Jacob.) Better some relationships than none, no?

Aidan was a young man who wore the aura of an old man. Crazy for a young man to carry himself like that, especially a good looking young man. Femi could tell that people noticed the contrast between her son's visible good looks and his ghostly aura. It made folk uncomfortable. She had observed them looking at him and then looking away, sometimes shaking their heads like they wanted to shake off the contradiction.

Aidan should have been a hero robed in kente cloth, one muscled shoulder emerging strong and beautiful from the parallel rows of woven color. Hadn't he done time without squealing on his homies? That counted for something on the street in Woodlawn. But doing Time had done him. He changed. Not just that he watched his back, distrustfully shifting his eyes to take in the panoramic. No, it was more than that. He was finding safety in hiding. In isolation. Fencing himself off from others.

Aidan's dreams were not just deferred; they'd been discarded. He wore "Ex-Felon" on his face as unmistakable as a tattoo.

Was Jacob right? Was Aidan following the path of the uncle he never met? Maybe Reggie's daughter wasn't the only one needing to know what had happened to Reggie.

At least she and Joan could give Reggie's child a chance.

Chapter 26

For the past two weeks Keisha had been researching her birth father's movements, working backwards from Maybe Crossings, Mississippi, where he had met her mother, to Chicago, where he had stayed while he worked with Dr. King, challenging segregation in Chicago's suburbs. Then to Philadelphia, his final stop.

She'd done her homework, confirmed in her email correspondence with Femi that Reggie had indeed died on the street in front of the MOVE house on May 13, 1985, arguing with the police, trying to halt their assault on the house at 6221 Osage Avenue.

His sister Femi wrote that she thought he had gone back to school in Philadelphia to earn a Master of Business Administration, but she couldn't remember which school he'd attended—Drexel? Temple? The University of Pennsylvania? Keisha had contacted them all, carefully scanning their lists of students enrolled in their business programs between 1970 and 1985. Eventually she found him.

He had been a student in the Wharton School of Business of the University of Pennsylvania in 1976 and dropped out in 1979, just before he would have received his MA.

She'd hunted for a retired professor from Wharton who might have known her father in the Seventies. Three days ago she located one of the few Black professors to teach in the business school.

That's when things began to fall into place. Dr. Walter Jones had joined the faculty in 1976, the same year Reggie entered the university. When she phoned him, he was eager to talk. He remembered Keisha's father as "that bright young man who finished his bachelor's *and* almost finished a Masters in Business Administration—all while managing the first Black-owned shopping center in America—and he did it all in three years!" He said this gleefully, with a deep, throaty chuckle. Dr. Jones seemed to be a man who took pride in another Black man showing what Black men were capable of.

That Reggie had managed the first Black-owned shopping center in

America was new information. It didn't take long for her to find articles online about Progress Plaza and the Baptist preacher who had started it, along with many other Black entrepreneurship programs. Reverend Leon Sullivan had been pastor of Zion Baptist Church in North Philadelphia.

Her grad students, Ronald and Cassandra, had each mentioned Reverend Sullivan. They were back in Chicago now, having completed their research in Philadelphia.

Twenty minutes after her phone interview with Professor Jones, he emailed her the name and contact information of a man who had been a classmate and friend of Reggie's, a man with whom the professor still maintained contact. He'd called George Marshall and Mr. Marshall was looking forward to talking with her when she was in Philly.

She had talked briefly with four people who knew her biological father: an email exchange with his sister Femi, phone conversations with Joan from Paris, Uncle Edward, and now Professor Jones. And her mother, of course, but her mother hadn't known him after 1964.

She had immediately booked a flight to Philly and made appointments to visit with the pastor at Zion Baptist and with Mr. Marshall. The pastor had arranged for her to meet with a group of his elderly parishioners.

Keisha walked rapidly down Broad Street in North Philadelphia, her heels clicking against the pavement. She felt hopeful yet apprehensive about what she might learn. How many more blocks to 3600 Broad Street, Zion Baptist Church?

One side of the church faced a highway, and its front faced Broad Street. It was a large building. Her research showed it had grown from 600 members to 6,000 members under its longest serving pastor, Rev. Leon Sullivan.

The exterior of the old building looked like its glory days had passed. It appeared worn and weary, and the cracked sidewalk leading to the front door was littered with potato chip singles bags and empty cola cans. Zion Baptist Church did not look like what she'd read about, when it was the center of Black community organizing to clean up Philadelphia and develop a phalanx of Black capitalists.

She'd read that the church had been one of Black America's lodestones from the mid-1960s to the early 1980s, attracting young folk from around the nation who were determined to grow their adult lives inside the American Dream, determined to make prosperity accessible to people of color.

Reverend Sullivan had retired in 1988, three years after Reggie's death. From what she'd read, Sullivan was a phenomenal man—nominated for a Nobel Peace Prize five times and author of five books, as well as the initiator of a program that Martin Luther King, Jr. borrowed in his early twenties to involve Black pastors in the economic development of their communities. Sullivan worked with King in Chicago for a while—*had he met Reggie in Chicago?* His success training Black entrepreneurs was legendary. His job training program had 20,000 graduates. And he'd raised the money to build the shopping center Dr. Jones said Reggie Lewis had administered. Keisha could probably learn a lot about her father from Reverend Sullivan. Except that the pastor had died in 2001, eighteen years ago.

Her thoughts about her biological father kept shape shifting. Sometimes she thought of him as her father. But that made her feel disloyal to Don Johnson, who had raised her and been her daddy for almost all her life. Other times, she thought of him as Reggie Lewis, the subject of her research. It was less confusing walling him off as a research project. What was he to her anyway other than the source of her DNA? (He and her mom, that is.)

One thing *was* clear as she stood on the sidewalk looking at Zion Baptist Church: What happened to Reggie Lewis was important to her. And in this year of so much loss, seeking the answers to her questions seemed to be the one thing that pulled her from her grief.

As she turned into the entryway to the church and started up the steps, she wondered why the promise of Zion Baptist and of Reggie Lewis had not lasted.

She stopped in the doorway of the locked building and dialed the number she'd been provided. While she waited for someone inside to pick up, she felt anxious. *Why was this so scary?*

A silky-smooth female voice resonant with—*What would Richard call it? Timbre?*—cooed "Zion Baptist Church. God's blessings on you today." She felt a crazy desire to curl up in the lap of that voice. Instead, she said, "This is Dr. Keisha Johnson from Chicago here to meet with Pastor Stanley."

"He's expecting you, child. I'll be right there to let you in." Within a few minutes Keisha heard a key turning in the old lock and the labored sound of the heavy door scraping across the floor. In the doorway stood a woman probably in her sixties, neatly dressed in a striped brown and cream pant suit that set off the chestnut tones of her skin and her dark brown, perfectly coifed hair. The warmth of her smile, the rich modulation of her voice, and her sophisticated suit suggested to Keisha that this woman ran the show at Zion. Was that how it worked in churches? She was out of her league in this environment.

The hand she extended to Keisha was warm, soft, and the nails carefully manicured, and the smile on her face was confident and welcoming. "Dr. Johnson. Very glad to meet you. I'm Ivy Diggs, administrative assistant here at Zion." As Keisha stepped in, Ms. Diggs relocked the door and gestured for Keisha to follow her to the left down a long hallway.

The room they entered looked like an enormous living room—or a showroom in a used furniture store. A profusion of sofas and overstuffed upholstered chairs, ottomans and sideboards, coffee tables and floor lamps artfully divided the space into conversation areas. At the far end, chairs and a sofa were arranged in a circle, each seat occupied by an elegant, well-dressed woman "of a certain age." Keisha checked them out quickly, trying not to be obvious. She guessed they were in their seventies, although a few looked older.

She didn't notice Reverend Stanley sitting in the midst of them, not until he stood and walked toward her, hand extended. He was a tall, thin, darker-complected man. Keisha felt a rush of longing for Richard's familiarity with this world from his two decades growing up in the church. Would he have known how to act in this Black church? She didn't know.

Reverend Stanley guided her to a large, striped, wing-backed chair, and she sank into it gratefully. The unfamiliarity of the situation had her flustered. The pastor smiled at the circle of women while he explained what they already knew, that Dr. Johnson was seeking information about a Mr. Reggie Lewis who had attended this church and been active in its outreach programs in the Seventies and early Eighties. "Now, I know you ladies remember Mr. Lewis, so don't all talk at once. Who wants to go first?" Pastor Stanley settled back into his chair and waited.

Keisha dug in her bag for her recorder, notebook, and pen. "Can I ask you to say and spell your name when you speak, please? And can you speak into the microphone and then pass it to the next person when you finish?" This was what she did, field research. It was her default, familiar. She began to relax.

But she could see from their faces that this was *not* familiar for them. The women's faces puckered. They looked sideways at each other, their readiness to meet her replaced by bored impatience. Their look communicated quite clearly that they had other things to do. Why was this woman wasting their time? Why couldn't she follow the script, exchange niceties and smiles before rushing into her cold, all-business work? Must be the white part of her.

Reverend Stanley, his intuition working overtime, inserted himself before the chill became a freeze. "I'm sorry ladies. I hadn't realized Dr. Johnson was using you for her *research*. Dr. Johnson, is it possible to proceed less formally? I am happy to make notes as to who is speaking, but I think a *conversation* will be more effective eliciting memories from so long ago than individual recitations."

Keisha felt chagrined and uncomfortable. "I'm so sorry. I am quite nervous. You are absolutely right. I would love to simply listen to your memories." She smiled tentatively at Reverend Stanley. "Thank you for taking down people's names for me."

She paused, debating about saying more, then, before she allowed herself time to recalibrate how to handle this important interview, her words tumbled over each other in a rush. Her heart overtook her head and came down on the side of utter honesty, which was her usual response, although in this situation utter honesty felt quite risky.

She heard herself confessing: "I am looking for information about my biological father." Every one of the women stared at her with new interest. "Reggie Lewis was my biological father, only I didn't know much about him until I was in college. He and my mother met in Mississippi registering voters as part of Freedom Summer. After that they lost touch. I've recently been seeking information about him. Which is why I'm here. And why your memories are so important to me."

She felt a wave of emotion and shook her head to force it away, but her hands holding the pad of paper and her pen were trembling. She heard a murmur or hum. It was the ladies now sucking their teeth with empathy for this woman with the wild hair who might be one of their daughters. A woman on one side of her patted her shoulder. The woman on her other side patted her knee and whispered, "It's going to be all right, child."

Suddenly Keisha didn't fight the tears. She let them slide down her cheeks. Is this what happened to Grandpa Arthur, she wondered. When he went to Nashville all alone, feeling his life was over, and Gran Cora took him to her church? They both had told her that story. How the people at that church had saved him—those people and Gran Cora. They'd offered him a Movement to invest his life in, a lifeline for a sinking man, and he'd reached out and held on. Gran Cora always said to look for the lifelines and hang on.

Some moments later, after Keisha had regained her composure, the women began to talk.

They told of a time long ago when the monumental men of the Sixties had been murdered—Malcolm X and Martin King and the two Kennedys. Fighting to overcome their collective grief, young people like them had turned toward their communities to bring the Movement home.

They spoke of Reverend Leon Sullivan, pastor here at Zion for almost forty years, a mountain of a man himself. They talked of Philadelphia's other Black heroes and sheroes, who'd combined the philosophies of Malcolm and Martin to build mammoth programs right here in this city, programs that trained young people to be entrepreneurs.

"You know your daddy was the administrator of the first Black-owned shopping center in the United States—seventeen stores, most of them Black-owned businesses, plus some major chain store franchises. Oh, yes, honey, Reggie Lewis was nearly as talented as his mentor, Reverend Sullivan. You can be very proud of him. Yes, you can."

That was the start, the statement that broke the ice. Soon the ladies were talking over each other as memories came back. There was elation remembering those years, the pride, the accomplishments, and the handsome young man who spoke English with just the slightest Jamaican accent, a buff young Black man they'd all had crushes on. "Oh, honey, your daddy was…I believe my granddaughter would say '*hot.*'" With that they all were laughing, the kind of contented chuckle that bubbles up when you recall something lovely that you've not thought about in a very long time.

The afternoon shadows leaned into the room and the women reached out to turn on the floor lamps. Still their conversation did not miss a beat. They'd gone on for more than two hours when Miss Ivy, the church administrative assistant, stepped into the room to tell them they'd probably best wind down their conversation or they'd be heading to their homes in the dark.

Cell phones began going off. Spouses or children wondering if they were nearly done, when did they want to be picked up?

Reverend Stanley brought the conversation to a gentle close. "Dr. Johnson—may I call you Keisha?—is staying in Philadelphia for a couple of nights. Perhaps if you think of other things, you could email or text her?"

Several of the women gave him a What-you-talking-about look and he amended his sentence. "Or you can write down your memory and give it to me to get to her, how about that?" Heads nodded.

"Reverend Stanley, you forget you've got a bunch of old ladies here," One woman said. "Now, I know it's easy to forget because none of us look our age—we're all so young and beautiful—but we need you to adjust your expectations." There was laughter around the circle.

Then one after another the women stood, some pushing on the chair bottom to raise themselves to standing. Some picked up canes, one unfolded her walker. One by one they moved to Keisha and wrapped their arms around her. For a moment it seemed to her that as they left their past, they suddenly aged.

"You're doing right, girl. Your daddy'll be happy to know you've come looking for him."

"Your daddy was a fine man. And you are a fine woman. He'd be proud."

"Don't you be sad, now. You are finding answers to your questions. You have children? Well, you can go home and tell them about their granddaddy."

"Reggie Lewis was close to as strong and smart a man as Reverend Sullivan, and that's saying a lot."

Reverend Stanley looked at the last woman to leave. "Ms. Alton, I do believe you'd be the last person to say good-by to Jesus!" They grinned at each other.

Ms. Alton had hung back so she would be the last to say good-by to Keisha. Her eyes commanded Keisha not to look away. "I was your daddy's assistant running the shopping center. I think he lost hope when all those programs—nearly fifty programs, as I remember, programs he and Reverend Sullivan started here—began to go broke. The Eighties were a hard time. During the Seventies the Black nationalists and groups like the Panthers scared the government so much that it gave money to our communities for anti-poverty work. Then Reagan was elected in 1980, and government and foundation money dried up—no housing assistance, cuts in food stamps and welfare, health care. I remember Reverend Sullivan kept preaching about it. He said Reagan was killing the hope of ending poverty in America. I think all that disappointment piled on top of your daddy and wore him down. He dropped out of the University and disappeared. We didn't know where he was. Not till the papers were full of stories about our terrible police chief and his men dropping a bomb on the roof of the row house where MOVE had its headquarters, where its people lived."

The old woman looked away. She was silent. When she turned back to Keisha her eyes were fierce. "I never will forgive Frank Rizzo for what he did to your daddy. And to those children. I said then and I say it now to you, *I hope he is burning in Hell.* It's not what I'd normally say in church, but you are your daddy's girl."

She reached for Keisha and enfolded her in a tight embrace. "I don't know what else you're working through, but I know you will come out all right. Don't let it break you, you hear me?"

Keisha, her face buried in the woman's soft neck, breathed in the smell of her perfume. She felt herself breaking right there, but she didn't want this woman to know. It sounded like the woman had had enough of pain and loss in her life. She didn't need to share Keisha's.

"I hear you. Thank you." she mumbled.

Reverend Stanley gave her a ride to her hotel. When she asked if he was free to have dinner with her, he declined, saying he had to be back at church in forty-five minutes for a meeting of the Deacons.

"What happened back there?" Keisha asked him. She felt overwhelmed by the outpouring of stories and affection and the passion of this group of elderly women.

"They were part of the Movement. Get those people together and they have stories to tell. They parted the Red Sea and waded through the muck, knowing it would return with a force that would lift them off their feet if they didn't move quickly. And in the past several years the Red Sea has come back. And their bodies are too frail now to do it again. They're torn up watching White Supremacists rise again. You gave them a special gift today—a chance to tell you their collective story, what they experienced standing against Evil and, at least for a time, overcoming it. Remembering what they did gives them—and me—hope. Their stories stoke the fires of resistance for me and the others that rise behind them. You too, I suspect. I'll send you their names. I'll include Ms. Alton's phone number. She was the last lady to speak with you. The look in her eyes when she talked about your daddy—like she was seeing him even now, after so many decades—it made me think she might have been in love with him… I hope you got what you were hoping for, Dr. Keisha Johnson. Here's my card. Keep in touch."

"I got so much more than I had hoped for, Reverend. Thank you." Keisha took the card and started toward the hotel. Then she turned back, taking a step toward the curb, but Reverend Stanley had disappeared in a blur of red taillights turning the corner of the night.

Keisha phoned her mom from her hotel room. Mom and Dad had flown from Cleveland to Chicago at her request when she told them she had to go to Philadelphia to meet with a person who knew her birth father. She'd expected her busy parents to suggest she wait a week so they could locate lower-priced tickets and rearrange their full calendars. But they made no such suggestion. Retirement had freed them to come at the drop of a hat, Mom told her. Dad added that their priority this year was to support her, however she needed them. They'd arrived at the house before Cora and Caleb came home from school, and Keisha had flown off to Philly the next morning.

On the phone she said little about her meeting at Zion Baptist Church. "I'm learning so much and people have been kind. I know you're eager to hear about Reggie, Mom, but I need to process it all before I can talk about it. Please don't be offended that I can't talk about it now."

Dad made a joke. "*Finally!* Keisha the Extrovert is behaving like *my* introverted side of the family, processing before she speaks. The girl knows how to bring her other daddy joy!"

They talked about how the kids were doing, and she promised to call tomorrow after dinner time to check in before the kids went to bed. After a round of "I love you," they hung up. She knew her parents both loved her. So why was learning about Reggie—who'd played no role in her life other than a gigantic question mark—so important?

Her night was fractured by fragments of what the women had said. When her alarm went off, she felt tired but eager to escape her broken sleep. She ate at the complimentary breakfast bar and then took a cab to the coffee shop where she was to meet George Marshall at 10 a.m.

It was called the Soul Food Coffee Shop. Scents of fresh brewed coffee and cinnamon and yeast bread met her as she opened the door. The name struck her as incongruous. On this weekday morning she was the only woman in the small restaurant. There were several tables of men who she thought must be the age Reggie would be now had he lived.

"Keisha?" A gentleman with salt-and-pepper hair and beard and a smiling face sat at a table in the front corner of the shop, beside a large window that overlooked the street. He stood and moved toward her. "George Marshall. Let's sit over here." They shook hands and he guided her to the table. Stop and start traffic interrupted the sunlight streaming in the window. Now and again she could see trees and a park a block or more away between the moving vehicles.

Mr. Marshall followed her eyes. "That's Cobb Creek Park. We're not far from Osage Avenue." Osage Avenue, where the MOVE house had stood before the police had burned it down with eleven people inside while her father lay dying on the sidewalk outside. "I thought you might want company seeing it for the first time. We can walk there once we've had our coffee and cinnamon rolls. This place is known for the best cinnamon rolls in Philadelphia."

She suppressed an urge to make a smart remark like, "Does the Soul Food Coffee Shop put greens and grits in their cinnamon rolls?" She didn't know this man and he might be offended by her sense of humor.

Mr. Marshall was tall and fit for an older man. He was dressed casually—ASICS walking shoes and a navy blue hoodie with "University of Pennsylvania" in crimson lettering.

"No Quaker logo?" she asked him. She was scrutinizing the embroidered shield affixed southeast of his chin—a chevron with three white circles in an upside-down V and, across the top, two open books separated by a dolphin. Before she could ask, he explained: "Books for learning, the dolphin from Ben Franklin's coat of arms, and the three circles from the Penn family coat of arms. You're inquisitive, like your father. I see him in your eyes. I suspect you don't like being uncertain about things? Neither did he."

His comment knocked Keisha off balance. For a moment she struggled to retrieve her calm, professional persona. She was determined not to be emotional with Mr. Marshall.

They talked for well over an hour, sipping the dark, strong brew and trying to make the enormous cinnamon rolls last. Richard would have loved this. Before they'd married, he'd bring her cinnamon rolls from the neighborhood bakery on Saturday mornings. He called it "one of my love rituals." Comforting to be eating them now, here, with Mr. Marshall, her birth father's friend.

Mr. Marshall told her that he and Reggie had bonded from their first meeting in Marketing 101 at the Wharton School of Business. They'd shared an apartment for two years. "Then Sharon came into my life." He opened his phone and showed her pictures of his wife, their children, and grandchildren. "Reggie was best man at our wedding. We'd meet for coffee weekly after he dropped out of the university." He grinned conspiratorially over his lifted coffee cup. "I teased him that he was following in the footsteps of that other Wharton drop out, that rich guy Donald Trump, our current President."

That was a different way to think about her father, a drop out from Wharton School of Business after a little more than two years *like Donald Trump,* only a decade later.

"We were both attracted to MOVE for a time. We considered changing our last names to Africa, or to X like some in the Nation of Islam were doing, but I'd worked too hard for my graduate degree. I told Reggie the MBA was more profitable than X or Africa." Mr. Marshall leaned back in his chair smiling. "After he left Wharton, we'd meet right here at this table most weeks. It was about halfway for both of us."

Here. Reggie had sat *here...*

"So you didn't really join MOVE?" She had taken out her tablet and was making notes, her curiosity fully engaged.

"No, never joined and left after they became more assertive. Osage Avenue was middle-class Black families living in row houses, minding their own business. It was also a community that held barbecues for Memorial Day, Labor Day, and Juneteenth. The kids played catch in the street and jumped rope on the sidewalk. It was a *safe* place, a good place to raise a family.... Until MOVE installed loudspeakers and harangued their neighbors to get involved challenging police brutality and the unjust incarceration of Black men. Don't get me wrong. Police brutality and unjust incarceration of Black men were real. MOVE was doing important consciousness-raising work, and they paid a very heavy price for their activism. Lots of folks agreed with them. *We* agreed with them. But other folks resented having their stable lives disrupted by high volume demands for action that came at any time of the day or evening. I got that. It was annoying. Some of their neighbors began doing what MOVE called for—moving their bodies to the street to protest. Only it was *MOVE* some were protesting, *MOVE* 'noise harassment.' Mind you, most MOVE members were doing their own thing—cultivating food so they could avoid the processed foods sold in stores, raising and rescuing animals—-goats and chickens, dogs and cats—and teaching their children inclusive American history and how to protect the environment."

Keisha listened, intent. "So, because of the loudspeakers you left the Movement?" She noticed the men at the tables closest to them had stopped talking and were listening to George Marshall, their eyes glazed, like they were seeing some long-ago familiar scene played out.

"It was more complicated than that." He poured more cream in his coffee and stirred it slowly. He appeared agitated and a bit uncomfortable.

"It was 1978. I was about to graduate with my shiny new MBA. Everything was ahead of me. I started to feel that the MOVE people were fixated on the past, how Black people had been treated, how MOVE people had been treated. To be fair, they had good reason. The police had blockaded their place for *nine months* and then raided it without a warrant. Cops arrested nine MOVE members and then bulldozed the house almost immediately, destroying evidence. All that was *WRONG!* But a police officer was shot during the raid and died, and you know what that means. The facts of the case made no difference. Witnesses said the shot came from the opposite direction, not from inside the MOVE house, and the investigation showed that MOVE's supposed weapons were incapable of shooting anything. Didn't mean shit. Excuse my language."

His face looked grim, angry. Keisha wasn't clear who he was most angry at—the city police? MOVE? Himself?

"You know how it is when a cop is killed. The police union was Hell-bent to punish someone, so nine MOVE members went to prison, sentenced to thirty to one hundred years, all nine charged with manslaughter. By law manslaughter would have brought a sentence of three to seven years, but the judge acted personally affronted by their claims of innocence. And when they came up for parole and still claimed to be innocent, parole was not granted. Two of the nine died in prison, and the other seven were imprisoned *for forty years and more years.* Hell, two are still in prison. It's shameful. There was talk the UN was going to investigate how the government treated them."

Mr. Marshall was working his jaw. "MOVE members on the outside were obsessed about the injustice their friends inside experienced. They worked hard to call attention to how their MOVE family was being treated in the City of Brotherly Love. You can't blame them for that. I guess I had too much going for me to languish in the past. I'm not proud of backing away from MOVE, but that's what I did. Your daddy chose to stay involved with them, though on the fringe. Seven years later, it cost him his life."

He stared out the window where kids rode bikes and mothers walked to their favorite stores, small children attached to one hand.

"The saddest thing to me about that first police raid in the summer of 1978 was the baby who was killed. An officer trampled her to death when they raided the building. He never was charged."

Keisha remembered hearing this from Cassandra. Nevertheless, she asked, "What happened?"

"MOVE didn't believe in government, called government 'an affliction.' They were for back-to-nature, live-in-intentional-communities. So, they had their babies at home and didn't register their births—or anything else—with the government. Kind of like the early Quakers. Keep government out of our lives. Sounds Republican, right? Because that baby's birth wasn't registered, the judge dismissed MOVE's case against the police for killing the child. Like she never existed. It was mean-spirited and just sad."

"Hang on," Keisha said. "Yesterday the ladies at Zion Baptist Church were telling me about all the good economic development work that was going on in Philadelphia around that time. But from what you're telling me, it sounds like the city government was terrorizing people in the MOVE community?"

"*Both* were happening. Reggie and I got interested in MOVE after the 1978 police raid. We got involved because we felt they'd been treated unfairly—they lost nine of their major leaders to police violence and court harassment for what turned out to be forty years! We wanted to help them recover. But I only stayed three years. Left in '82, years before the second police attack on MOVE in 1985." He was shaking his head slowly. "When that happened, I questioned whether I'd made the right decision in leaving. I was messed up for a while after that, thinking I was a sell-out who might have been able to save all those people if I'd stayed. Especially my best friend."

"How did you recover?" Her voice was thin, and her question was personal.

"My wife stayed with me. She and others of my family helped me through. Honestly? I don't know how I recovered. I just know one day I woke up and knew I could go on. Been full of gratitude since then. You know, counting your blessings." He excused himself and walked back to the bathroom. Keisha wondered if he was all right; the conversation had gone so deep.

He wasn't gone long. When he returned he'd reassembled his face.

"You ready to walk?" he asked. He'd become again a man successful in his career and confident in his family life.

She nodded and collected her things while he moved to the cash register and paid their tab. He motioned for her to join him, and they left Soul Food Coffee Shop, crossing the street, and walking toward the park.

"All of this was burned down on May 13, 1985, you know. Sixty-one homes of middle-class Black families. That fire burned three blocks and the fire department made no attempt to stop it... A person could get bitter, but bitter is not better. Better keeps going. Counting the good things. Realizing the work of the kingdom is long haul and needs all of us."

"You sound like a preacher."

"No, Keisha, just a survivor who chose life." He wasn't smiling.

Osage Avenue bore the scars of fire and destruction even now, thirty-four years later. They walked the blocks that had been destroyed by the bomb the Philadelphia's Police and Fire Department dropped on the roof of the MOVE house. "The police had evacuated the area. They'd been ordered to 'Let it burn,' but I don't think anyone was prepared for the size and force of the fire that consumed the community and left only rubble."

George Marshall shook his head. "The families relocated, sucked up their losses, and regretted demonstrating against MOVE. Damn shame. Travesty." Mr. Marshall and Keisha walked toward a major street that formed the western boundary of the eight streets that had comprised this neighborhood. Across Cobbs Creek Parkway lay Cobbs Creek Park, a verdant grassy area shaded by large trees. George pointed to a sunny expanse of grass not yet in the shade. "That's where the MOVE children and their neighbors played. In the sunniest part their parents grew vegetables."

The sun-saturated August day felt incongruous as the images of May 13, 1985, streamed in Keisha's head. She saw the flames lighting the night sky and heard the sounds of shooting and battering, hundreds of policemen laying siege, and the terrified cries of children and adults unable to escape the fire. She pictured the homes of more than sixty families who thought they'd achieved the American Dream caving in, smoking, gone.

"So unnecessary," George repeated, shaking his head.

They were approaching the house—to be accurate, the lot—where the MOVE house had stood. Newer red brick homes built by the city squatted along Osage Avenue now. He told her the city sold the replacement homes to developers for $1 apiece, and the developers sold them to people for $250,000 apiece—bougies, he called the buyers. When she looked puzzled, he explained. "Middle-class folk, bourgeoisie. In the Sixties we called them bougies. Guess I'm dating myself." He chuckled and she imagined he'd have been a good man to have as your best friend. Maybe Reggie was, too.

"They used C-4, you know, that plastic explosive terrorists around the world use, terrorists and the military."

Late that afternoon back in her hotel room Keisha researched C-4 on her laptop. She found a document the General Accounting Office prepared for Congress in 1990. She read that C-4 is a military weapon that can live forever if properly stored. It is cheap and powerful and stored across the U.S. on military installations in twenty-five U.S. states. Its one serious disadvantage is that it is easily pilfered. It often goes missing from military bases and production facilities. A quantity that would easily fit in a duffel bag can do incredible damage. It can also bring big money. Plenty of domestic and foreign terrorists are now and were then happy to pay for it. *Why would the Philadelphia Police Department be using this weapon of war on a small group of Black people who were at worst a cult and at best a utopian community?*

Keisha called home before ordering dinner from an Indian restaurant that delivered. Caleb was eager to tell her about a science project that Granddad was helping him with. How could your science project fail when a respected physicist was your assistant? Ann reported that Cora was going to a school dance on Friday with a girlfriend. Gran Ann planned to take her shopping for a new outfit tomorrow, most likely jeans and that Pink hoodie she'd been wanting. She didn't put Cora on the phone. Her parents sounded happy, enjoying this time with the kids, although their voices seemed a bit forced.

Keisha was glad she could be here in Philadelphia for these three days while her folks were with her children. "I can't thank you enough," she told them. "I'm going to beg off and go to bed. I didn't sleep much last night." She hung up before Mom could question her. She wasn't ready to share what she was learning.

Chapter 27

"*Why did she leave?*" Cora's voice was metallic and full of rage. "*Why did she leave us? Now? No explanation.*"

"Honey, she had a chance to go before her classes start and follow up contacts with people who knew her birth father. She wasn't *leaving you*. She made sure Granddad and I would be here. And it's only three days."

"Gran, I don't mean to disrespect you, but she did leave us with no explanation. And it's typical. It's how she's behaved since Dad died. She's supposed to be the grownup, but she just wallows in her feelings. And I hate it. *I hate her.*"

Cora ran up the stairs to her room, slamming the door behind her.

Her thoughts swam frantically, unable to find a place to land. She wanted out of her house, her family, her life. She wanted to disappear.

She gathered a change of clothes, her phone charger, and the money she'd squirreled away in her sock drawer for a new phone. She shoved it all in her backpack along with her blankie, the tattered remains of the quilt she'd slept with since she was a baby. She cracked the door to her room and listened. She could hear Gran Ann and Granddad in the kitchen talking, voices hushed. She was sick of people tiptoeing around this house, whispering, avoiding real contact, afraid they'd add to Mama's troubles. She was sick of taking care of Mama, of being the responsible one. For once they'd have to worry about *her*.

She had no idea where to go, but she knew how to leave the house without anyone knowing. From the tiny balcony off Dad and Mom's bedroom, she could climb down the wrought iron fire escape that led to the driveway. No window from the kitchen looked out on the driveway, only the back door, so Gran and Granddad wouldn't see her leave.

She took a last look around her room, grabbed her toothbrush, a hand towel, and a picture of Dad that she kept under her pillow. Then stealthily she left her room and entered her parents' bedroom, careful to open the window to the balcony and to close it behind her without making a sound. Down the fire escape. Through the shrubs that shadowed the driveway. Down the alley. Lake Michigan was only ten blocks away. There she sat on a rock sorting her options.

When no clarity came, she lay back on the rock and closed her eyes, letting the sun's warmth sink into her face, her arms, her legs. The advance of afternoon brought partial shade to dapple her body. It felt comforting to lie there away from all of them on this mid-August day. The turmoil inside banged around for a while and then subsided.

She must have dozed off. She heard someone calling to her. She opened her eyes and sat up to see an old woman pushing a grocery cart along the asphalt path behind the rock where Cora was resting. "You okay?" The woman called again. Her face had a large purplish mark that ran from her forehead down her cheek. Cora felt uneasy. "I'm good," she said, hoping the woman would go away.

"You live around these parts?"

"No," Cora lied.

"You hungry?"

Actually, she was, but she didn't want to admit it.

"I got some bread. You can have some."

Indecision. Was this someone she could trust? She'd never had a one-on-one conversation with a homeless woman before. Mama would say "houseless," but Cora was angry at Mama and didn't autocorrect herself.

"I know this part of Evanston. The police patrols don't come this way for another couple of hours. We can share some bread and then I can show you where you can sleep tonight and not be bothered."

The woman dug into the heap of stuff in her cart, what looked like blankets and clothes, assorted finds she had probably pulled from trash bins. She came up with a loaf of raisin bread dented on one side as though some canned goods had sat on it. She carried the bread to Cora's rock, walking slowly and minding her steps. There were sweat stains on her green shirt—under the arms and across her back. Her hair was wrapped in a colorful head tie, and she wore blue sweatpants and red sneakers. She smiled warmly at Cora as she settled herself on the rock beside her and opened the plastic bag, offering Cora some bread before she helped herself.

"You got plans?"

Cora shook her head no.

"Gotta have plans, young girl like you. Got no family?"

Cora chewed the bread. It tasted really good, especially the raisins. Eventually when the woman kept looking at her waiting for an answer, Cora spoke.

"My father's dead and my mother went away. It's just me and my brother." She was feeling sorry for herself so decided to leave out Gran and Granddad.

"And you be the oldest, I bet. Just like me. My daddy died young, too. A whole lot to cope with when you're… What are you, seventeen?"

It pleased Cora that the woman thought she looked that old. Maybe she'd let her think that. What did it matter? She nodded.

"I'm glad to hear that, young lady. 'Cause at seventeen you can get into shelters and find a safe place to stay." Her comment alarmed Cora.

They ate more bread. Cora wished she'd remembered her water bottle.

"What happens to younger girls?" She tried to sound nonchalant.

"Oh, the ones fifteen and younger get picked up by the police and, if they don't have a safe home to go to, they take them to juvie. Lock 'em up there till they figure out what to do with 'em."

"What choices do the younger girls have?"

The woman chuckled. "No choices, child. They stay at juvie or the state sends them to a foster home. Even the programs for runaway kids won't take them overnight if they're that young." Behind them the sky was streaky, and it cast an orangey-pink light on the lake water. The woman gazed at the lake. "Pretty out here. I think I'd like to live here."

"Where do you live?"

"Wherever. I been on the street for three years now. There's a freedom in it, and you learn how to get by—which restaurants throw out their leftover food, where you can dumpster-dive without being seen by the cops, where you can lie down for the night and not be bothered, where the public toilets are that aren't locked up at night, and where they have paper towels so you can wash yourself."

"Do you like being homeless?"

"Let's say I've mastered it. Somebody try to mess me over, I go all crazy on them. It scares them and they back off, most of the time. There are skills to learn whatever your life brings you." She was chuckling again.

Cora was beginning to be glad the woman had spoken to her. It felt companionable and safe, safer than being hauled off to juvie, although she hadn't a very clear picture of what that would be like.

"How did you become homeless?"

"That's a long story but, long story short, I married a man who started drinking ten years in. He'd spend all the money we both earned on booze. He got into trouble with the law, added drugs to the booze, and after some years started beating on me. Didn't know what to do, but I figured life had to be better than that. So, I left. We hadn't had kids, so I was on my own. Had no papers, no money, no nothing—just what I could carry. Took the L as far north as it went and began my new life." Her eyes, still on the lake, were unfocused, like she was fishing, and nothing was biting. "Winters are rough, but I stay in shelters when it's bad cold. Haven't figured out another way than this. You have any ideas?"

"Don't you have other family somewhere you could go to?"

"Really, I don't know. Haven't had a phone number for a long time, or any addresses. My parents are long gone. My brother and his wife was on the South Side, but they was about to move when I runned away. Like I said, I don't have any kinfolk who'd know where to find me."

Cora's eyes went wet.

"Now, don't you be feeling sorry for me. I have angels looking out for me. One of them directed me to walk this way today and look what I found!" She was looking straight at Cora.

The woman swiveled her head to scan the sky. "Guess we better be thinking where we're going to sleep tonight. You want company?"

Cora nodded. "Is that okay?"

"Of course. Don't forget your fancy backpack."

When Cora didn't come down for dinner, Gran went up to her room and knocked on her door. No answer. "Your mom's coming home tomorrow evening, honey." Gran called to her before going back downstairs. *Better to let her sleep off her funk*, she was thinking.

In the morning, Gran returned to Cora's room. She'd slept intermittently, worried about Cora and what they should do about her. This time she opened the door.

Ann and Don tried Cora's cell phone. Nothing. Must be dead. Then they called the police, who told them runaways usually return within twenty-four hours. They should wait it out. Department policy was not to start looking until at least twenty-four hours had passed.

They discussed whether to call Keisha, but there was nothing she could do from Philadelphia, and she'd be back in Evanston tonight. They would have to sit tight. At least Caleb was all right. He'd gone off on his bike before Gran had discovered Cora was missing. He'd agreed to be home by five. And she had his phone number.

Gran began phoning shelters for runaways—she could locate only one, and it would not allow fifteen-year-old kids to spend the night. Don drove Keisha's car around the neighborhood looking for Cora. She wouldn't have had the resources to go far, would she?

Chapter 28

They'd "slept rough" in a secluded corner of the neighborhood park. Cora used her backpack as a pillow and lay close to the woman. She was surprised how the ground retained the day's heat so she wasn't chilled.

The woman and Cora exchanged names—Lucy Jordan seemed happy enough to have Cora with her. When they woke up, a man was sleeping nearby. "Al" and Lucy greeted each other. Cora bought breakfast for the three of them at McDonalds, although Lucy seemed really nervous that someone might take her grocery cart that she'd parked behind the McDonalds, hiding it as best she could among the dumpsters.

Cora was still puzzling what to do. The morning passed in casual conversation, the two adults sharing a park bench and talking comfortably about their lives while Cora sat yoga-fashion on the grass in front of them listening.

At noon Lucy said it was time to get to work and they headed out for Lucy's favorite dumpsters. Cora watched her cart while Lucy dug through the refuse, coming up with dinner rolls and a Styrofoam container of half a hamburger, someone's leftover lunch. Underneath all the greasy paper, paper cups, and containers was another Styrofoam container with a full order of pancakes. "Person must have changed their mind. No sign anyone has even tasted this! I hit the jackpot!" Lucy exclaimed.

They moved on down the street to a bakery. The clerk was just throwing out stale bread from two days ago. She did a doubletake seeing Lucy and Cora. "Got your granddaughter with you, Lucy?" Lucy was clearly a regular.

"I wish." Lucy threw Cora a conspiratorial grin. "This is a good woman. Tuesdays she feeds the homeless outside St. Marks."

Cora was beginning to think being homeless might be fun.

"Have you seen Harvey lately?" the clerk asked Lucy. "He's not showed up the past two weeks."

"He's been in the hospital. Got roughed up pretty bad. His kidneys were damaged, is what I heard. Some kids on fentanyl wanted money from him. Imagine that—money from Harvey! Poor man wouldn't hurt a fly, and he'd have given them the shirt off his back, wouldn't know any better. They kicked him till he was half-dead! I was on the next block when it happened. Saw the ambulance." She turned to Cora.

"Don't you forget. Everybody on the street isn't like me and Al." Her face looked stern.

They said good-bye to the bakery lady and kept walking.

"You gotta plan yet?"

"No."

"Think maybe you should go on home? I'd be glad to go with you, make sure you get there in one piece."

Despite the heat of the day, Cora felt frozen.

Chapter 29

George Marshall had suggested Keisha talk with the MOVE survivors who had been released from prison in the last few months. Her last day in Philadelphia she planned do that, if she could locate them. He'd supplied phone numbers for Ramona Africa and for the daughter of a MOVE member who died after getting out of prison. Ramona Africa was the only adult to survive the fire set by the police at the Osage Avenue house in 1985. Keisha texted both women asking to talk. Neither had replied.

She brushed her teeth and fell into bed, without the energy to hang up her clothes. She was exhausted and overwhelmed. She would try the women again in the morning.

When she awakened, there was still no response from either woman. She had five hours before she had to be at the airport for her flight home. Over breakfast she perused brochures on what to see in Philadelphia. Remembering that Ronald had said the African American museum was well done, she left her bag at the front desk of the hotel. It was an easy walk to the museum.

The exhibit on the ground floor drew her attention. Glass boxes held life-sized mannequins of Black historical figures from the nineteenth century "talking" about their lives. It was interesting and well done, but she kept wondering what Reggie Lewis would say about his life. Why don't museums include people like him, people who invested their lives to better the world but were cut down in their prime?

Still no texts from the MOVE women.

She returned to her hotel, retrieved her bag, and settled in the business area of the lobby, deciding to spend the remaining hours before her flight researching. There were books on MOVE she hadn't read, and she ordered two, including a book by the founder's sister. There were interesting reports in the media about the fifteen-month stand-off in 1978 between MOVE and Philadelphia's then-mayor, Frank Rizzo.

George Marshall said Reggie and he were drawn to MOVE because of what they perceived as a giant miscarriage of justice. The two friends were outraged when eleven MOVE members were arrested August 8, 1978, and nine of them were sentenced to thirty to one hundred years in prison for the murder of a police officer. They'd wanted to help.

Following up on what she'd learned from Mr. Marshall, she sat before the computer reading articles and watching the raw film footage of the 1978 police attack on the MOVE house.

For months MOVE had been demanding the release of four of their members from prison. The Philadelphia PD had demanded MOVE leave the old Victorian house that was their home because it violated city codes and was an eyesore in the neighborhood. Police barricades had encircled the property. Although eleven children lived inside, the police had cut off food and water to the building. They prevented other residents from entering the building, although a city councilman and some negotiators got in. The councilman reported the interior was clean and the people intelligent and articulate.

After fifty-six days, an agreement between MOVE and the city gave MOVE ninety days to find new housing and leave. But on the ninety-first day, MOVE said they could not cooperate with the eviction order. They had been unable to locate new housing and needed more time.

That's when Frank Rizzo, who dominated Philadelphia politics from 1967-1980 as police commissioner and then mayor, ordered an assault on the house.

The computer screen showed police and fire department officials pumping water into the basement of the house, where children and adults huddled. One MOVE adult reported standing in chest-high water holding her child up to keep her from drowning. Keisha remembered Cassandra telling her about this. The details were shocking.

Someone fired a gun from inside the house, according to police officers. A police officer was killed, and others hit. Several reporters said the gun shots came from across the street. That one bullet set off a barrage of bullets from the police, then more water from the fire hose poured into the basement. Finally, the eleven MOVE adults and eleven children inside surrendered. Film footage showed Delbert Africa climbing out of the basement window, unarmed, hands up, and several policemen stomping and beating him. Rizzo had ordered the house bulldozed immediately, defying a judge's order and destroying evidence.

For more than two hours, Keisha watched part of the trial, heard the nine young adults—the MOVE Nine--sentenced to thirty to one hundred years each, heard Rizzo saying they should get the electric chair and he'd throw the switch. She read what had happened to them. Merle and Phil died in prison. Debbie gave birth in prison, and she and her partner, Mike, were released in 2018, after forty years and multiple denials of parole. Janine, Janet, and Eddie were released in May and June of 2019, two months ago, but Delbert and Chuckie remained in prison. She learned that several of the men were veterans.

She located a YouTube *Skin Deep* video of Debbie and Mike Africa, interviewing each other about their lives after forty years of separation, but she was out of time. She saved the link, logged out of the computer, and hurried to catch the train to the airport.

Chapter 30

Dark was taking over the sky. Ann and Don sat on the porch where they could see the front of the house. They were watching for Cora and waiting for Keisha's Lyft to arrive from O'Hare.

They'd phoned the police at four, approximately twenty-four hours after Cora had left, by Ann's calculation. They'd told Caleb, when he came home from a friend's house, that his sister wasn't back yet. They'd ordered pizza. A large box of meat-lovers supreme lay on the porch floor with several uneaten pieces. Ann and Don had not been hungry, and there was only so much a fourteen-year-old boy could consume at one sitting.

A dark blue Honda pulled up, and Keisha got out and made her way up the front walk, pulling her roller bag behind her. Caleb got to her first. "Mom! Cora's missing. She left yesterday afternoon and hasn't come back." His face looked desperate. "You can fix this, right?"

Keisha dropped the handle of her bag and it fell over, smacking the pavement. She reached for her son and held him tight. All the words about her experience in Philadelphia were gone now, irrelevant and unimportant in the face of this terrifying news.

She felt her dad towering over them, enfolding them in his long arms. "Come inside. We'll explain what's happening. The police are looking for her."

It was ten o'clock. Don had put on the evening news. Ann had called the hospitals. Keisha had called the police. Again. She knew the number by heart. Caleb had retreated upstairs to his room to play a video game.

A light spread across the front window and Keisha heard an engine turn off. Then a car door open. And another car door. Steps up the pavement. Someone's finger pushing the doorbell.

Don was there first, after Ann, peaking through the curtains, identified the car as belonging to the Evanston PD. The officers stepped inside, removed their hats, and shook hands with them. Behind them stood

Cora, her face streaky with tears and snot.

"I think this young lady belongs to you," said the officer.

Gran fixed lemonade and brought glasses cloudy with condensation to the family room. They sat there listening to Cora until the hall clock chimed midnight. Cora told them how angry she was, that she was tired of being everybody's caregiver when she needed caregiving, too. It spilled out of her—why she'd run away and what she'd experienced. Except for Lucy Jordan. She didn't tell them about Lucy. Lucy was hers. Dad would say Lucy was her guardian angel.

Keisha kept reaching out for Cora, touching her hand, her hair, until Cora crossly told her to stop it and pushed her hand away. Cora did tell them about Al and the woman at the bakery. Maybe she would tell them about Lucy later. Or maybe never. For now, she wanted them to picture her staying on the dangerous streets alone because she was so sick of being neglected.

Her mother heard her.

When Cora finished talking, Keisha collected the glasses and carried them to the dishwasher. Tomorrow she would tell her parents how grateful she was that they were here. Should she tell Cora that her running away clarified for Keisha how self-absorbed she'd been these six months? Apologize? Right now, she would accompany her children upstairs and tuck them each into bed despite their protests that they were too old for that.

Chapter 31

The next morning, Keisha lay in the king-sized bed in their spacious house in Evanston. Her eyes were closed, and she was caught up in a strange dream. The past and the present danced together in her head, spun and stomped, kicked and wiggled. Fit young adults, Black and white, danced together, Irish step-dancers and Nigerian highlife dancers, faces shining, showing off their best moves. Counter rhythms, some strong on the downbeat, others leaning into upbeats, delaying with deliberate hesitation. The balls of their feet hit the ground, bodyweight on their toes, turning and sliding, shuffling and spinning, arms moving too, and fingers snapping, sharp and clipped like needles hitting a tin roof in the midst of a rainstorm. She felt liberated and slightly anxious as the physicality of their movement sucked her in. She was moving too, her head and her body rocking side to side. The repetitive motion was both comforting and exciting. She felt wild and giddy with gratitude.

"Mama! What are you doing?" Cora stood beside the bed watching her mother. Her cry brought the rest of the family to the room, their anxious faces ringing Keisha's bed. Reluctantly Keisha opened her eyes, left her dream, and returned to her bedroom and her family. They looked cartoonish, those four faces arranged in a zigzag around her bed—Caleb, who was nearly six feet now, down to Mom, who was the shortest, up to Cora, who came to her granddad's shoulder, and finally all the way up to 6'3" Dad. They made a wobbly V-shape. This hovering V of perplexed faces struck her as somehow funny, and she laughed out loud.

"Are you OK?" Caleb's voice wavered like he might be near tears.

"Of course I'm OK. Come here, baby, and give me a hug."

Their eyes looked questions at each other. This was not the mom who had inhabited this house the past six months in misery and silence, barely acknowledging her children's presence.

"Mama, are you really back? Don't set us up and then disappear again. You've had us really worried." That was Cora, straightforward and tactless like her mother.

Keisha pulled herself up to sitting and patted the bed on either side of her. "It's dawning on me the price you've all been paying for my grief. This bed is big enough for all of us. I guess it's time for a talk," she said.

The four of them moved toward her, sitting on the bed, the kids on either side of her, Ann and Don leaning against the footboard. They all looked wary. Hope, that thing with wings, uncertain whether to stay or fly away.

"What happened in Philadelphia, Mom? And why did you leave us?" The room was quiet with waiting.

"I guess I owe you some explanations. Now's as good a time as any, right?" With that she launched into an account of her trip, the church ladies, George Marshall, Osage Avenue, and what she had learned about "your other grandpa, Reggie Lewis." It took a while. She didn't tell them about the MOVE members imprisoned for more than forty years or about the C-4 explosive the city dropped on their rowhouse. They simply listened.

Later, gathered in the kitchen, ravenous, they rummaged in the refrigerator and the cabinets for food. Keisha felt she was really seeing them, this fragile group of people who loved her, and who had been secretly terrified they had lost her.

Still later—after they'd stuffed themselves with chips and ice cream and Oreos and slices of bread thickly spread with peanut butter—they sprawled in the family room in front of the window that looked out on the back yard. Don in the middle of the sofa, his long arms resting on its back, Cora and Caleb on either side of him, Ann beside Keisha on the loveseat rubbing Keisha's shoulders. Five pairs of legs stretched out into the space between them, at ease. They were chatting about the small things that make up family life—what the kids did today, whether the mail had arrived, what they needed from the grocery store, who would vacuum the living room. "I'm sorry," Keisha interrupted, but no one heard her small voice. She decided it didn't matter. She had said it and she meant it. As hard as it would be, she would remember their need for her to be present. In time they would know she was sorry for leaving them. They would see she was paying attention.

She was learning that grief was a two-steps-forward-and-one-back dance. You made progress in re-entering the world only to be pulled back into desolation. Tonight, a crack of light in the darkness pulled her onward, lending temporary laughter and delight. She knew it would not last. Tomorrow she—they—might be swamped by darkness again. Temporary darkness? That was a new thought.

She stood to close the curtains, catching a glimpse of what her mom had called the Cheshire Cat's grin when Keisha was a child. She beckoned to her family to come see the sliver of new moon smiling down on them.

Cora, standing behind her, was saying something. Keisha turned to her daughter, "Say it again, honey, I missed what you said."

"Gran Cora told me that even when the light seems nearly gone, the star you see through a cloudy night sky or a sliver of moon are signs to give us hope. Do you believe that, Mama?"

Keisha's voice was wistful. "I'm not clear yet what I believe. Gran told me I must *practice* affirming that I will make it through, *practice*, and practice will make it so."

"I thought 'practice makes it perfect.' Isn't that what you say, Granddad?" Caleb was teasing his grandpa, trying to lighten the conversation so the actual fun they'd been having together wouldn't evaporate.

"Perfect is a lot to ask, but making it through? That's a reasonable request." Don reached for Ann's hand and draped his other arm across Caleb's back. After a moment in the moonshine, they returned to their seats.

Keisha leaned back against Ann's hands and let her mom knead her shoulders till she felt as relaxed and limp as a rag doll. She consciously banished the voice in her head that said no one gave back rubs as well as Richard. *That was Then. This is Now.*

After the kids went to bed, Keisha found her parents playing cards in the family room. "Mom?" she slid onto an empty chair. "I didn't tell Caleb and Cora anything about how Reggie died. I thought it would be too much for them to handle. Is that why you didn't tell me? I owe you an apology. And I need your advice. Should I tell them?"

"That's a heavy question. Didn't he say several months ago that his other grandpa was shot by the police? I thought then that he already knows. But we don't know what he knows and how accurate it is." Ann was mulling. Keisha had just acknowledged that it might have been out of love that Ann had withheld information from her about how Reggie had died. Her words implied forgiveness.

Don stood abruptly. "Some things are better left unsaid." He folded his cards and left the room.

"Is Dad all right?"

"Are any of us?" Ann answered.

Chapter 32

Ronald strolled down the street toward Grandma's house preoccupied. His research trip to Philadelphia had ended, and he was back in Chicago, back in the Woodlawn neighborhood, back with Grandma. She had informed him that she had survived his absence quite well and was perfectly capable of living by herself, although she was glad he was home.

He was glad to be home, too, glad she was safe, glad for all he had learned. He loved hearing about the successful hard work of the folks he'd interviewed. It felt like his mind was expanding so rapidly that it crowded his skull. But what he was learning also troubled him. Did history repeat itself? Why hadn't the progress of Black Capitalism in the Sixties endured?

On this end-of-summer afternoon, Ronald was thinking about how much had changed since he'd entered graduate school, a young Black man whose confidence was derived from his grandmother—and from eight years living with a Black man serving as President of the United States. A Black President who led the country through a devastating recession with no scandals to tarnish his presidency. For nearly half Ronald's life a Black family had lived in the White House. He'd felt so proud and empowered by their example! He'd believed Grandma's encouragement that he could aspire to anything.

Then, with the election of 2016, Ronald felt he was riding a racial rollercoaster. His hopes and expectations spiraled downward as President Obama was replaced with a president whose goal appeared to be keeping America white and native-born, a president who didn't try to hide his disrespect for women, people of color, gays and lesbians, immigrants and asylum seekers, environmentalists and human rights advocates.

Ronald had felt so excited about his future when he'd entered grad school, so proud that he would soon achieve the highest educational benchmark, a PhD. He was so happy that he lived in the 2010s and not the 1960s. He'd heard Grandma's stories about what his relatives experienced in Georgia, how she and his grandfather had moved to Chicago to escape White Supremacist violence, to get better jobs, and to vote. That was long ago. But it felt like that past had come back, like those scenes in horror movies where the monster the audience thinks is dead rises up from its grave seeking vengeance. He couldn't deny that White Supremacy was rising. Was believing he was immune to it with his educational accomplishments a delusion?

He had learned to function in a hope-for-the-future world. Was his faith in the future a sham? How did one behave in an America where, once again, race was one's most determinative characteristic?

He was almost to Grandma's house. He could see the red geraniums that marked her place. Walking toward him was a Black man who appeared to be his age. The man looked at him and then away. On the sidewalk between them a cluster of Crips jostled each other, jive-talking.

Instinctively he and the other man crossed the street. They passed each other, not making eye contact. Ronald walked faster. Down the block and up the front steps. His questions were derailed by the presence of the gang members.

Chapter 33

The early September sun strode into Keisha's room like a conquering hero, riding roughshod over her resistance and demanding her attention. The carpet was dappled with light, and dust motes rose sparkling from it. She tried to remember being delighted when seeing this as she stepped out of bed in the mornings. Now she simply observed the dancing motes and the dappled carpet. Delight was fickle. That she noticed at all would have to be enough for now.

The filmy white curtains hung from their rods overlooking the back garden, listless. Where they parted, the scent of the last roses drifted into the room. She had never been clear whether she liked that fragrance. She associated it with funerals—her grandparents' funeral, after they died in a car wreck when she was in college, and Richard's.

She told her brain she was changing the subject, retrieved her laptop, powered it on, and went directly to email. *I can make choices*, she reminded herself, *even small choices will make me stronger*.

There it was, an email in response to Keisha's hesitant reply to Reggie's Chicago sister, Femi. The woman was inviting Keisha to come to her house in Woodlawn, downtown Chicago. "Of course, we'd love to meet your children, but we will understand it that feels too much too soon," she'd written.

She keyed in a reply and plunged her forefinger onto SEND.

The following week on a glorious fall Saturday afternoon, she took the L downtown, exiting near the University and walking several blocks to the red brick row house, following Femi's directions. The woman who came to the door had beautiful, wrinkle-free mahogany skin, and her face lit up when she saw Keisha standing on the other side of the screen. "You have his eyes!" she exclaimed and her own shone. "Come in, come in."

They moved through the tidy living room with its finely carved wood furniture and elegant, tufted sofa and matching armchairs. The dark wood arms curved out, undulating along the back of the sofa and ending in curling spirals that invited your fingers to follow their whorls. The blue Jaccard velvet upholstery gave the room a formal, British-colonial feel.

They passed through the equally formal dining room and into the kitchen, where most of the space was taken up by a large, round, oak table. Femi indicated Keisha should sit. Two ancient photo albums lay on the table, brown leather covers laced at their spines with strips of rawhide. One was open and Keisha could see some photos inside held in place with shiny black corners.

"Would you like coffee or ginger beer? I got out the albums. I thought they would illustrate our conversation." Femi was smiling again. Was she a woman full of smiles or did she smile to hide anxiety? "It will just be the two of us this first time, though, knowing my Jacob, he may sneak in to take a peek at you."

Keisha was absorbing her surroundings, struggling to stay calm, but feeling emotional.

Femi brought her an iced ginger beer and a plate with sweet rice cakes. "Where shall we start?"

For the next two hours the women talked about Keisha's biological father's family. Femi did most of the talking, turning the pages of the albums to locate photos to illustrate what she was saying: Their mama and papa, brothers and sisters clowning and showering each other with seawater on a Jamaican beach the one time they had visited Jamaica as a family; graduation photos of each Lewis sibling, serious in caps and gowns; and babies and toddlers of the next generation.

Keisha asked questions. It was her familiar mode of operation. At first, she made notes in the spiral notebook she always carried. Then she set it aside and simply listened.

As Femi predicted, Jacob arrived, ostensibly for a beer and to check what time dinner would be. They heard him calling from the front hall, pausing, then the click of his shoes on the hard wood floor as he walked back to the kitchen to apologize for interrupting them. "Where's the young woman Mr. DNA says is our niece?" he called out before emerging in the doorway, tall and strong and with a small paunch that pushed out his shirt. He looked to be in his sixties, and, from his manner, Keisha concluded he was a kind man. He reminded his wife that she needed to let *Keisha* talk. His face showed his curiosity.

"I suppose you're wanting to join us?" Femi indicated the chair between the two women and Jacob sank into it, throwing her a head nod that she knew meant he wanted her to get him a drink and a snack. Which she did. She brought a plate of fried plantains she'd warmed in the microwave and set it on the table next to a stack of paper napkins. "You've had plantain, right? They can ooze oil and we don't want oil on these precious photographs." She patted the slices of plantain with one of the paper napkins.

Not long after they'd consumed the plantain and wiped their fingers to Femi's specification, the conversation turned to Keisha. She said little about herself, only that she'd grown up in a loving family with her mom and stepdad, that she taught history at Northwestern, that she was a single mom with two children, a girl fifteen and a boy fourteen. She didn't mention Richard.

When the light poured horizontally through the kitchen windows, Keisha said she needed to get home. Her children would be wondering what happened to her.

On her way out, she surprised herself by asking if she could hug Femi. Femi's arms enfolded her for more than the requisite few seconds. She smelled of lavender and cooking oil.

Walking back to the L, Keisha reviewed her time with them. Femi and Jacob were unpretentious people—except for their formal front- and dining-room furniture—and warm and welcoming. The kitchen visit had been enjoyable. She felt slightly guilty that she had not mentioned Richard.

Back home in Evanston, she phoned her mom to report on the her time with Femi and Jacob. Of course, Ann wanted to hear every detail and Keisha obliged her.

When the conversation wound down, Keisha noticed that Cora had taken a seat behind her where she could listen unobserved.

Keisha turned to her. "Let's get some supper ready. How about spaghetti carbonara?" Cora showed obvious surprise at this proposal. As they moved toward the kitchen, her arm around her daughter's waist, Keisha saw her reflection in the hall mirror. She looked more closely. "You've got his eyes!" Femi had said. She stared at her eyes.

Why didn't I tell Femi and Jacob about my trip to Philadelphia and what I learned about Reggie? I guess I need to know them first, to trust them. I

think I can do that. Just not yet. But why didn't I mention Richard? I should
have told them about him. Maybe I need a place where Richard…and his
murder…isn't part of the picture of me.

Chapter 34

Having no appointments for the rest of the day, Keisha had come home after her last class. The kids were still at school. Among the unwanted catalogues and appeals for contributions pooled on the floor beneath the mail slot, there was an overstuffed manila envelope from George Marshall, Reggie's friend in Philadelphia.

Before opening the envelope, she made herself a coffee, then settled in the family room's overstuffed armchair, the one they'd kept from Richard's bachelor apartment. She stretched her legs, took a deep breath, and slid her finger under the fold.

Dear Keisha,

Since meeting you I've been going through a box of things from the 1980s to see if I have anything of Reggie's I can share with you. Voila! I found these photos and clippings. I've written on the back of the photos who is whom. I hope they help.
So glad to meet you! Let's stay in touch.

Cordially,
George

As she pulled the assorted clippings from the envelope, several slid away from her onto the floor. Gathering them up, she moved to the table, spread them out, and began to order them chronologically. She could feel her heart racing. The earliest were dated 1968, clippings from various Chicago newspapers. One described "A Marshall Plan for the Ghetto," laying out proposals by President Johnson's advisor for entrepreneurial development in Black center cities: grants from the federal government's Economic Development Administration, industrial bonds for ghettoes, tax privileges and incentives to attract private capital to invest in these areas, housing programs, and the creation of community development corporations.

An article from *U.S. News and World Report,* dated September 20, 1968, compared the views of the presidential candidates, Hubert Humphrey (Democrat) and Richard Nixon (Republican) on Black Capitalism. Another quoted from a Nixon speech that April: "What most militants are asking is not for separation, but to be included in—not as supplicants, but as owners, as entrepreneurs—to have a share of the wealth and a piece of the action. And this is precisely what the Federal approach ought to be. It ought to be oriented toward more Black ownership, for from this can flow the rest—Black pride, Black jobs, Black opportunity, and yes, Black power, in the best, the constructive sense of that often misapplied term."

Keisha was intrigued. She had known that Dr. King had voted Republican in 1956—the year he led the Montgomery Bus Boycott. Then he'd become a Democratic Socialist. She hadn't realized that Nixon had vocally, publicly supported Black Capitalism. Nixon's speech was given a few weeks after the assassination of Dr. Martin Luther King, Jr., after many cities across the nation experienced outbursts of frustration and despair that brought out national guardsmen and even military tanks.

She had been barely three, but she had a vivid memory of her mom Ann and Don, her new stepdad, glued to the television watching the King funeral, weeping. And they were *whites.*

In the stack of clippings was a picture tagged "Reggie Lewis and Rev. Leon Sullivan at the opening of Progress Plaza." She peered at the yellowed newspaper photo, trying to bring the slightly blurred image into focus. It showed Reggie, a well-built, dark-skinned man with a confident smile, nearly as tall as Reverend Sullivan. No wonder the women at Zion Baptist Church had found Reggie Lewis so attractive.

Caleb and Cora burst into the house. She heard the door bang and their animated chatter. They were talking about something that had happened at school. A student in ninth grade had brought a gun to school and another student reported him to the assistant principal. Police cars had roared to the school, lights flashing, and officers in body armor had marched the young man out of the school and into a police vehicle, his wrists behind him bound in white plastic ties.

The kids were in the kitchen raiding the fridge for drinks, talking nonstop. She set the clippings aside and joined them, sitting on one of the bar stools at the island, ready to listen and pushing down the terror she felt hearing their accounts of this might-have-been tragedy. She resisted pulling them into her embrace. They were alarmed enough by their own imaginations.

Cora said the armed student was in her class. A geek like her, only, "He has more courage than me—he wears a nose-ring and dresses goth, even when he was inducted into the National Honor Society. I've always respected him," she'd asserted, waiting for Keisha to disagree with her.

"Why?" Keisha asked.

"He told me he wanted to demonstrate to all the parents that you can be smart and punk at the same time."

"Did you know he had a gun?"

"No."

Keisha asked if other kids they knew had guns. "Yeah, Mom, of course!"

"Do any of them carry guns to school?"

"Yeah. In their cars. The ones who have their own cars." Caleb looked uncomfortable. He and Cora got quiet and exchanged looks that said it was time to change the subject. They took their snacks upstairs.

She waited a few minutes and then followed them. They were in Cora's room sitting on the floor and talking quietly, which was unusual.

"Mom's really freaked out."

"She's probably afraid for us. Do any of your friends have guns?"

Keisha stood unseen in the hallway listening.

"Yeah. Bruce. He showed it to me, let me hold it. His dad got it for him for Christmas. But I don't go over there anymore. He's into some bad stuff."

Their conversation shifted to the guy taken away by the police and Keisha crept back down the stairs. Her hands were trembling.

That evening after she cooked dinner and cleaned up, she returned to the stack of clippings. Among them was a handwritten letter from Reggie to George dated December 17, 1971. A yellow sticky note dangled from the first page. George had written, "Maybe this was the beginning of his shifting ideology? Just a thought."

Reggie's letter was short:

Dear George,

Remember my telling you I'm reading James Forman's latest book, The Making of a Black Revolutionary? *Well, I'm learning a hell of a lot. The man is brilliant! Unlike you and me, he grew up dirt poor in Mississippi, then moved to Chicago in 1934—the guy is a decade older than us!*

He writes about meeting Robert Williams, head of the NAACP in Monroe, North Carolina, of learning from him the necessity of arming ourselves for self-defense. We need to talk about this.

Forman is complex. His children are by a white woman from the famous British Mitford family. But complexity is typical of him, I think. His intellect doesn't recognize boundaries. Wish I was more like him.

Let's talk.

Reggie

She could hear his voice in this letter—how he constructed sentences, his admiration for Forman… She'd attended a lecture by James Forman, *Jr.*, a professor at Yale whose book on the criminal justice system won the Pulitzer last year, and she knew of his famous activist father. To read that her biological father admired him raised Forman, Sr. higher on her pantheon. There was something else important in this note. *Reggie didn't criticize Forman for having mixed-race children. Like me.*

She finished looking through the clippings, and returned to the two grainy photos of Reggie, the second taken at the MOVE house and undated. His face looked different in the second photo. Gone was the confident smile that showed fine white teeth with a small space between the front two. His mouth closed over those teeth and his eyebrows pushed toward each other, his dark eyes intent and serious. His hair was in locks in the second picture, and he was casually dressed. No business suit like he wore in the photo taken of him with Reverend Sullivan.

She could sense someone standing behind her.

"Caleb? Want to see your birth grandpa?" She felt his hand on her shoulder and put hers over his. "Sit here." She indicated his dad's armchair. "We can look together."

Instead, Caleb settled on the sofa beside her. He smelled of popcorn and melted butter from his after-dinner snack.

"Do you think my chin is like his? I think you have his eyes, Mom."

"I was thinking the same thing," she told him, putting her arm around him. "Are you okay? It sounds like a scary day."

"Yup." He was quiet overlong, and his eyes, though staring at the photos, were slightly out of focus. "I'm glad you were here when we got home, Mom."

Did "here" mean downstairs? Not hiding in her room? Listening?

"I'm glad, too," she said. "I don't want anything to happen to you. I love you so much. You know that, right?"

Caleb's smile resembled Reggie's, wide with just a hint of space between his front teeth.

After Caleb went upstairs to finish his homework (or play a video game?), Keisha got on her laptop to look up James Forman, Sr. Reggie's letter enthusing about Forman was the only personal note in the stack of papers in the envelope. But it was a place to start.

She ordered Forman's book in ebook format, then emailed George Marshall thanking him for sending the papers.

After saying good night to the kids, she got in bed and began reading Forman's book on her phone. At 4 a.m., she turned off the light. She had finished reading Forman's vivid account of his 1961 visit to Monroe, North Carolina, with other Freedom Riders. What she read left her unable to sleep.

She read about Robert Williams—the leader of the local NAACP—defending a Black doctor, Albert Perry, who was imprisoned for two years on a fabricated charge of assisting a white woman to have an abortion.

She read about Williams' campaign to integrate the local swimming pool. He'd assembled a picket line of Black and white Freedom Riders and local Black folk who stood outside the chain-link fence holding hand-lettered protest signs. A mob of over seven thousand angry whites had surrounded them, threatening to lynch the local protesters and the Black and white observers from elsewhere who'd arrived on the Freedom

Riders' bus and joined the protest. One white man, who appeared drunk, held a gun to Forman's head promising to execute him.

She read how the local police arrested dozens of protesters and forced them into crowded jail cells with no mattresses or water.

She read about the kangaroo court trial that swiftly brought guilty verdicts and sentences of two years in prison for nonviolently protesting. The government later expelled the protesters from the state of North Carolina.

She read Robert Williams' historic statement in May 1959, the statement that had motivated Forman to visit him. After all the KKK threats and violence and the injustice perpetrated by all-white juries, the final straw for Williams came when a white man who attempted to rape an eight-months-pregnant Black woman was found not guilty. Robert Williams had served in the Marine Corps. After these experiences he concluded that his country had no place for him and would never bring Black people freedom.

His words stunned her: "We cannot take these people who do us injustice to court and it becomes necessary to punish them ourselves. In the future, we are going to have to try and convict them on the spot. We cannot rely on the law. We can get no justice under the present system.... If it is necessary to stop lynching with lynching, then we must be willing to resort to that method." Williams, Forman, and the members of MOVE all became advocates of self-defense as necessary to preserve Black lives. Did Reggie also advocate self-defense?

Even after she fell into a restless sleep, the title of Forman's autobiography kept circling her unconsciousness, *The Making of a Black Revolutionary*. Was this Reggie's story, too?

She awakened an hour later. Forman's book included an address, where he had lived from age six here *in Chicago*--6108 Prairie Avenue on the South Side, not far from Femi and Jacob. She would find the place the next time she visited Femi. She would make a kind of pilgrimage to honor this man, these heroes, who found the courage to remain in the struggle.

The world of privilege she grew up in and in which she raised her children was vastly different from the world of default violence and gratuitous cruelty that these men experienced.

She awakened a few hours later from a terrifying dream in which

Cora and Caleb were cowering under the desks in their classroom, hands over their heads, which were turned toward her. A fellow student held an assault rifle that he swung side to side, forefinger on the trigger while he barked angry commands she could not understand.

Chapter 35

In late September, Keisha made the trek by L back to the home of Femi and Jacob in the Woodlawn neighborhood of Chicago. This time Cora and Caleb accompanied her. The kids had wanted her to drive, but she insisted the L would be easier.

Once on the L, Caleb found this "field trip" exciting. Cora, not so much. She couldn't forget that her father was murdered on a train like this. Caleb, typical fourteen-year-old boy, teased his sister. "That dude is looking at you, Cora. I think he thinks you're *hot!* Oh, wait—it's the girl *behind* us he's flirting with. Sorry."

"Mama, make him stop!" Cora was shrinking into her seat with embarrassment. When Caleb kept playing her, she shifted to an empty seat across the aisle.

Keisha barely noticed Caleb's banter. She was thinking about her dad, Don, the man who had raised her. Last night she had called him to reassure him. "Reggie is my biological father. I am curious about him and ready to learn about this part of my family that I never knew before. But I don't want you to feel threatened by this, Dad. *You will always be my dad. Always.*"

She could tell, by his silence and then by his passing the phone to Mom while he blew his nose, that her words moved him. Mom had had several miscarriages, never after Keisha able to carry a baby to term. Keisha was Dad's only child, or the only child he ever knew.

When Keisha had been in her mid-thirties, Dad had learned he had a biological child he had never known about. The woman had placed the baby boy for adoption. Did her dad think about that son? Had he tried to locate him? She made a mental note to ask him when next they talked.

So much family trauma in her dad's life! He was twelve when his alcoholic mother removed his father—Grandpa Arthur—from his life. They had found each other decades later—the same year Dad learned he had a son somewhere in this world.

Despite his difficult childhood, Don had been a wonderful father to

Keisha. His love for her and the kids—well, that was one of the things that kept her—them all—going. She should regularly remind him how much she loved him. Mom had said he still lacked confidence in his dad role.

"Mom! Isn't this our stop?" Caleb stood and moved into the aisle. "Come on, Cora."

They scurried out the door of the car just as it was sliding closed.

"I guess you're good for *some*thing," Cora snarked, still irritated by his teasing.

From the L they walked down South Champion Street, Keisha first, the kids following, bodies leaning into the wind off Lake Michigan that nearly blew them off their feet.

"OK, we're almost there. It's the fourth house on the left."

Femi and Jacob stood together in the doorway watching the threesome climb the steps to the small porch. This time Femi ushered them to the formal living room. Cora surveyed the room with its framed photos, colorful paintings, bric-a-brac, and ornate furniture. Her eyes studied the particulars.

Jacob invited Caleb to play a game of pool in the basement. The two guys conversed with surprising ease as they moved down the stairs to the lower level. Her son was not cautious like his sister.

Femi brought a plate of gizzada tarts and slices of toto cake into the living room. Cora said she could smell the coconut.

"And the rum?" Femi was teasing.

Cora smiled at her first bite of gizzada. Femi and Keisha exchanged a look of relief. Both knew it wasn't easy to meet relatives you never knew, especially *older* relatives from a branch of the family you hadn't heard of until recently.

Femi brought out an album. Pushing the plate of treats aside, she set it on the table in front of Cora. "We're going to introduce you to some kinfolk," she said. "Don' be 'fraid now, as my mama used to say. They be good folk, like you, sistren. I don't usually talk Jamaican, but it's part of your heritage, Cora. I owe it to my brother to teach his grandchild some patois!" Keisha and Cora smiled hearing the traces of Jamaican creole in Femi's speech.

For the next hour, Cora and Keisha, with Femi between them, sat on the elaborately carved sofa with its tufted velvet upholstery looking at photos. The photos prompted stories from Femi about life in the Lewis family when she was growing up. Suddenly Femi stood up. "Now's the time," she said walking upstairs. She returned carrying a small, carved, wood box and placed it on Keisha's lap. "Cooyah. Open it," she urged.

Inside was a lock of tightly curled black hair, three inches long, tied with a red satin ribbon.

"Mama said she cut it when he went to school, said he needed to look respectable, and besides, it would grow back. *I* think she wanted a lock of her baby boy's hair to keep. I've done the same with my three boys. That hair is from your other grandpa, Cora."

Femi's eyes overflowed suddenly, and she sat down on the armchair. "I'm not sad. Just so glad my favorite brother lives on in you both." She shook her head to banish her tears, regained her composure, and changed the subject.

"Cora, I want to know about *you*." To Keisha's surprise, Cora did not hold back. Keisha was glad to see her children were comfortable with these people. While Cora told stories of school and her upcoming orchestra concert, the books she was reading, and the cooking that had fallen to her these months, Keisha fondled the lock of toddler Reggie's hair, only half-listening.

Dark came early. Autumn was shortening the days and cooling the September air. Femi and Keisha moved to the kitchen where Femi had been cooking a Jamaican feast for her new family. Caleb and Cora stood on the back porch under the porchlight watching Jacob cook jerk chicken and pork in a pit in the back yard. The smells of the spices floating up from the coated chicken made Caleb hungry.

The gate to the alley swung open suddenly and a tall person in a hoodie walked into the back yard and toward the house, following the sidewalk that divided the yard in two.

"This is our youngest son, Aidan," Jacob told them. "This is Cora, and this is Caleb, your cousins." Aidan's face was in shadow. He stuck out his right hand and Caleb stepped closer to shake it.

"Glad to meet you both. I'm going up to my room," Aidan said.

"He doesn't talk much," Jacob told them as Aidan took the steps to the kitchen two at a time.

Watching the interaction between father and son, Cora sensed neither man was happy with their relationship. She wondered why. Why was Aidan so uncommunicative? She hoped he'd stay for dinner. Caleb was more interested in how things worked, but Cora enjoyed figuring out how *people* worked.

When the chicken and pork were properly jerked, Femi called them to the dining room table. The large table was covered with dishes of steaming food, "dirty rice," fried plantain, greens, yams, chicken, pork, and two kinds of bread. Aidan arrived after they were seated, and Femi introduced him to Keisha and said that Cora and Caleb Allen were his cousins once removed.

Cora thought Aidan was "Fire,' as her girlfriends called hot boys. He was tall and well proportioned, with intelligent eyes that appeared to take in what was around him and hold it in some place no one else could enter.

"What do you do, Aidan?" Keisha asked, and the room went quiet.

"Aidan's looking for a job right now," Jacob answered for his son. Aidan looked away and reached for more yams. It was awkward, and Cora felt the discomfort. It made her more curious about her new cousin.

When the meal ended, Cora offered to help with dishes. "That's Aidan's job until he can contribute to the household," Femi told her.

"Maybe you'd like some help?" Cora's voice wavered a bit. Her boldness surprised her. Aidan must be a lot older than she was.

Aidan smiled at her. "Sure, you can help," he told her.

Thirty minutes later Jacob was nodding off in one of the armchairs, Caleb was playing video games on his phone, and the women were drinking coffee and finishing off the gizzada tarts in the dining room, their conversation comfortable, their voices low.

In the kitchen, Aidan was engaging Cora in conversation, showing more personality than he had before. "So, do you have a dad?" he asked her.

"My dad died last April," she replied. It was not something she talked about, and she didn't want to have to acknowledge how he died.

"What did he do?" Aidan seemed interested, and Cora got few opportunities to talk about her daddy.

"He was a composer, Richard Allen. He teaches at Northwestern and performs with a band. I mean, he *did*. He was an amazing person." Her eyes showed pain. She couldn't control them.

Aidan seemed to be debating which way to take the conversation. He changed the subject. "Are you a musician, too?"

"I want to be. I play violin in the orchestra at school."

"Was your dad white?"

"Yes."

"I think I read about him online." He stopped himself from going further. Cora seemed vulnerable. He changed the subject. "What are your favorite bands, or do you only like classical music?"

While Jacob sprawled uncomfortably in the formal armchair, dozing, Femi took Keisha upstairs to show her something she'd discovered among her mother's things. She pulled out the bottom drawer of her dresser and lifted from it a worn manilla folder full of papers. REGGIE was written on the tab in a shaky hand.

"Mama kept these articles. I think Reggie sent them to her when he moved to Philadelphia so she'd know why he was going there and what he'd be working on."

One article was from *Forbes* magazine, September 1966. The other was a front-page story in the *New York Times* from the following year. Both were about Selective Buying Campaigns spreading rapidly from Philadelphia across the nation's cities. Dr. Martin Luther King, Jr. had endorsed them and the central person behind them was the pastor of Zion Baptist Church, Reverend Leon Sullivan.

Keisha could hardly contain her excitement. "I went there last month," she told Femi. "I met with some of the elders, women mostly, who knew Reggie. One of my grad students is doing his dissertation on Black Capitalism which Rev. Sullivan—his group and hundreds of other Black clergy—ignited. They got major industries to agree to hire and promote Black workers and set up training centers to equip thousands of students with the skills to do *skilled* jobs. They started a Feeder Program to teach them basic literacy and—get this—*Black history!* Actually, the history of all minority groups. Being a historian, I was particularly interested in that. Their Feeder Program provided literacy and the social skills to succeed in a white work environment. The governor of Pennsylvania opened a state armory for them to use for their program after the synagogue they were using burned down."

Femi was laughing. "I've never heard you talk so much. It's good to see you so animated."

"These clippings are more evidence that Reggie was involved in Reverend Sullivan's programs. I met with one of his friends from when he was in grad school who said something must have happened to him to make him suddenly leave the entrepreneurial programs that Sullivan was building. Something that explains why he dropped out of Wharton School of Business and got involved with MOVE."

"Could that have happened in 1979? That's when we saw a change in him. I remember because that was when Jacob and I got married and he didn't come to our wedding. He just stopped coming home. Only came for one Christmas in four years. Broke Mama's heart. We all knew he was her favorite."

"Mom? Are we going home soon?" Caleb was calling from the bottom of the stairs and Keisha startled when she saw how late it was.

Femi put her arms around the younger woman and patted her back encouragingly. She intuited that the tension she could feel in Keisha's body meant the woman had been through some kind of trauma, something more than growing up without Reggie in her life. "Just leave these on the bed and I'll make copies for you. Oh, Keisha, I am so glad we found each other!"

"Me, too."

"Aidan?" Jacob called from the front room. "Cousin Keisha is ready to leave. Could you please drive them back to Evanston? It's not good for them to be out alone at night in this neighborhood or riding the L."

"Yes, Papa."

Aidan welcomed the diversion. After he and Cora had finished the dishes, they'd remained in the kitchen, seated at the round table talking. Sometimes not talking. He sensed the girl was on the edge of memories so painful they could leave her in a puddle. He didn't want that. Didn't want to think about what he'd remembered reading online about a Dr. Richard Allen who taught at Northwestern. He didn't want to go there.

He extended his hand toward Cora's shoulder to give her a pat of encouragement, then quickly pulled his hand back before he touched her. She was a young teen, might take it the wrong way, might not want to be touched at all. "Thank you for helping with the dishes," he said and smiled with what he hoped she would read as appreciation.

Aidan was a careful driver. Once Keisha, Caleb, and Cora said some socially scripted words about being glad to meet his family, they were mostly quiet on the drive to Evanston. Until Caleb broke the silence. He told Aidan he thought Jacob was a dope dad. Jacob had taught him some boss tricks playing pool. Caleb loved the idea of pit cooking. He announced his intention to dig a pit in their back yard so he could jerk some chicken. Maybe Aidan's family would come teach them how to do it? He asked if there were cousins his age in the family. He asked if Aidan smoked. If he'd ever done drugs. He said he was glad Aidan was his cousin.

Cora rolled her eyes. Keisha just let him babble on, glad he wasn't noticing his sister's reaction to him. Keisha expected Cora to lecture her brother: "He's *Mom's* cousin, dummy. He's our *first cousin once removed.*" But Cora didn't correct him. She didn't say anything.

Aidan patiently answered all of Caleb's questions and asked some of his own. By the time Aidan pulled into their driveway and opened the car door for Cora and Keisha, Caleb, like Cora, had become an Aidan fan.

Chapter 36

Aidan sat on the back steps of his parents' house in Woodlawn. They were at work. He was not, of course. Raking the leaves was one of his responsibilities since he'd returned from prison, payback for the rent he couldn't pay.

He'd spent an hour corralling recalcitrant leaves into orderly piles and shoving armloads of them into black plastic trash bags. They were brittle and brown, and they smelled of decomposition and death. The rake lay on the grass where he had tossed it in frustration after a breeze off the lake swept across the yard, disassembling his mounds of leaves and tossing them into the air.

Is this all there is? The question had been stuck in his head for months. During his years in prison, his tentative belief that things would get better rested on being released. Occasionally a bird sailed the air of the prison, and he'd imagine himself riding on its back, flying free beyond those walls. There were no walls confining him now. He was "free," yet depression had settled on him, rooted in him. Bone had warned him about that.

Bone was the old man, the only person he talked with on the inside. Bone told him to not give up when he was released and met his demons on the Outside. "Getting out takes a lot of brothers deeper into the Pit than they've ever traveled, thinking they're worthless, can't do nothing, can't find work, leeching onto family, no one of them able to understand what you been through. The *isolation* of being Outside—it's why so many give up and do something crazy to get back inside. Don't you be doing that, Aidan. You're too smart, got too much potential. Don't go falling into that trap." But Bone admitted he himself wasn't one to talk. "Why you think I know so much about it? Been out and back more times than I can count. I'm like those September flies that chase the warmth of indoors even though they know a flyswatter death waits for them inside."

Bone. He missed Bone. The old man had befriended him early on and kept an eye on him for five years. He introduced Aidan to his favorite authors, told him stories. Some of them stuck. Bone had told him of Sisyphus rolling the heavy rock up a steep mountain, reaching the top breathing heavily, sweat pouring off him, then the rock beginning to roll back down the mountainside, gathering momentum as Sisyphus tried to stop it. And failed. He'd asked Bone if the story meant everyone was fated to live that life, trying and almost succeeding, then watching achievement roll away out of reach. Having to try again, perpetually.

"Sisyphus had offended Zeus, the god of gods. He was a greedy dude, treacherous. Not everyone is like that. It's a choice for most people. Some choose meanness, deception, greed, and Sisyphus is their story. Others choose kindness, truth, and generosity. You're that kind of man. I can see it."

Sitting on the step facing the back yard with its storm of swirling leaves, Aidan's eyelids burned. Bone believed in him. More than his father and even his mother. Bone believed he was a good man. Was he?

After a while Aidan retrieved the rake and went back to work.

Aidan avoided the Crips. He stayed to himself, like he had in prison. When Femi sent him to the store to pick up something she needed, he might run into one of his parents' friends who would attempt to engage him in conversation. His voice, he noticed, sounded gravelly from lack of use as he responded to their questions. Yes, his parents were well. Yes, it was a beautiful day. No, he didn't know when his mom was planning to retire from teaching. No, he had no lady friend. Monosyllabic answers most of the time. Except when he gathered his plastic bags of purchases and excused himself: "Gotta get this back to Mama. Good to see you, Mr./Mrs. ________."

Without friends or a job, with nothing meaningful to do, time sat heavily on him. Only the household chores he did to help out and video games occupied his time, but they were not enough. Sometimes it felt a lot like prison.

Chapter 37

At fifteen, Cora was in the throes of teenage angst. A solitary girl, especially since her father's death, she allowed her imagination to compensate for her loneliness. Mom's cousin Aidan had sparked her imagination. He was handsome, melancholy, independent, and caring—characteristics she found attractive—and he was *older*. She could tell all that from that one dinner and their conversation doing dishes together. Mama said she imagined her birthfather looked like Aidan. They had the same coloring, both dark with large, sensitive eyes. Cora was thinking that they both were tragic figures.

She wanted to see him again. Maybe she could tell him about Dad, and he'd tell her why he and his father were estranged.

One afternoon after school, she went online to see what she could learn about him. To her surprise a mug shot popped up. *Aidan had been in prison for armed burglary for five of the six years of his sentence.* Most of her classmates would be scared off by this piece of information. But Cora lived in a family that talked about the need to reform the criminal justice system. Before Dad's death, they'd have conversations at the dinner table about how many Black men were in prison for using drugs, while whites, who used drugs at the same or higher rates, got off with warnings. Cora could recite the litany of young, unarmed Black men shot and killed by police. She knew their names and circumstances. It was part of what made her odd to her friends. This information about Aidan made him even more intriguing.

Aidan was twenty-one, and had been out of prison for a year, so he would have been fifteen when found guilty, but *he was charged and sentenced as an adult!* This injustice tapped her sympathy and her outrage. She wanted to see him and tell him how unfair it was that he was sent to prison as an adult at fifteen. *She* was fifteen.

Next to the phone was a notepad on which Mama had scribbled Jacob and Femi's address and phone number. When no one was near, Cora dialed the number hoping to hear Aidan's voice. She hung up the minute she heard Femi answer.

Cora developed her own narrative about Aidan. Unjustly treated by the prison system, he'd spent half his teenager years behind bars, a source of embarrassment to his parents. He had missed the last years of high school and lived among a rough and brutal crowd of older men in prison, probably tormented and abused by them. She knew Mama would be sympathetic to Aidan's situation but decided not to tell her about his time in prison. And she *would* see him again.

She dreamed of Aidan, of his smile and his dark, intelligent eyes, of his body—yes, even that. Thoughts of him kept her preoccupied when her life felt too predictable.

Chapter 38

Aidan waited to come downstairs until he heard the front door close with the familiar solid thunk. He heard his mama say to his papa the words that were part of their morning off-to-work ritual. "Jacob, when you going to plane that door? Every fall you tell me it swells up because of the humidity of summer and will soon un-swell. Please, husband, fix the damn door!"

Jacob's reply was the reprise of their ritual. "Woman, that thunk is God reminding you you're not in charge of everything." Then Aidan's parents would chuckle, and he'd hear their laughing recede as they headed off to work, leaving the house bathed in quiet. He felt nostalgia for his younger years when their banter and general good humor had made their home a safe place of love and protection, not criticism and disappointment.

Aidan kept thinking of something he'd seen in early April while walking home from a visit to his parole officer. He'd been hurrying and took a shortcut through Washington Park. A weird spring snowstorm had dissipated, leaving a layer of thin, treacherous ice on the sidewalks. He walked on the rough grass to avoid the icy paved paths. That was how he came upon them, a half-dozen young men huddled around a long black bag that, from its size and shape, might hold an assault rifle. He modified his direction to avoid them, but the image had remained in his mind. Along with the sense that he was witnessing something illegal and dangerous.

Last weekend, when the family threw a birthday dinner at Mom and Dad's for his brother Barron's thirty-second, he'd recalled what he saw in Washington Park that cold April afternoon.

Femi and Jacob had presented Barron with a Gator gig bag for transporting his keyboard. Barron had been talking about wanting one to carry his Yamaha keyboard to his friend's house where his band practiced. Aidan found it amusing that Barron, at his advanced age, performed in a band that still dreamed of making it big.

Barron had been excited about the gift and demonstrated the features of the long, padded, black carrying case with adjustable straps and multiple large pockets. The bag triggered Aidan's memory of the group in the park. *That's* what they'd been gathered around, a keyboard carrying case. Weird that they would be clustered around a carrying case for a digital keyboard.

He'd assumed they were drug runners. Of course, he knew that, like most big U.S. cities, Chicago had a deadly drug trade. Young men, on the South Side of Chicago and in the Austin and Woodlawn neighborhoods, mostly Black, were recruited by the mob to distribute drugs. That was common knowledge. He suspected the carrying case had held drugs.

He remembered hearing on the news at the start of April that a professor in the music department at Northwestern, returning on the L from a gig in the city late at night, had been mugged and murdered. Could that have been Cora Allen's father? Was he carrying a digital keyboard in a gig bag? His questions took him to the family computer to read online about the murder.

Yes, it was Dr. Richard Allen, and he *had* been carrying his digital keyboard, which his assailants took. No mention of a carrying case, but how else would he carry his keyboard and music to a gig?

Might Richard Allen have been mugged because he was transporting drugs?

Aidan opened a story about a major drug bust in late May. Seven heroin deals had occurred in the 5300 block of West Washington Boulevard, allegedly by members or associates of the Four Corner Hustlers gang. One of the purchasers was an undercover federal agent. The drug bust occurred near where he had seen the dudes in Washington Park. The head of the drug trafficking organization had been arrested, along with a group of his subordinates.

But those sales were in Chicago. Richard Allen was *leaving* Chicago heading north to Evanston. Was he crazy to be wondering if the group in the park might be responsible for Cora's father's death?

There were so many drug-related deaths in Chicago and the suburbs, and so many gangs involved in distributing heroin, cocaine, crack, and deadly fentanyl. The route from Texas to Chicago was a major drug pipeline. He read an article on the honchos at the top, mostly white and rarely prosecuted.

Allen wouldn't have *knowingly* been transporting drugs in his case, would he? If he was, he'd have known he was risking his life. Although it wouldn't be surprising if the Northwestern campus had a drug distribution operation.

When he'd seen the men last April, he hadn't seen anyone's face well enough to recognize them. He was on parole, trying to keep himself clean and separate from that world. Best to forget about it. There was nothing he could do. But if Cora's father had been transporting drugs, was his family safe?

He warmed up a cup of Papa's strong coffee and returned to searching. The story about Dr. Richard Allen's brutal murder had been easy to find. He followed links to read more about the man and his family. He found several articles about his compositions and their premiers. More articles about his wife's career. Dr. Keisha Johnson was a recognized scholar of African American and Indigenous history, making her mark as one of the few American historians who studied both groups, comparing their experiences. Aidan found links to her books and to articles that he couldn't access without a university credential. He went to her author page and recognized her from the book jacket photo on her 2016 book. She looked older now, worn, even haggard. He guessed the murder of her husband accounted for the change.

After he closed the browsers and turned off the laptop, he sat for a long time staring into space. Eventually his eyes found the photo of his family on the desk beside the laptop. It was taken on his fourteenth birthday, when he was Caleb's age, the year before his life began to collapse. In the picture, his nuclear family gathered around him, Mama beaming and Papa less effusive, of course, but still smiling, everybody touching someone, except him. It seemed a lifetime ago.

Later that week, Aidan left home carrying only the duffel bag he used when he went to the gym. He didn't know where he was going or what he was doing. Somehow, he found himself on the L riding the train to Evanston and walking the six blocks from the stop to the Allen-Johnson house. He felt uncomfortable. He didn't want them to see him. He just wanted to see them, to observe life amongst the grieving. He wanted to make sure they were all right.

There was nowhere he could stand or sit on this suburban street without looking odd, without generating calls from neighbors to the police about "a suspicious Black man," so he kept moving, passed the house, and walked on to Northwestern University.

He hung out in the library, roaming the stacks to locate Keisha's books. He sat at an empty carrel desultorily leafing through them, stopping when something attracted his attention. One was dedicated to "the love of my life" with a small oval headshot of a white man wearing glasses who looked nerdy and wore a doofus smile. He stared at it a long while.

When the library closed at five, he walked back to his cousin Keisha's house. By now the lights were on downstairs and dark silhouettes passed back and forth in front of the windows. He thought he heard violin music, faint but melodious. When a biker in a helmet and hoodie almost collided with him while turning into the driveway, he jumped out of the way keeping his head down, hoping Caleb wouldn't recognize him. It wasn't safe to hang out there any longer. He walked back to the L.

He was thinking about Cora and how hard it must be on her, losing her father, losing him so brutally, and watching her mother suffering from the loss. He'd overheard his parents talking about Keisha and the children, his mom sucking her teeth with that sound she made when she felt saddened by another's plight. Mama said it was obvious the woman carried a heavy burden of pain. Papa said you could see it in Caleb's eagerness for attention. Aidan could have added, in Cora's sad eyes, too.

At the subway station, he stood conflicted. Where should he go? When two trains pulled up, their doors sliding open almost simultaneously, he boarded the one headed west, away from Chicago.

When Femi and Jacob returned from work, the darkness was lowering over the neighborhood's homes. Femi opened the front door, called out "We're home!" and went straight to the kitchen to begin supper. There was no answer when she called Aidan to come eat. No answer when Jacob knocked on his youngest son's bedroom door. They ate without him. It was not unusual. He was, after all, a man now.

Three days later, on Friday, Aidan returned home. His parents had not realized he was gone.

Chapter 39

Edward called Keisha's cell phone in the middle of the day. "Have you seen the news? A twenty-eight-year-old premed student was shot and killed last night by a police officer in Fort Worth. She was babysitting her eight-year-old nephew, playing games with him. Neighbors had called the police to report that her front door was open and an officer who'd been on the force a little more than a year went to her house, stood outside on the lawn, and shot her through a window."

"Oh, no! *Not again*. It doesn't seem to matter if you are educated and middle class—the only thing that matters is your color. Remember that accountant killed last year by an off-duty Dallas cop?"

"I've been keeping a list. Jean Botham."

"I'm worried about Cora and Caleb, how to protect them. Can you come for supper tonight? I can drive you home. This is another 'talk' I need to have with the kids and your presence would help. Also, I have news about Reggie that I haven't told you yet."

Uncle Edward arrived carrying canvas grocery bags with the fixings for pork chops with mango chutney, oven baked sweet potato chips, green peas, and baked apples stuffed with walnuts and cranberries. He was a firm believer that a delicious meal helped one cope with any situation. The two of them worked at the kitchen island cutting sweet potatoes into wafer thin slices and preparing the apples. While they worked, she told him what she was learning about Reggie's work with Progress Plaza, Reggie's note to Mr. Marshall about James Forman, and about Philadelphia's treatment of the MOVE 9.

When everything was in the oven, Keisha poured them wine that they took to the sofa in the family room, along with her laptop.

"So much of what I find about MOVE paints them as a back-to-nature, environmentalist cult. They eat raw food, oppose additives and guns, practice healthy living—no smoking, drinking, or drugs—and keep themselves physically fit. They know how to talk trash, but they take in people in need of a place to stay and consider their members 'family.' They all take part in raising their children. They get called Black Nationalists, but they have white members living with them who are part of the MOVE family and who also use the surname Africa. They don't trust the government or big corporations, but that's true of a whole lot of people. I found a video on YouTube that has changed how I perceive them. It's a conversation between Debbie Africa and Mike Africa, lovers separated by more than forty years in prison. They were released last year. Can I play it for you?"

"Of course."

The video showed a man and woman in their early sixties seated facing each other. They were a handsome couple, their bodies fit, their faces loving. Each had a stack of 3-x-5 cards before them on the low table that separated them. The cards held questions they wanted to ask each other. Cameras focused on each face, while another camera captured the long view, both profiles, looking at each other. As the video played, each spoke of their love for the other, for their MOVE family, and for their children, from whom they had been separated for more than four decades.

Keisha was crying softly.

The man said that no one wants to be a revolutionary, that most people, including the two of them, would much rather be at home with their families. But sometimes injustice forces you to speak out. They were grandparents who had missed their children's and grandchildren's growing up, birthdays, holidays, vacations. They had missed experiencing this huge portion of their lives because their love didn't stop at home.

"Their son, Mike Africa, Jr., grew up visiting them in prison. He worked for twenty-five years to get them released. They haven't seen each other for forty years, yet they're not bitter. They radiate so much love." Keisha's voice trailed off.

"Sounds like the Reggie I knew and loved." Edward spoke quietly. "It seems his journey from SNCC to MOVE was not abandoning his values, just following them down another path. Until he ran into a literal dead end in the form of a police bullet."

"You're saying his sympathy for MOVE was consistent with who he was? There is comfort in that." Keisha reached for Edward's hand.

"Maybe he wasn't lost, just *moving.*"

The fragrances of pork, apple, and cinnamon had brought Caleb and Cora downstairs and into the kitchen. They greeted Uncle Edward and pitched in to get the food onto plates. It was another "Feast of St. Edward," as Keisha called the meals he cooked for them.

"Mom, we want you to invite Femi, Jacob, and their kids to our house for dinner. Uncle Edward, too. It's time our families came together here, in our home." Caleb spoke with authority.

"Don't forget to invite Aidan." Cora was trying to sound nonchalant.

Later, in the safety of her car as she drove Edward back to his apartment, Keisha confessed something to her uncle. "I'm not sure I know how to raise Black children at this time in history. I grew up protected. I never faced what Black young people are facing today."

His answer surprised her. "Maybe Femi and Jacob can help you with that."

Chapter 40

Cora's mind kept getting stuck on her newly discovered first-cousin-once-removed. Like the antique record player on which Dad used to listen to his father's collection of 33 1/3 LP jazz albums. He kept the albums in their aged cardboard covers lined up on the shelves beside his worktable and had listened to Ella Fitzgerald scat singing "How High the Moon" so often that the needle stuck when it reached "somewhere there's music, it's where you are." It would repeat and repeat that line, and if Mom was in the room, Dad would grin at her in that special secret look-language they used. Then he'd lift the needle and place it at the start of the next song.

Cora loved Ella Fitzgerald's rendering of that song, and she loved Dad's delight in the liquid, cascading voice—"Her voice is a whole orchestra!" he would say each time, as though it was the first time he was noticing.

Cora was stuck on Aidan, her needle repeating the moments in Femi's kitchen when he'd looked at her with such sympathy, when they'd been doing the dishes and Dad had come into their conversation.

This morning, she stood in her kitchen looking out on the back garden. It looked gray. The persistent rain had extinguished the fall colors as it pummeled the litter of leaves covering the grass. Cora had decided to ask Mama what she thought of her tall, thin cousin with the intense eyes and gentleness lurking behind them. Did Mama recognize the gentleness? Or was she put off by Aidan's withdrawal in the presence of his parents and his obvious discomfort when Mama asked him what he wanted to do with his life?

The second Saturday in November, Uncle Edward, Femi and Jacob, and their sons, daughters-in-law, and grandchildren gathered at the Evanston house for a getting-to-know-you evening. Femi and Edward were both outstanding cooks, so when each offered to bring a dish, Keisha accepted. The meal would be spectacular.

It had turned cold, so they would be indoors.

Once the awkward moments of introduction were passed, the

group broke into twos and threes, conversing. It seemed surprisingly comfortable, even though it was the first time Ajani, Barron, and their wives and kids had met Keisha, Edward, Caleb, and Cora.

Cora was assigned the job of giving a tour of the house. After the tour, when the kids wandered off with Caleb to his room and the adults returned downstairs, Aidan and Cora were left alone in Cora's bedroom. They sat on the floor, backs against the twin beds, across from each other, and began to talk. Like last time, Aidan asked good questions and Cora opened up. She told him about her continued worries about her mom.

"Have you made friends at school you can talk with now?"

"Not really. Everyone treats me one of three ways—either like I'm broken, or like I'm invisible, or like if they get too close, they'll catch my bad luck. Like their fathers will be murdered, too! It's easier to stay by myself. There is one girl who's also 'broken' who talks with me sometimes. Her mom died of cancer and her grandma is raising her."

"So she can understand how lonely it feels to be different?"

"I guess. Do you ever feel lonely, Aidan?"

"A lot of the time." He took a deep breath, as if he was about to dive into a very deep pool. "I don't know if you know this, but I was in a gang when I was your age and got in trouble and was sent to prison for six years, adult prison. It was lonely and dangerous. Surprisingly, my gang buddies deserted me, which meant I didn't have anyone watching my back. It's not supposed to work that way. When I got out, I thought it wouldn't be as lonely. I was wrong. The kind of people I'd like to hang out with now don't want to hang out with an ex-felon. I'm beginning to think that Life is lonely."

Cora felt so attracted to this man who spent time with her and took her seriously. The air in her room felt different, magical, and she sat up straighter, pulling her shoulders back, pushing her chest out, breathing in her new woman-ness. She felt ready to change. Her cheeks flushed and her eyes softened as they looked at Aidan. She wanted so for him to touch her. She wanted to jump the chasm separating childhood from womanhood and throw herself unreservedly into what came next. She scooted so she was beside him rather than facing him. They were leaning against the same twin bed. Where their shoulders touched, she felt his warmth.

Aidan took her hand and held it in his. He looked at their hands, his chestnut brown, hers mocha. She thought the colors looked beautiful together.

Cora let her body overtake her mind. She wanted this. She was ready.

Chapter 41

Downstairs the adults were deep in conversation. Femi had asked Keisha to share what she was learning about "Uncle Reggie's" years in Philadelphia and how he came to be part of the community headquartered in the house on Osage Avenue.

When Keisha finished speaking, Barron, Femi and Jacob's middle son, spoke. "Why do they hate Black people so?" The question hung suspended in mid-air, like a guillotine blade ready to fall. "All these terrible murders officially sanctioned and excused. It's still happening, and it's still being covered up."

"Violence is as American as apple pie." Uncle Edward's comment met silence.

Jacob changed the subject. "Keisha, maybe you have a book to write from all you're learning. What will you title it? 'Distinguished Historian Researches her Roots and Discovers Historic Police Violence?'"

Jacob's question drew attention. The others weighed in with possible titles, some of them funny. There was relief in playing this game, ooo'ing and applauding each suggestion:

"'With Dr. Johnson in Darkest Philadelphia.'"

"'How Did a Well-Educated Jamaica-Born Man Go Wrong?'"

"'From Non-Violence and Black Capitalism to the Philadelphia PD.'"

"'One Woman's Search for her Birth Father.'"

"'MOVE-ing the Truth.'"

"'Who Killed Reggie Lewis?'"

"'Finding your Father in the Ashes of Osage Avenue.'"

"'My Father was Not a Terrorist.'"

"That is the point, isn't it?" Keisha jumped in, "The people in MOVE were not then, and are not now, terrorists. They are part of an American tradition of free thinking. The Puritans separated themselves from their society to live out their own beliefs in New England. Quakers and Shakers and all sorts of utopians did the same. Why were all those Black towns built across the U.S. after the Civil War? Folks were looking for a safe place to live out their values.”

Uncle Edward was a news junkie. He wanted them to pay attention to the international context, too. “One person’s freedom fighter is another person’s terrorist—the Irish fighting the British, the African National Congress in South Africa fighting the white minority government, refugee communities like the Rohingya in Myanmar.”

“The Ghost Dance Movement of Native Americans. Another group of people seeking to follow their beliefs and shot down.” That was from Keisha. The others had no idea what she was talking about.

“Lots of groups face persecution and violence. Some take up arms in self-defense.” Ajani’s wife was from the Sudan and this conversation was directly relevant to why her people had fled their country.

“What about the Palestinians?” Barron’s company did business in the West Bank.

“Or the Maroons back in Jamaica, hey? Escaping slavery and determined to never go back to it, fighting from their mountain hideouts against the British planters.” Femi made stern eye-contact with her sons. “Don’t you forget your people’s history.”

New insights sparked more parallels. They rode the conversation like a rollercoaster. It was exhilarating. Keisha was in her element, intellectually stimulated in a community of like-minded people.

No one noticed that Aidan was not there. He had been “not there” since before he was sent to prison.

Chapter 42

Cora rested her head on Aidan's shoulder, her eyes closed, waiting for him to kiss her. They could hear animated conversation wafting up from the living room and the chatter of the younger kids down the hall in Caleb's room. Aidan gently moved her head off his shoulder, stood, and walked to the doorway. He closed the door to her room and then took his seat on the floor beside her. Cora waited, like Janie Crawford in the book she was reading that lay on the table beside her bed. Like a blossom on a pear tree waiting for a bee.

"Are you reading *Their Eyes Were Watching God?*" Aidan reached for the book and opened it. "'Janie saw her life like a great tree in leaf with the things suffered, things enjoyed, things done and undone. Dawn and doom were in the branches.'" He was reciting from memory. Then he began to read to her.

> *It was a spring afternoon in West Florida. Janie had spent most of the day under a blossoming pear tree in the back yard. She had been spending every minute that she could steal from her chores under that tree for the last three days. That was to say, ever since the first tiny bloom had opened. It had called her to come and gaze on a mystery. From barren brown stems to glistening leaf buds; from the leaf buds to snowy virginity of bloom. It stirred her tremendously. How? Why? It was like a flute song forgotten in another existence and remembered again. What? How? Why? This singing she heard that had nothing to do with her ears. The rose of the world was breathing out smell. It followed her through all her waking moments and caressed her in her sleep. It connected itself with other vaguely felt matters that had struck her outside observation and buried themselves in her flesh. Now they emerged and quested about her consciousness.*

She was stretched on her back beneath the pear tree soaking in the alto chant of the visiting bees, the gold of the sun and the panting breath of the breeze when the inaudible voice of it all came to her. She saw a dust-bearing bee sink into the sanctum of a bloom; the thousand sister-calyxes arch to meet the love embrace and the ecstatic shiver of the tree from root to tiniest branch creaming in every blossom and frothing with delight....Oh to be a pear tree--any tree in bloom!

"I love that passage. Is that how you're feeling right now?" He watched her closely.

Cora nodded smiling dreamily. He understood! She felt giddy with anticipation.

Aidan stood and set the book back on the table. He turned to face her, and his eyes took in her eager young face. "Cora, you are a beautiful young woman, intelligent, caring, graceful, attractive, and loveable. I like you very much. And I respect you. The time for bees to meet your blossoms 'frothing with delight' will come, but now is too soon. Besides, you're my *Cuz!*" He lowered himself to the floor to sit facing her. His eyes held hers with tenderness, watching the tears traveling down her cheeks.

"You have suffered a terrible tragedy. You yearn for closeness. I get that." He kept his eyes on hers. "I hope you will let me be your friend. Friends are rare in both of our lives right now. Friends are very special. If you push me to 'enter your blossoms' we won't be able to remain friends. Do you understand, Cuz?"

She didn't understand. Disappointment and confusion produced more tears. Was he not attracted to her? Did he have a girlfriend? Was it because they were cousins? Was he gay?

She wouldn't understand for many years. But she knew she would love him all of her life.

Then he asked her to tell him about her daddy.

Chapter 43

Femi and Jacob's family stayed until after midnight. They took Uncle Edward with them so he wouldn't have to take an Uber. Keisha lay in bed watching the haloed full moon over the back garden and feeling grateful.

Cora also was awake. She was reviewing what had happened in her room with Aidan. She might still be a virgin, but something inside her had changed. And, despite her disappointment, that felt good.

Caleb slept.

It was nearly Thanksgiving. Time for the annual pilgrimage to Ann and Don's home in Cleveland. Caleb looked forward to the extended weekend with Granddad and the other men. Sometimes he resented being the only man in the house. Cora looked forward to seeing Gran Ann and Gran Cora especially, but she pictured Dad's empty chair and that made her teary. Keisha wished she'd get sick so they could cancel the trip.

None of them were prepared for the surprise awaiting them.

Chapter 44

The week before Thanksgiving, Dr. Johnson had asked Ronald and Cassandra to meet in her office.

Ronald was early as usual. Cassandra was late.

Dr. Johnson looked better. The dark circles under her eyes were nearly gone, and she appeared to be putting herself together with more care. He was glad.

Before they talked about their research, Cassandra pulled up a breaking news story on her phone. Former police officer Jason Van Dyke, who had been found guilty of second degree murder a year earlier and sentenced to six-and-three-quarters years in prison, had just been released from federal custody and would be freed next week, on November 26th, after serving one year and one month. Van Dyke was the first police officer in fifty years convicted of murder for an on-duty shooting. He had shot a Black teenager, Laquan McDonald, sixteen times while Laquan walked away from police.

"Remember last month when the Inspector General released a report about sixteen Chicago police and supervisors who covered up how Van Dyke killed Laquan?" Ronald had followed this local news and had hoped Van Dyke's prison sentence was a sign the Chicago police would be reforming how they treat people, especially people of color.

"I remember seeing that dashcam footage. This kid walking away from the cops, never turning toward them, and Officer Van Dyke pumping *sixteen shots* into his back, most of them after he was lying on the ground. He was only seventeen." It was not like Ronald to talk this much and this forcefully. "My grandma lives a few blocks from where it happened."

Cassandra passed her phone to Keisha. "The footage is replaying here."

"I remember. Didn't it take more than a year for the dashcam video to be released?"

Ronald's face was ashy. "Then, after five years, the report is released that says the supervisory officers covered up the destruction of notes made of civilian witnesses' testimony, testimony that disagreed with

Van Dyke's account. Those officers and supervisors had lied in signing off on a statement that Laquan had moved toward Van Dyke, threatening him with a knife."

"My cousin died that way about five years ago." Cassandra was shaking her head, the small beads in her braids bumping against each other like wind chimes.

This is the same police department that is supposed to be finding the killer of my husband. The same police department that tells me each time I call that it's unlikely they'll ever find out who murdered Richard. And I haven't paid attention to what's been happening right here where we live for seven months. Listening to the two of them, Keisha felt sick and ashamed of her inattention.

Ronald was bitter. "He's getting out after not much more than a year. One of my cousins has been incarcerated for *five years* for possession of a sandwich baggie of weed. I expected them to say Laquan died of sickle cell disease. The police have been using that excuse a lot of the time when their victims never had sickle cell."

"At least the mayor is trying to clean up the police. Without her pressure, the Inspector General's report would not have been released to the public. Let's hear it for Lori Lightfoot, our Black lesbian mayor."

Keisha appreciated Cassandra's persistent determination to find a smidgen of hope in everything. Now she pulled them back to the reason for their meeting. She was considering writing a book about a Black professor searching for her biological father in the ashes of Osage Avenue. She wanted to include their research and, of course, would cite them. Would they give her permission to do that?

She had their full attention. She had never mentioned a personal connection to their research.

"Are you going to write a novel?" Cassandra was direct.

"No. It will be more like a memoir, if I actually write it. It's my story. My biological father died May 13, 1985, on Osage Avenue."

Cassandra and Ronald were silent, staring at her. Keisha felt vulnerable. She rarely shared her personal life with students.

Then she continued. "This story must be told while there are living, breathing people who remember it and can fill in the details. It must be told, including the memories of people who knew MOVE and, hopefully, people who continue to belong to MOVE. My approach will be different from yours, not scholarly, more personal. With Black Lives Matter raising consciousness to the disproportionate number of unarmed Black people killed by police, it seems a good time for a book that provides a historical perspective and tells the Philadelphia story."

"There are already a number of books and a few films available on MOVE," Ronald was cautious. Most people thought MOVE was a crazy cult. Wouldn't a personal book about her connection to MOVE backfire, damaging her credibility as a historian? He didn't want his professor to be surprised by a tsunami of criticism. He had experience with disappointment and unintended consequences.

Cassandra had no reservations. "Way to go, Dr. J! How can we help?" She fist-bumped Dr. Johnson with enthusiasm.

That evening, Keisha and the kids began packing for their Thanksgiving trip to Cleveland. They would leave the next afternoon.

Chapter 45

Dozing in his chair, Arthur took a sudden deep breath, then exhaled audibly. Gran Cora, seated beside him, heard a low rumbling sound. That was all. It was enough to tell her he had gone. She sat in her chair beside him, holding his hand, and talked to him as the afternoon sun faded through the blinds. *We've had a good life, dear friend. We found each other after we'd both been battered by loss and made a new life together, helping each other carry our burdens. We've truly been blessed.*

She patted his hand with its familiar brown spots and skin so fragile she could see his veins.

Remember how the neighbors gossiped when you began coming to see me, driving all the way to Nashville from Buffalo, New York for a one-day visit? Remember when your daughter Mi-Young first arrived from Korea? How much joy you brought me letting me raise her! How much joy she brought both of us.

Then you moved to Nashville. You were a hot mess, hardly functioning. You slept all day in Edward's room, rarely emerging, not bathing, sunk in depression, until we threatened to evict you. Then all the prayers sent up for you started working. You came to church with me, and you found yourself in the Movement, going with me to protests and trainings.

And we became a family, a skinny white guy from New York who'd been my husband's best buddy in Korea, my son Edward, your Korean daughter Mi-Young, and me, an overachieving Black woman leaning on the Lord to get her through. Oh, Arthur, we made a way out of no way, and it's been good!

Then, after so many years of separation, Don found you. Brought his wife Ann, bless her, and Keisha into our lives. You got a second chance to be Don's dad, and you both made up for the lost years.

She shifted in her chair and leaned toward her deceased husband, kissing his cheek and stroking his hair. *I thank the Lord for giving me second chance at love. And I thank you, Arthur. We've loved each other well and long, my friend. Please don't go too far away. I'm counting on talking things over with you and I need you to still listen.*

She sat half-smiling, holding his hand, her face wet, reluctant to let this holy time end.

As dusk settled over their apartment the phone rang. It was Don calling for his 5 p.m. weekly chat with his dad.

"His body is here, Don, but he's moved on. Just an hour ago. I'm going to put the phone to his better ear so you can tell him whatever you want. I knew you'd call, and I knew he'd not want to miss you." She heard Don crying as she tucked the phone between her husband's ear and shoulder. She sat beside Arthur, one hand holding the phone in place while Arthur's son spoke to his daddy.

When the phone began beeping and a digital voice said, "Please hang up and try your call again," she knew Don had finished. She rang Don and Ann's number. "Thank you," Don said before passing the phone to Ann.

Then Gran Cora phoned her son Edward with the news.

Arthur had wanted to be cremated, his ashes to remain with Cora until her death when they would be buried with hers in the plot beside Booker--Edward's father, Cora's first husband, and Arthur's best buddy. When the family next gathered in Cleveland—which would not be this Thanksgiving, after all—they would hold a memorial service. Meanwhile, Edward and Don would fly to Nashville to be with Cora.

Arthur's passing was as gentle as the man himself.

Chapter 46

On Wednesday, the day before Thanksgiving, when Femi returned from the corner store at 1 p.m., their landline answering machine was blinking. Aidan's probation officer had left a message reporting that Aidan hadn't shown up for his weekly appointment. Did they know where he was?

Femi checked Aidan's room. The bed was made up and his duffel bag was missing from the closet. Then Jacob called their other sons, Ajani and Barron, his voice sounding tight, scared. Ajani said he'd be there in thirty minutes and instructed his father to wait until he talked with them before returning the probation officer's call. Ajani was a lawyer and well aware of the consequences of missing your check-ins with your parole officer.

They sat at the kitchen table, neglected cups of coffee growing cold while they talked. Jacob alternated pacing and sitting, his face grim and angry. "What was he thinking? This could land him back in prison."

"What happened before he went missing? Tell me everything you remember." Ajani's voice sounded worried. His tone caused Femi's anxiety to surge.

"Everything seemed all right when we all were at Keisha's. That was the last time we saw him." Jacob looked at Femi, who confirmed what he remembered.

"That was four days ago." Femi's hands were holding up her face.

"Let me look at the laptop. Maybe his browsing history will tell us something." Ajani waited for his father's nod and then took the stairs two at a time to fetch the laptop, bringing it back to the kitchen table. He found the sites Aidan had visited in the previous weeks and showed his parents. A number of articles came up about a murder on the L last April. The victim was a composer and professor at Northwestern with the same surname as Keisha's kids

"Did you know Keisha's husband had been murdered?" Jacob asked Femi. It was unlike her to keep something like that to herself.

"No! She never spoke of him. I didn't ask. I thought maybe they were

divorced. Oh, that poor family, God love them, they've been through Hell, that's certain." Femi was distracted from her own fear as she took in what had happened to Keisha's husband.

Ajani alternated pacing the kitchen with sitting on the edge of his chair, scrolling his phone. His face was intent.

"You're scaring me, son."

"Could Aidan have known something about Keisha's husband's murder? It happened the first week in April. Aidan was released a year ago, so he would have been out and living here at the time."

"He's been so lost since he was released. I don't know how he has used the time while we're at work. He seems to hibernate, no friends, no social life. We've worried about him." Femi silently summoned her ancestors, God, and whomever might bring aid.

"I know my baby brother would never participate in murdering someone. Never. But he might have heard something on the street. He might know something about who was involved. That could put him in real danger. I know you both know that. It could put you in danger, too. The Crips are King of the Hill in this neighborhood right now. And he's stayed away from them since they abandoned him when he was on the inside."

Femi was glad Aidan had confided in his big brother something about his prison experience. He'd said little about prison to his parents. "What should we do?"

"Where could he have gone?" Now Jacob was pacing.

"Mom, Dad, this is important. *You cannot lie to the officer.* It's Thanksgiving weekend so the office will have closed at noon. Maybe call on Monday and say he's been depressed and hasn't slept at the house this week. Meanwhile, let me talk to my friend at the court. I can sound her out, all hypothetical. The police are probably already tracing his phone with GPS. We need to buy some time. If he is in danger, perhaps they wouldn't count his running against him."

They knew he was grasping for straws and that his straws were all they had to hold onto.

Chapter 47

Femi phoned Keisha later that day. "I know it's the day before Thanksgiving, and I'm calling with very short notice, but Jacob and I wondered if you have plans for tomorrow?"

"That is so kind of you. We always go to my parents' home in Cleveland for a family reunion, but yesterday my grandpa died, and Dad is on his way to Nashville to be with Gran. I've canceled our tickets."

"I'm so sorry about your grandfather. May he rest in peace. Was it a surprise?"

"Death is always a surprise to me. He was 94, so we knew he might die any time. He died in his chair with Gran in the room. Gran says it was a peaceful and painless transition. They were lucky."

Knowing what she now knew about Keisha's husband's violent death, Femi felt the emotion behind Keisha's words.

"Would you like to come to our home tomorrow? The boys go to their wives' families for Thanksgiving and come to us for Christmas. So it will only be Jacob and me—and your family, if you can come."

"Thank you. That is very kind. We'd love to come. What can I bring and what time?"

It was raining and the sky was dark with storm clouds. Cora, Caleb, and Keisha dodged puddles as they followed the sidewalk to Jacob and Femi's front porch, avoiding the sodden, swollen grass.

When Femi opened the door to greet them, the Woodlawn house exuded fragrant smells, the scents of a blended Jamaican/American Thanksgiving—cinnamon and oranges, oil frying plantains, sage in the dressing, and bacon in the greens. Jacob challenged Caleb to another round of pool, and Keisha joined Femi in the kitchen. Nothing was said about why Aidan wasn't joining them.

Cora felt keenly disappointed. She sat in the living room on the overstuffed chair beside the window, hunched over her book, while the women finished food preparations. The world through the window was bleak and blurry, a monotone of grayed browns.

From the kitchen both women could see down the hall to where Cora huddled, could see that Cora was near tears.

"Hormones?" Femi asked.

"Probably. It's her first Thanksgiving without her daddy," Keisha replied.

Keisha thought Femi and Jacob looked weary. As the women sat at the kitchen table chopping onions and crying from their smarting eyes, suddenly Femi laid her knife on the table, took Keisha's hands in hers, and plunged ahead to ask a question that had haunted her the past twenty-four hours. "You've never spoken of your husband. If you don't mind, I'd like to know what happened to him."

"He died. Was murdered on the L returning from a gig late on April 5th. The police have given us no information about who killed him, just that they think it was a gang." There, she'd said it, had told these new family members the central horror of her present life.

Femi didn't speak. In time Keisha deluged her with words she had not spoken to anyone, describing what she knew of that night, describing the police arriving at their home the next morning, describing identifying Richard's body, describing her rage that the police had not apprehended his killers. All the while Femi listened, holding her hands.

The feast they shared in the formal dining room sometime later tasted delicious, flavored with tears and melancholy and sweet attachment.

After the meal Femi, Jacob, and Keisha sat in the living room talking. Cora and Caleb were playing pool in the basement.

"I wanted to tell you that I have two students doing their dissertations on what was happening in Philadelphia from the late 1970s till 1985. Have I mentioned them before?"

"No." Jacob looked uncomfortable, wary of another Reggie conversation.

Cora and Caleb came upstairs, arguing about whether Caleb cheated on a shot. Cora slipped into an armchair, and Caleb stood in the doorway smiling at Jacob, who was looking for an excuse to leave the women's talk. Jacob smiled back. "Did you bring the design for your rocket you were telling me about?"

Caleb reached into his backpack and pulled out a notebook covered in drawings. "Yeah. I'm building a rocket strong enough to travel ten miles. Wanna see!" The males escaped downstairs. Femi and Keisha barely noticed them. They were focused on Keisha's story.

"My student has discovered that the federal government was interested in supporting Black economic development in the late Sixties, about the time Reggie moved to Philadelphia. The Small Business Administration had programs to make loans available to those seeking to start Black-owned businesses." Keisha rifled through a stack of papers in her large shoulder bag. "Here they are!" She passed a stapled report on yellowing paper to Femi. *A National Strategy for Developing Minority Business Enterprises*, dated February 14, 1968, and another report dated a month later titled *A National Program for Promoting Minority Entrepreneurship*.

"I think the motivation for these programs was partly to avoid urban unrest by giving Black folks a stake in the economy so they wouldn't take to the streets. Philadelphia was the city most involved. Republicans and Democrats, Richard Nixon and his rival Hubert Humphrey, were supporters."

"How does this relate to Reggie?"

"Maybe it doesn't, but I'm thinking it might have been why he was drawn to Philadelphia, to work with Reverend Sullivan's programs. They were doing exciting organizing of the North Philly community. I told you about my visit with the elderly women at Zion Baptist Church who knew Reggie."

Their conversation branched and Keisha told Femi she was thinking about Jacob's suggestion last weekend, the night they were at Keisha's house, that she write a book about her search for Reggie. They had all joked about possible titles, and it had all been in fun. But the idea had intrigued her.

The women's conversation veered this way and that. Keisha felt relieved that she'd been able to share with Femi what she'd been going through without being asked too many questions. On this difficult Thanksgiving, with nothing familiar, she felt surprisingly thankful. It was odd and not what she'd expected.

On the way home Cora, trying to sound nonchalant, asked, "Why didn't Aidan come?"

"They said he was away looking for a job," Keisha replied.

Chapter 48

Ajani had checked with his contacts in the federal District Attorney's office, but they knew nothing about Aidan. Ajani was confident one of his friends there would let him know if Aidan's disappearance meant he'd entered witness protection, been assigned a new name and identity, and relocated out of state. Ajani told his parents that lots of people who enter witness protection can't take the isolation from friends and family and leave the program. He cautioned them that it was equally possible Aidan was lying in a ditch, or in a morgue. Femi and Jacob refused to entertain that possibility. At least for now.

On the Saturday after Thanksgiving, Aidan showed up at the house. He had tried to run away, but he was no better at running than he was at finding employment. At some point, he gave up.

Jacob was furious with him. Femi simply wept.

They sat at the kitchen table. It was the family comfort place where family secrets were shared and tears shed.

Aidan's eyes were resolute as he raised them to look at his parents. "I had to see if I could live in a new place as a wholly different person and not have contact with you. I guess you can tell, I can't. Didn't make it even a week."

"You were in witness protection?"

"No. I was testing if I could do it."

"Why the hell didn't you tell us? Your mama has been so worried."

"And you, Jacob? Tell him how worried *you*'ve been. Don't go all macho. He's your son too."

Jacob muttered something under his breath and fetched the coffee pot, clearly agitated and uncomfortable.

"I *couldn't* tell you. I know you are doing a lot for me by letting me stay here, and I know there's no way for you to understand how hard it's been for me. I thought going away might make it better for all of us. By staying here I could be endangering you. And that's the last thing I want."

"How would you be endangering us?" Femi reached across the table, and he gave her his hand.

"Gang membership is a commitment for life. But I broke with them and have avoided all contact with them on the outside. You don't do that. But I did. Like I said, I can't stay here, for my sake and yours."

It was Femi who raised the option of moving to another city while retaining his identity. She had a former student who'd gotten himself into trouble with the law and, after he got out of prison, he had taken the bus south to Atlanta (or was it Austin?) where other members of his family took him in to help him start over without "felon" causing prospective employers to say the job had just been filled. She texted Ajani, telling him the prodigal had returned and did he know anything about a relocation option less extreme than witness protection.

"I think we still have some of my Daadie's people in Kingston who'd take you in." Jacob was on it like a dog on a bone.

"Husband, going South to kinfolks for this family would require a *boat* as well as a bus!"

"I don't think you can leave the country while you're on parole." Aidan avoided his father's eyes. He wasn't disrespecting his father. There just was a lot that families of immigrants, families with no experience "in the system," didn't know about the American criminal justice system.

Ajani texted back that he'd found a possibility and would come by after work.

Several hours later, Ajani dropped by with a document that explained how an ex-felon on probation might be able to leave Illinois. Jacob, Femi, and Ajani again sat at the kitchen table as Ajani went over what he'd learned. The fourth chair at the table was empty. The others didn't seem to notice that Aidan stood in the doorway, left out of the animated conversation his parents and oldest brother were having about him. It was like he wasn't even there. *Is that how they see me? Like a ghostly presence floating through their house with nowhere to settle?*

The flyer was titled, An Interstate Compact Transfer. He said that since 2008, the federal government had allowed interstate transfers through a legal agreement between states. They weren't always granted, but they could be. Ajani was serious, like he always was. Aidan observed to himself that the family's oldest child seemed to have missed their parents' humor genes. Their youngest child, also.

Ajani read out loud to them from the Interstate Commission for Adult Offender Supervision (ICAOS) pamphlet:

- The defendant must have family in the receiving state (such as a parent, grandparent, aunt, uncle, adult child, adult sibling, legal guardian, or stepparent) who has resided in the receiving state for at least 180 days and is willing to assist in supervising the defendant, and the offender must gain employment or have a means of support; AND
- The defendant must be in compliance with all the rules of probation from his state at the time of the application for transfer.

Femi screwed up her face in concentration, taking an inventory of their relatives. "Aidan has no living grandparents, no stepparents or out-of-state siblings, no adult child. He does have an uncle in New York, my brother, and your sister in Dallas." She was looking at Jacob. "They're the only family that meet the requirements." Ajani nodded and entered notes in his phone. Aidan felt invisible.

It was at least a possibility. As they weighed the merits of Aidan's New York uncle and Dallas aunt, Jacob's sister Eve seemed to be the best bet. She was five years younger than Jacob, divorced, and worked for American Airlines. But they hadn't told her of Aidan's incarceration. They had told very few people.

When Aidan was a little boy, his Aunt Eve was a flight attendant and came to Chicago regularly, staying with them during layovers. Aidan had captivated her. When they talked on the phone, she often recalled those days, quite openly calling Aidan her favorite nephew.

The dozens of nights she had spent on their pull-out sofa—the predecessor of their elegant, tufted divan—might make her glad to help. She'd said for years that she'd be happy for Aidan to stay with her if he ever got to Dallas.

Jacob was tired of Aidan's gloomy, brooding presence in their house. He was eager for a quick solution that would bring back their empty nest without putting Aidan back in prison. "Doesn't she have one of those fru-fru dogs that requires a lot of attention? Maybe it would help her to have Aidan there while she's on the road?"

Aidan's time in lockdown humiliated Jacob, embarrassed him. Jacob didn't know that Aidan could see how his father felt about him, which increased Aidan's alienation and shame.

When Aidan spoke, all three turned to look at him, as though surprised by his presence. "Can we call Aunt Eve and see what she says?" He didn't say what he was thinking: *I'm as eager to get away from here as you are to have me gone.*

"Okay, but you do the talking, Femi. You're more persuasive and she likes you—you didn't leave a dead mouse on her pillow when she was five."

"That's a lot to get past, husband. If she says no, we know who's to blame." Femi swatted him affectionately as she moved into the living room to place the call in private.

Aidan sat with his father and brother. The men strained to hear, their faces cycling from hopeful to discouraged and back as they tried to interpret the fragments of the conversation that they could hear. Aidan watched his father scratch a hangnail until it bled, then reach for a paper napkin and wrap it around his leaking forefinger.

After ten minutes, Ajani got up to grab a ginger beer from the fridge.

"Woman! Don't leave us hanging. Get on with it." Jacob muttered under his breath.

After twenty minutes, they heard the familiar ritual ending of a conversation. "I love you, too. We'll get back to you." Femi returned to the kitchen, her face hard to read.

"Wah gwaan, woman? Tell us?"

"Jacob, what's wrong with your finger—it's bleeding!"

Aidan could tell his father was exasperated. "*Nuttin* wrong wit me! Wah gwaan wit me sistah?"

Ajani tossed Aidan a slight smile. When Papa resorted to patois, they knew he was upset. The sons found these interactions between their parents funny, even now.

Femi took her time, enjoying Jacob's distress. She poured a cup of tea for herself and wiped the counter before taking a seat. She cocked her head to one side, speculating, and then, finally, spoke.

"'Yu sistah'"—she was mocking him; Femi the teacher never used patois except to tease Jacob. "She has her own problems. New grandbaby coming soon, and her daughter hasn't located childcare so she can go back to work. Sistah's new man doesn't like how much she is working. Rumors are American Airlines may make cuts."

"Didn't you ask her about taking Aidan?" Jacob was pacing again and Ajani, who had returned to the table, no longer wore his impassive, lawyer face.

Aidan just watched.

Femi's smile gave away the pleasure she was taking from drawing this out. "Auntie loves her nephew Aidan and was glad I was telling her the truth about what happened to him." She reached for Aidan's hand, laughing. "Honey, she'd heard you'd been taken to Guantanamo and might never return!"

Her face settled down. "Of course, your Aunt Eve will invite you to Dallas. She started telling me the friends she could approach to hire you. She says if Ajani will draft letters for her to send, she can start the process this week."

"Not a done deal, remember," Ajani cautioned. "But very good news, very good. I can draft a letter for her tomorrow and Aidan can fill out the forms that are online.

Aidan felt a rush of emotion. His family was funny, sometimes irritating, but they came through. Even for him. "I'll get started," he said heading for the stairs to his room. Then he turned around, and returned to stand in the doorway, hesitant and humbled. "Thank you," he said before escaping. He stopped halfway up the stairs to hear what Ajani was saying.

"You know he'll have to be on his best behavior." Ajani's authoritative, big-brother tone annoyed Aidan. "The law says that 'duly accredited officers of a sending state may at all times enter a receiving state and there apprehend and retake any offender under supervision.'" He was reading from the statute. "In other words, Illinois can take him back. This is an agreement between states. Individuals have no standing, no constitutional right to transfer out of Illinois. Interstate transfer of supervision is a *privilege.*" Ajani returned to reading the document: "'Individuals cannot appeal a rejection…[I]t helps to have a solid job offer, suitable residence, completed treatment, all fines, court costs and restitution paid, and a favorable history of supervision. Even if all of the previously mentioned steps have been taken, there are no guarantees that a discretionary transfer will be approved.'"

"So it could take months for this to be worked out?"

"Yes, Mama, and he'll have a one-in-three chance of being accepted by Texas, so don't get your hopes up. But I think it is our best option."

The three in the kitchen were quiet. Aidan imagined what Ajani and Papa were thinking: *This is the best solution to my baby brother's reckless behavior that got him into trouble and embarrassed the family. This is the best option to my son's laziness about finding a job here in Chicago.*

Aidan heard what they were not saying. He couldn't dispute their allegations. He blamed himself for getting involved with the Crips and spending the best years of his young life behind bars. And for not finding work on the Outside. Would his family ever see him differently? *Dallas is my chance to reinvent my life. I know I can do this. Just give me that chance.* he prayed.

He paced himself as he climbed the stairs to get to work on the forms. He didn't want to appear overly hopeful.

Chapter 49

A few days later, Femi's sister Joan, the family celebrity, arrived in Chicago from New York where she'd been performing at the Blue Note. Femi and Jacob were at O'Hare to meet her. Femi played at being jealous.

"Now don't you go gawking at her, Jacob. You are *my* man and Joan is a married woman." It was another family ritual, and Jacob played along.

"Your baby sister is one gorgeous woman. Ain't no man alive not going to notice her." Jacob loved to tease Femi about her sister, mostly in fun, but there was a smidgen of meanness in his teasing. It came with being married for almost four decades.

Joan's French husband had remained in Paris working and would fly to Chicago to join her in time for Christmas. It would be a major family reunion with Femi and Jacob's sons and their families. And Joan would meet Reggie's daughter and her children.

Joan was looking *fine,* her hair in braids threaded with gold ribbons and tiny beads, her posture as erect as ever, and her body shapely, despite her sixty years. Femi told herself Joan's body was the product of the daily exercise that her career required.

"Teachers like me are saved from that kind of discipline, thanks be to God," she told Jacob.

The sisters fell into each other's arms. *Mama would be proud to see how happily her youngest daughters greet each other,* Femi thought. "Tonight you will meet Reggie's daughter and grandchildren," she announced. Jacob waited patiently for his hug.

They were seated around the dining table of Femi and Jacob's house in Woodlawn. Femi and Joan had spent several hours catching up on family news, especially the story of Dr. Keisha Johnson and her entrance into their lives.

When they needed a break, Joan pulled up *The Chicago Tribune* on her phone. "Can you believe it? There's a story here on the fiftieth anniversary of the murder of Fred Hampton. I remember him. He was a friend of Reggie's."

"Keisha told me she discovered that Reggie was a mentor to Hampton in 1968, when they both joined the Black Panther Party in Chicago. Hampton became the leader of the Chicago Panthers."

Joan read aloud from the *Tribune*. "'Hampton was assassinated on December 3, 1969, while asleep in his bed with his pregnant girlfriend.'—Didn't Reggie leave Chicago and move to Philadelphia about then?"

"Yes, I think so." After talking with Keisha, Femi had been piecing together more of their brother's timeline.

The doorbell interrupted their conversation, and Keisha, Cora, and Caleb appeared on the threshold. Awkwardness receded as the three women talked. Caleb watched them. Jacob was right. Aunt Joan was gorgeous, for a sort-of-old woman.

The conversation turned to Reggie, and Joan pulled up on her phone the newspaper article she'd been reading. "I saw an article in today's *Tribune* about Fred Hampton. It said he brought 700 youth into the NAACP, and then became the leader of Chicago's Black Panthers. We were talking about it when you arrived because Reggie talked about Fred a lot."

Femi added, "We were wondering if Fred's murder by the Chicago PD was the reason Reggie left Chicago for Philadelphia."

Joan read from the article that at 4:30 a.m., fourteen police officers had raided Hampton's apartment building and fired at least eighty-two shots into him as he lay sleeping. "How traumatic that would have been for Reggie!"

Joan continued. "The article says Fred's fiancée testified at a criminal trial that officers pulled Fred from his bed and *shot him dead after the group had surrendered!* He was so young, only twenty-one!"

Keisha was familiar with the story of Fred Hampton's murder, although she hadn't known Hampton's connections to Reggie until talking with Uncle Edward. She had something to add: "Also, the Chicago Panthers were targeted by the FBI's secret COINTELPRO operation that was set up to discredit and silence activist Black organizations and peace groups. They were afraid of Fred's charisma. He'd been working to attract gangs to the Panthers and get them involved with the Panthers' feeding programs. He was building relationships between rival gangs and enlisting them to keep the peace here in Woodlawn and other neighborhoods."

"Lord have mercy, Fred was a brilliant young man."

Keisha had never seen Femi so emotional. There was a heaviness in the room that Keisha wanted to dispel. She changed the subject.

"I have been wanting to ask your help," she said to her aunts. "I need to prepare Cora and Caleb for the world they live in as young, mixed-race people who are viewed as Black. I grew up in a protected environment in a Cleveland suburb with white parents. I knew I was Black, but being Black wasn't particularly dangerous for me—awkward sometimes, but I always felt safe. Can you advise me on what I need to tell my children to prepare them to live safely in this country, with White Supremacy on the rise again?"

Femi stood and fetched a bottle of merlot and more ginger beer. Then she sat down heavily and sighed. Her right forefinger rubbed the grain of the oak table as she collected her thoughts.

Finally, she spoke. "We felt safe when our boys were young. Actually, until Aidan turned fifteen. Till he began hanging with the wrong group of kids, the wannabe tough guys. Once he got in trouble, and the system sentenced him like an adult, though he was only fifteen, well, we've not felt safe for Aidan since then. He's been lost since he got out of prison, unable to find a job, lonely, trapped in this house with his aging parents. We gave him 'the talk' just like we gave it to Barron and Ajani: If stopped by the police, keep your hands in the air and visible to the officers, don't talk back, be respectful, don't carry drugs or guns, don't wear gang colors or associate with gang members, etc., etc., etc."

"But he's doing well now, isn't he?" Keisha wanted to reassure Femi. "You said he's found a place to live and a job in Dallas and may be moving there, right? I don't know if you know this, but he's been really helpful with Cora."

"Yes, he's found a job in Texas working for his cousin, taking care of her yard and driving for her boss, and he can live with Jacob's sister, if the state of Illinois approves his application. But because he was sentenced to prison for six years when he was Cora's age, his choices are really limited. I don't think I can advise you what to say to Caleb and Cora when my youngest son has been so lost and alone."

Joan jumped in. "But Aidan's life is not over. You need to remember that. Like Keisha says, he is a bright young man and caring."

Joan took a swallow of her ginger beer before saying more. "I think being forced to change direction happens to most folk. Our life's road divides and crisscrosses. We think we're heading one way, and that way is suddenly blocked. We must take a detour. But we still have choices. Take me, for example. In a miserable first marriage, walking out when my son was little and not knowing how I would survive. Then finding my way as a singer, performing, moving to Paris, and meeting Andre. Even Reggie, who was nearly killed in Mississippi, found other places to use his brilliance right up to the time of his death. Do you agree, Keisha?"

In the living room Cora sat cradling her book and straining to hear the women. She was listening for her mom's response. *Does Mom think she has choices now?*

"I'm looking for those other paths. One of them led me to you all, and for that I'm grateful."

Cora wanted to challenge Aunt Joan and her mom. Did they really believe that people like Reggie and Cora's father, Richard, had choices when their lives ended so abruptly and violently?

Chapter 50

Just before Christmas, Aidan received authorization to relocate to Dallas on the Interstate Compact Transfer Program. He was to arrive by the first of the year. Numerous phone calls between Aunt Eve and Femi worked out the details. He felt hopeful, a feeling so unfamiliar that he distrusted it. Then he remembered his old friend Bone's advice to not be seduced by the familiar. Hope*less* was his familiar. Yardwork and chauffeuring were not the vocations he had imagined for himself, but he should be able to make it work. He'd probably have time to take classes online to help him identify what he wanted to pursue as a career.

Aunt Joan had reserved seats for the whole family to hear her sing at the Jazz Showcase. This would be his last chance to see Cora before he moved to Dallas. She was going to Cleveland with her mom and brother for Christmas, leaving the following afternoon.

Aunt Joan looked glamorous, leaning against a high stool and moving from one side of the small stage to another as she sang. Her voice filled the room. She cradled the sounds in her throat and the music that came out was transformative. Aidan noticed Cora get emotional listening.

At a break, he asked if she'd like to step outside with him. He asked how she was doing.

"You know my dad was a musician, piano mostly. Joan's voice brings him back. I miss him so much. Sometimes I wonder if I will ever stop missing him so."

"What hurts the most?"

"Dad and I shared our love of music and we also shared… I don't know how to describe it. A sense of there being something holy in life? We had started going to church before he died. Church isn't Mama's thing, but Dad grew up in a minister's family. And when we went together, I felt something pulling on me or in me. Gran Cora, Mama's grandma, is really religious. She has a way of making the bad times seem like just a prologue, not the whole story. She is so confident that God is real and that God talks with her. I think I want that. Does that sound crazy?"

"No. So can't you have that if you want it? What stops you?"

Jacob stood in the doorway to the Jazz Showcase calling them. It was time for the second set. They returned to their seats, Cora puzzling over Aidan's question.

When the evening ended, Joan had a surprise for Keisha and her children. "Come to Paris over spring break. You can stay in our flat, if you don't mind a bit of a squeeze, and I'll show you the city of my heart." Cora was thrilled.

When she got home, she had a text from Aidan with his new contact information and one line: "Stay in touch, Cuz."

Chapter 51

Christmas in Cleveland without Richard and Arthur was subdued. For Ann there was an added sadness. Her daughter was finding her way through her grief by building relationships with her biological father's family. While Ann's mind said that was good, she envied the way Femi, Jacob, and their sons had embraced Keisha and the kids, how often they saw each other, how easily they'd become family.

Christmas afternoon, after cleaning up from the big meal, Keisha and Ann stood in the kitchen. Keisha was telling stories about Femi and Jacob and Joan. She finished with a big reveal: "Joan's invited us to go to Paris for spring break! The kids are really excited."

Ann turned away and began briskly wiping the stove, hiding her hurt.

"Mama, I want you to come with us. Will you? Please? Joan would love it."

"Really? There is room for me, too?" Ann's voice was tentative. Her face as she looked at her daughter looked vulnerable, waif-like.

"Mom, of course there is room for you. There is always room for you. You're not Richard, but you're the next best thing." Keisha knew that was an exaggeration, and the part of her that valued honesty above all other virtues felt exposed and uncomfortable.

Then Ann dropped the dishrag and reached for her daughter, enfolding her in a fierce hug. Keisha wondered why her mom was so emotional.

In the living room, Don and Edward sat talking. Don was grieving his father and his son, and Edward was the only person who knew the truth of Don's relationship to Richard. The fire in the fireplace crackled and spat sparks. Scented candles augmented the light in the otherwise dark room.

"This is my favorite time of day," Edward said, taking off his shoes and stretching his stockinged feet toward the fireplace. "I have something to say to you, my brother. I've been thinking about this ever since Richard and Keisha's engagement, and I better get it out now while I still remember it…" Jokes about their advanced age came more frequently of late. Edward sipped from his mug of spiced cider before continuing.

"Life gives us opportunities to love." Edward spoke slowly. "Some we seize, some we let pass, some we never resolve how to handle, never. You never resolved the secret that lay between you and Richard, between you and Keisha, and Ann also. But you did seize the opportunity to love him, and he knew it, felt close to you, said how fortunate he was to have you for his father-in-law."

Don was leaning forward in his chair. "Just what did he say?"

"At his father's funeral, Richard told me how grateful he was for his relationship with you. In the midst of his grief, he said that knowing that you and Ann loved him 'like a son' gave him solace. That may not be enough, but it is important, brother."

In Don and Ann's family room, Cora and Gran Cora sat together on the sofa. Cora was leaning against her great-grandmother, breathing in Gran's scent of vanilla.

"You doing all right, child?"

"Getting there. Lots of changes. How about you?"

"Getting there. Grandpa is still hanging around, so that's good for me. He'll probably move on one of these days, but that's all right. So will I."

"You feel him near you?"

"Yes. And I'm trying to let go and give him back to God."

"Will God take good care of him?"

"Oh, yes. The best care."

"I want that for my dad. But we only went to church for a few weeks before he died."

"Going to church isn't the important thing, Cora. Love is. You may be a person like me who is fed by going to church. Or you may be a person like your mama who isn't. Either way it's loving that matters. I know you know how to do that. Your daddy knows it, too."

Cora asked if she could tell Gran a secret. Then she told her about Lucy Jordan, the woman who befriended her when Cora ran away from home.

Gran asked if Cora had thought that Miz Jordan might have been an angel sent to her by her daddy.

Cora said she would have to think about that. That sounded like magic to her.

"And what is love, my dear girl, but magic?"

Chapter 52

Two months after they returned home from Christmas break—in late February 2020—they sat in the kitchen talking about the breaking news that a dangerous virus called COVID-19 was rampaging across the world, bringing terrible deaths, especially to older people. Cora said she was worried about Gran Cora, Gran Ann, Uncle Edward, and Granddad. She didn't say it, but she was also worried about Lucy Jordan. She hadn't seen her since she'd run away from home, but once Cora had found a bouquet of weeds tied with a scrap of fabric on the front porch. She had a feeling Lucy Jordan had left them for her.

The new virus worried them all. Cora could see that they were all trying not to panic.

"Nothing like this has happened in Gran Cora's lifetime, and Gran Cora is, let's face it, really *old!*" Caleb scrutinized his mom, his face puzzled, looking more mature than his years. "Mom, promise us you won't die on us."

Cora was watching her brother. Given the sarcastic way she often related to him, her expression was surprisingly respectful. "*What?*" he asked her. "Why are you looking at me like that?"

"I'm glad you said that. I've been thinking the same thing but didn't have the nerve to say it." A smile flickered momentarily.

Caleb changed the subject. "Mom, you seem to be better. Are you over Dad?"

"No, Caleb. I will never be over your dad. I think about him every day." Her son's honest question deserved an honest answer. "I will always miss him. Probably I'll always talk to him in my head."

"Like you used to talk to Ida B. Wells-Barnett?"

"Something like that, but more special. Sometimes I feel overwhelmed with missing your dad. I wonder if I'm crazy. Then those times pass for a while, but I know they will return."

"Do you think you'll ever get married again?" Cora locked her eyes on her mama's.

"I don't know. If that ever happens, it would mean the other person would be able to accept that I am two people in one body, your dad and me, forever."

"I hate it when people ask me if I am over Dad's death. I still miss him so much."

"We won't ever 'get over' anything about Dad. We will hold onto what we have of him, of his life, and never let those memories and that love go." They sat in silence while the spring rain hummed as it pelted the ground.

Several days later it was still raining. Keisha awakened to the sound of rain and the smell of earthworms. She'd left the window open, and the rain had released these smells into her room. She remembered similar mornings from her childhood, when the sweet smell of newly washed dirt with its cargo of curling, pink worms had fascinated her. *My childhood was lovely and prolonged. It feels like I spent a lifetime just growing up. I wish my children did not have to grow up so quickly. In one year they have had to become young adults.*

Her adult years had been too crowded with activity, with work and responsibilities, for her to notice much, but now she noticed. The smells of her childhood tugged her to arise. She sat up suddenly, swung her legs out of bed, and stepped into her jeans. She headed out of her room, down the stairs, and out to the back yard, pulling a rain parka over her head and moving quietly, so she would not awaken the children.

She knelt on the shiny grass that was marbled with last fall's maple leaves. She thought they resembled hands face up to the sky in supplication. There beside the garden bed, where they'd planted bulbs in another lifetime, she watched the rain pit the earth and bounce up, watched the worms floating in small ponds and streams that had formed on the surface of the soil. She knelt and looked.

She felt the cold damp on the front of her calves from the wet ground. Felt it spread out from her knees. She was observing something ancient: The sure coming of spring with its onset of soaking rain, tufts of new green, and worm-scent rising.

It was enough. Enough, even in this terrifying time of pandemic, when she could not see her parents, or Gran Cora, or Femi and Jacob, or Uncle Edward, except on Zoom calls. Their trip to Paris was canceled—

postponed, Joan said. Her students and her children were learning online, physically separated from each other. And so many people, especially old people, were dying horrible deaths on ventilators in crowded hospitals, without their family members near them.

Later, after she'd washed the mud from her clothes, showered, and washed her hair, she knew that something in her had changed.

She had a Zoom appointment with one of her grad students that afternoon. On the monitor, she could see the woman's face glowing with excitement. What she'd been learning poured out of her. She could have been Keisha twenty years ago.

Keisha listened and felt the familiar thrill of discovering the past. It was like reuniting unexpectedly with a long-lost friend.

When the session with her student ended, she phoned Ann. "I smelled the worms this morning, and the rain, and got excited about what one of my grad students is researching."

She could hear the smile in Mom's voice. "That's good news, honey. I'm so glad you called."

Then she called Gran Cora. "How are you doing, Gran? I know you must miss Grandpa terribly."

"That I do, child. But sometimes I see him sitting in his recliner reminding me to take care of myself."

"Are you taking care of yourself?"

"Yes. I know my time here is limited. Everyone's is, but... But it is so *good*, this life, and I want to live it as fully as I can while I am here. What about you, Keisha?"

"You said I should call you when I saw a crack in the darkness. I saw one today," she reported.

"Remember Leonard Cohen, the Canadian composer? Do you know his song 'Anthem?'" Gran began to sing across the miles. The strength of her voice surprised Keisha:

> *"The birds they sang*
> *At the break of day*
> *Start again*
> *I heard them say*
> *Don't dwell on what has passed away*
> *Or what is yet to be...*

Like a refugee

Ring the bells that still can ring
Forget your perfect offering
There is a crack, a crack in everything
That's how the light gets in."

You asked for a sign, Cora, and you got it. The light that came through the crack. It's just a little light, but praise God for small signs."

"Thank you, Gran."

The box and the note sat on the table next to Richard's side of the bed, where they had lain for nearly a year. That evening, before she turned out the light, Keisha moved them to the top drawer of her dresser. Richard was right. People eventually "recover," but she would never use that word. "Move on into my next life," was what she said, "and carry you with me."

Chapter 53

On the anniversary of Richard's murder, Keisha sat in the family room looking out at the back yard. With the sun hiding behind heavy clouds, everything looked gray and monochromatic, dreary and unattractive. Her garden lay dormant under half an inch of an unexpected late spring snow. Not enough snow to be beautiful. Just enough to render the view depressing.

It was fitting, the scene she looked out upon. It matched her gray life during this year. At least she was no longer awash in tears. Only a perpetual dull ache of sadness.

I'm like Humpty Dumpty, she thought, fallen, cracked open, *unable to be put back together again.*

> Humpty Dumpty sat on a wall,
> Humpty Dumpty had a great fall;
> All the king's horses and all the king's men
> Couldn't put Humpty together again.

She opened her laptop, curious about the origin of this Mother Goose rhyme, hundreds of years old, that named her state of mind with such concise accuracy. Within seconds her screen showed results for Humpty Dumpty: "a sly allusion to King Richard III, who died in the Battle of Bosworth in 1485. During the battle King Richard III fell from his horse, who was named 'Wall.' He was so severely beaten his men could not save him. When his skeleton was exhumed from a shopping center parking lot in Leicester, England in 2012, his skeletal remains showed eleven wounds, eight of them to his head."

The parallels were disturbing. Her Richard had been attacked and bludgeoned. The coroner's report identified eight blows to his head as the cause of death. If he had somehow survived, he would never have been the same mentally, the homicide detective had told her. He meant to be comforting, implying it was better for Richard to die than to live as a vegetable.

She partially agreed. Better that he be changed in form and moved to another planet where his beautiful mind could continue to sing. But he was destroyed. Where now is his intelligence, his capacity to love, his music? She had not found the detective's words comforting.

She had never told the family what the coroner's report said. She glanced out the window at the beds she and Richard had planted with tulips. He'd been excited, imagining the tulips standing tall and straight and blooming in red profusion in the coming spring. He hadn't lived to see them. She wondered if the tulips would survive this winter. They'd been beaten down by the elements and pushed aside by the perennials that replaced them. Were they finished? Or dormant?

Her mind turned to that word, dormant. She consulted the online dictionary. "Dormant: 1) having normal physical functions suspended or slowed down for a period of time; in or as if in a deep sleep. 2) temporarily inactive or inoperative."

Her Gran would say Keisha was dormant this year, *temporarily* inactive or inoperative. Would she also say Richard was dormant—his normal physical functions suspended? Or would she say that Richard was finished, had moved on, taken another form—Einstein's theory that all energy and matter are constant, just changing form? Gran might call it a resurrection.

Since Richard's murder, Keisha had not consulted Ida B. Wells-Barnett, her first go-to for insight. Now she felt the need to summon her. What would Ida do? Keisha cast her mind into the waters of memory, recalling Wells-Barnett's autobiography.

Ida had been a journalist living a happy life in Memphis, Tennessee. Then three of her close friends, who ran a store across the street from a white-owned store, were seized by a mob, beaten, and hanged, *murdered*. Before their murders, Ida had believed the generally accepted excuse for lynching, that any Black man lynched had raped or attempted to rape a white woman. But Ida knew these men, loved them as dear friends, was godmother to their children. She knew they were lynched for being successful businessmen. She recognized that she had believed a lie, the Big Lie told to justify lynching. She wrote a scathing editorial that exposed it and left Memphis for a church meeting in Philadelphia. She was just ahead of a lynch mob that came for *her*. In the midst of her grief, she found a reason to live. She began researching and exposing the practice of lynching that had taken the lives of at least 4,000 innocent Black men (and women), murdered by mobs of white men.

Ida Wells-Barnett had not written about her *grief*. She found her way through her grief by investigating and writing about an evil of her time that had touched her life. That's what Ida would do, what Ida *did* do.

In a moment of insight, Keisha realized that's what she also had begun to do. She'd begun investigating the Philadelphia police campaign to destroy the MOVE organization.

She could not put Richard back together. She could not bring her biological father back from the carnage of May 13, 1985. She could not put herself back together, not as she was before. Each of them had "moved" on. "Moved." The word was MOVE's mandate, not an acronym but a directive, a command. *Keep moving.* Make a path forward.

She picked up her laptop and carried it upstairs to her bedroom. The door to the walk-in closet was open. Richard's favorite flannel shirt hung on a hook watching her. She entered the closet. His clothes still lined up against one wall. They'd been a daily reassurance that he had been here, a regiment of regret. She lifted the flannel shirt off the hook and put it on. Then she began lifting Richard's shirts, slacks, and sports coats, still on their hangers, off the rod. She lay them gently in a pile on the floor beside the bedroom door. Tomorrow she would take them to Goodwill. Others could use them. But not the flannel shirt.

When his side of the closet was empty, she moved some of her clothes there. Then she returned to her laptop. She sat at the table that faced the back yard and opened her computer.

She had saved dozens of documents to her laptop. She had a notebook full of handwritten notes of what she'd learned during these months since meeting her birth father's sisters and going to Philadelphia to learn and see for herself. Several books on MOVE sat beside the bed with sticky-pad notes marking passages she wanted to be able to find easily. She shifted the books to the table and stood them up, so that their spines faced her like soldiers in close formation.

What would Ida do? *She* would not stop with finding answers to her personal questions. She would *write*. She would tell the world.

Keisha opened a blank Word document, stared at the empty page for a moment, then keyed in one word at the top of the page: MOVE. Then she began to write.

"Reggie Lewis was a brilliant man who journeyed from registering voters in Mississippi, to working alongside Martin Luther King, Jr. in Chicago, to developing Black-owned businesses in Philadelphia while studying for his master's at Wharton School of Business. He was a man who cared deeply for the world and for its future. He supported the utopian community called MOVE because MOVE shared his love for people and animals and his concern about police brutality, corruption, chemical pollution, and the Big Lies people were being told.

"Reggie Lewis did not deserve to die trying to stop the police from murdering five children and six adults living in a Black neighborhood of West Philadelphia in 1985. And they did not deserve to be reduced to ashes by a bomb dropped on their residence by the city of Philadelphia. His death on May 13, 1985, was part of a long line of lynchings and murders that are part of the history of this nation. This is his story, an American story. Yours. And mine."

Epilogue

Don and Ann sat side by side on the bed, leaning against the pillows. Ann was reading a novel. Don had been scanning email on his phone. Now he set the phone down and reached for Ann's hand.

"There is something I want to tell you. Can I interrupt your reading?"

"Of course." She closed the book and set it on the nightstand, half turning to see his face.

"Remember when Connie died, and I went to her funeral? Remember when we first met her daughters and set up the fund for their children's education?"

Ann was nodding. Attentive. Connie had been Don's first love. When he learned that she had died, he'd also learned she had given birth to a son, *his* son, and that she had to place the boy for adoption. It had been a traumatic time in his and Ann's marriage, but they had made it through.

"I discovered where my son was just about the time Keisha and Richard decided to get married."

Ann's face tensed, alarmed, worried. Where was this revelation taking them?

"I learned that… that *Richard* was my son. I wrote it in my will for him to learn upon my death. I was afraid it would upset his and Keisha's commitment to each other, that it might give him misgivings about going through with the marriage, although there was no blood relationship between them. Then Richard was murdered…

"I don't want family secrets, but I feared if I told you and Keisha, it would disrupt your grieving. So I kept my secret. But I don't want secrets between us, my love. Not any longer."

"Why tell me now?" Ann had that look that said she was trying to stay calm while processing this new information.

"It's been a very hard year. We are in the midst of a worldwide pandemic and can't travel to see Keisha and the kids."

Ann interrupted him. "Keisha sounds much stronger and her relationship with Cora and Caleb appears to be restored."

He continued. "I wanted to tell you and my father, but I kept putting it off and now he is gone. I'm telling you because I need the love of my life to know what I've been going through." He didn't tell her that he'd been talking with Edward, the only person who knew that Richard was his son. He knew she would feel hurt that he'd confided in someone other than her, and he didn't want to hurt her.

Ann was patting his hand. "So, you lost your father *and* your son this year. That is so hard. I have some idea what that's like from when my parents were killed. You held all that pain inside and protected the rest of us from this additional layer of trauma." Her face crumpled suddenly, and he was surprised to see tears in the eyes of his stalwart, fearless wife who rarely lost control. Was she angry with him?

Her voice cracked as she continued. "I can see why you kept your relationship to Richard secret all these years, but the thought of you bearing his death alone, with none of us supporting you—it breaks my heart. Thank you for telling me now."

They sat without speaking. He passed her his handkerchief as she cried. "You're not angry with me?"

"No. Just very sad for you and amazed by your strength. Will you tell Keisha?"

"I don't know. I'm worried how it might affect her. How is it affecting you?"

"I loved Richard like the son I never had. And I loved what he meant to Keisha. It's weird to think of your son marrying my daughter. But not so weird to think of them both as our children."

She stood and walked to the bathroom, returning to perch on his side of their bed and hand him a glass of water. Then she wrapped her arms around him and held on. He had to listen closely as she spoke through her tears.

"This year brought so much change—Richard's murder, Keisha's despair, her discovery of Reggie's family and his story. You lost Sam the Dog, your father, and your son. And now we're quarantined, and people our age are dying by the hundreds of thousands across the world. Our daughter and grandchildren are worried about whether we—and Gran and Edward—will survive the Corona Virus. If it's not one thing, it's another, right? Maybe our job now is just to nourish our love for each other—and, long distance, for Gran Cora, Edward, Keisha, and the kids."

"I'm grateful we got to meet Femi and Jacob and Joan and their families at New Year's. And I'm grateful Keisha has them in her life along with us."

"Have I ever told you how amazing you are, Don Johnson?" Ann kissed him gently on the lips.

"I figure we don't know what else we may have to face. But we do know we've come this far, and mostly it has been good."

"What is it Gran Cora says?"

"When the options are hope or despair, choose love."

The End

Study Guide

1. Which character/s did you most identify with? Why?

2. There is a family secret that runs through this novel. Should Don have told Keisha that Richard was his biological son? Why or why not?

3. Should Ann have told Keisha the truth about her birth father's death when Keisha was in college? Should Ann have told Reggie about Keisha's existence?

4. There is a lot of history in this novel. What was new to you?

5. Which historical figure was most interesting to you and why?

6. This is a story of coping with the sudden death of a close family member. If you have gone through this, what parts of Keisha and her children's experiences felt familiar or "true"? What would you have said to Keisha about recovering from gigantic loss?

7. This story takes place in 2019. How do you think the characters' lives will be affected by the pandemic and the political polarization that increased dramatically in the following years?

8. Femi and Jacob have two children who are "successful" in their careers and families, but Aidan is "lost." Why is Aidan's life so hard? What do you think will happen to him? If you ever experienced estrangement from your family, how did you get through it?

9. What insights did you get from this novel about race in the U.S.?

10. At the end of Chapter 49, Cora questions whether her mother and Aunt Joan really believe that people like Reggie and Richard found other paths when their lives ended so abruptly and violently. Are Joan and Keisha trying to sugar-coat violent deaths? How would you answer Cora?

11. At the end of the book, some things remain unclear. Keisha has started down a new path. What about Cora and Caleb?

12. What do you think about the Black Capitalism? Is it a viable solution to poverty? Why or why not?

Historical Notes

In 1969, Reverend Leon Sullivan wrote *Build, Brother, Build,* a book arguing for Black entrepreneurship in response to the riots of the 1960s Sullivan founded OIC, a series of training schools aimed at putting African Americans to work in various industries, in 1964. By 1969, it had about 20,000 people enrolled in its job placement programs. OIC still operates in 22 states and Africa. Sullivan opened Progress Plaza in 1968. It was the first African American-owned shopping center in the U.S. Sullivan organized the "Selective Patronage" campaign, pulling together 400 ministers and their congregations to boycott major companies that refused to hire Blacks.

In 1971, Sullivan became the first African American to join General Motors' board of directors, where he served until 1991. While he was on the board, Sullivan took his fight against racial injustice international. In 1977, he drafted the Sullivan Principles, guidelines for American businesses operating in South Africa during apartheid, a system of institutionalized racial segregation that existed in South Africa from 1948 to 1994. A state historical marker in Philadelphia honors the late Rev. Leon Sullivan.

Another marker along Cobb Creek Parkway notes the destruction of the MOVE house by Philadelphia police and the bomb that started a fire that destroyed 61 homes and three blocks of West Philadelphia.

Acknowledgements

A number of people carefully read drafts of this historical novel, gave feedback, and suggested edits. My deep gratitude goes especially to Reginald D. Jarrell, Primus Singleton, Ronda Miller, Avery Marshall, Lois Ruby, Michael Poage, and Blue Cedar Press's managing editor Laura Tillem, each of whom strengthened the trajectory of the plot and the development of the characters.

Reggie Jarrell , author of *Thirty-One Days [Nights]: Memoir of Living Black in America* (2022), noticed places where my wording or description of a character's behavior was "off" or insensitive.

Avery Marshall, Front of House Supervisor of the Bob Dylan Center in Tulsa, a songwriter, and performer, taught me about emo, led to my writing the Prologue, and strengthened several scenes.

Ronda Miller, a life coach and trauma counsellor who is also a prize-winning poet with five published books of poetry. taught me how teenagers experience traumatic loss, leading to fuller depictions of Cora and Caleb.

Lois Ruby, author of over twenty young adult novels, identified what needed clarification.

Primus Singleton, who grew up in West Philadelphia, introduced me to life there in the 1980s. His close reading and extensive notes helped me develop Aidan's story and sent him South to stay with family and start over.

Laura Tillem, the managing editor of Blue Cedar Press, was as always "spot on" in suggesting improvements for some sentences and identifying what was extraneous. She also suggested that the next novel in this family saga focus on Cora, who will be twenty in 2024. Cora's Crossings is begun! Stay tuned.

I am immensely grateful to my writer-husband, the poet and brilliant teacher of writing, Michael J. Poage. His wisdom and knowledge challenges me to keep growing in my appreciation of the potential and beauty of the English language. Shortcomings and errors are mine alone.

As many novelists do, I fell in love with these characters. The pre-quel to this book, *Maybe Crossings*, tells of Ann, Don, Reggie, and Edward in the Sixties and what happens when they reconnect in 2003, which is when Richard and Keisha come together.

Finally, thank *you* for reading this book! I welcome feedback through bluecedarpress.com.

About the Author

Gretchen Eick is a professional historian and a writer. In addition to two prize-winning histories, she has five published novels and writes for an online newspaper. Her work has appeared in assorted anthologies and her short plays have been performed by a school and a congregation. She was named Prose Writer of the Year by the Kansas Authors Club in 2021. She and her husband, the poet Michael Poage, live in Wichita, Kansas, when they are not living and teaching outside the U.S.